Advance Praise for
The Extraordinary

"A family already living on the edge of disaster plunges into despair when the father, a Marine Corps captain, returns home from Iraq with both legs blown off by a suicide bomber. More devastating damage follows, much of it self-inflicted. Brad Schaeffer's novel recounts the sense of loss, terror, and pain through the eyes of fourteen-year-old Wesley, the family's youngest member, who suffers from autism. Schaeffer doesn't avert his gaze from the hurt that members of this wounded family cause each other, yet never loses his compassion for his characters. The result is an intimate and compelling tale of vulnerability, endurance, and forgiveness."

—GLENN FRANKEL, Pulitzer Prize-winning journalist whose most recent book is *Shooting Midnight Cowboy: Art, Sex, Loneliness, Liberation, and the Making of a Dark Classic*, published by Farrar, Straus and Giroux

"A fascinating and touching view of life, seen through the eyes of a very special young man, as told by an author who himself is blessed with a gift for storytelling that brings this wonderful novel to life."

—ERIC L. HARRY, author of *Arc Light*, *Invasion*, and *Pandora: Resistance*

ALSO BY BRAD SCHAEFFER

Of Another Time and Place

the Extraordinary

a novel

Brad Schaeffer

Post Hill
PRESS

A POST HILL PRESS BOOK
ISBN: 978-1-64293-942-2
ISBN (eBook): 978-1-64293-943-9

The Extraordinary
© 2021 by Brad Schaeffer
All Rights Reserved

Post Hill Press
New York • Nashville
posthillpress.com

Published in the United States of America
1 2 3 4 5 6 7 8 9 10

For Marge

ACKNOWLEDGMENTS

A work of fiction doesn't just emerge from the mist, but is often a reflection of the people, places, and events that shape an author's outlook and ignite his or her hidden passions. In the case of *The Extraordinary*, there were many who encouraged me to take a germ of an idea and develop it until it became what you have before you. I thank my daughter whose in-depth and insightful collegiate study on autism sparked in me a deep appreciation for what the estimated 1 in 54 children on the spectrum confront every day…and the trials and triumphs of their families who are by their sides. My appreciation extends to my son as well, whose interest in learning about his grandfather, a Marine combat veteran of the Korean War, stoked my desire to understand better his thirty-year battle with PTSD. I also deeply appreciate Bob Thixton of Pinder Lane & Garon-Brooke, my diligent champion of an agent, for his unwavering support of my writing endeavors, wherever on the page they may take me. Additionally, I wish to acknowledge Maddie Sturgeon, my editor at Post Hill Press, for her patience and professionalism, as well as Simon & Schuster for bringing my voice to the public at large. And, as always, I am grateful to a loving God, not just for the many blessings of my life, but also the disappointments and challenges I have faced over the years that ultimately forged within me a stronger and fuller—and I hope better—man.

TABLE OF CONTENTS

THE DREAM

I'm starting to wonder if I'll ever see Dad again. The dream starts off the same. The darkness; the scrape of blowing, twisted branches on the window, like the tapping fingernails of a giant. It wakes me and I try to open my eyes, but all is black. I hear the rain falling. A rushing of sound as if my bed's in a cave hemmed in by a waterfall pouring past the only exit to the outside world. I must walk through it. When I get to the other side, wet and cold, I find myself at a gate. My white hands grip the rusting bars and I pull with all my might, but the chain and padlock holding the doors closed won't give. I see my dad through the bars. He walks upright, his legs intact, and wears his dress blue uniform, white gloves, and hat. He smiles. I reach through the bars and then he's gone. I look down into my hand, up to the forearm through the gate, and open my fist to reveal a tiny sand crab. It lies on its soft shell on its side; its legs, like the teeth of a translucent comb, are stiff and lifeless.

Then I wake up.

SAND CRABS

"The waves. What do you think, Wesley?"

Dad smiles as I stare down at the wet sand covering my bare feet. The cool seawater feels good against my ankles as the brine rolls over them. Dad crouches down and looks into my eyes. I look away. I don't like to meet others' stares. Not even his. Faces bother me. I don't know why. There's a lot I don't know. But there's a lot I do know too. Dad understands. He's the only one in the family who understands. He digs his thick fingers into the soupy wet sand and takes my hand. I usually don't like to be touched. I sometimes panic, and it makes Mom very angry with me. Dad never gets mad. He scoops a handful of grainy porridge like a steam shovel and lays it into my palm. The salt water drips through my fingers. Something tickles. I stare at the mound as it moves. "It's a sand crab," he says with a smile. "See?"

As the sand drips away, the little creature emerges. He looks panicky. I know the feeling and I feel compassion for the animal the size of an almond. Whirring legs under a soft shell. I touch it with my finger. I want to smile. But I just can't. So I stare at the crab until Dad gently removes it from my hand and lays it back on the sand. It frantically burrows into the earth and disappears. My father puts his hands on my shoulders. I look away to the haze of the horizon. What's beyond the edge, I wonder?

Dad smiles. "I thought you'd like that. There are thousands of them down there, Wes," he says. "Do you see? You never know what lies beneath the surface."

He stands up tall and straight. A military posture about him. Even people who first meet him when he doesn't wear his uniform know he's special. A Marine. An officer. He runs the house like he runs his unit. Tight and in control. I like that. I like to know I can lean on him. He is my pillar under my very shaky world. I'll miss him when he goes away tomorrow.

I briefly glance up at him. I'm fourteen, but Dad says I'm still growing so I won't catch up to him for another year. He always tells me I'll be tall like him. "A height to match the man," he says. "And you are my man, Wes. I know you hear me."

I do. Which is why he reads my thoughts now. "I'm sorry, Son. I have to go. It's, well, it's my job. There are bad people out there, and I have to stop them from hurting good people. It's hard to understand. Even for the Ords." "Ords" is his term for people who aren't special like me. He calls me an "Ex." "You're extraordinary. Unique. A gift to me," he would say. He briefly catches my eye. It's a fleeting moment. Like a rare bird that flits past an otherwise ordinary landscape and then is gone. "I'll miss you too. But it's just one tour."

One tour. I know that means one year. Three hundred sixty-five days, three-sixty-six during a leap year, but this isn't one of those. Like the song my mom likes to listen to when she cooks. Five hundred twenty-five thousand six hundred minutes. I sometimes try to count them down when he's gone. It's a long time to be left alone with my family.

I want to hit my head with my hands when I think about it. I want to scream at the ocean. It's such a chasm between where I will be and where he is going. Dad sees my fists clench. He looks around, and then quietly says, "Fight it, Son. You'll be okay. Breathe in." People walking past us on the water's edge glance my way as I shout out in protest. But then I'm calm again. My scream is carried away by the salty air to the far shore beyond the edge of the world.

"Come on. Let's go back to the house. I'm hungry. Aren't you?" No, I think. I'm lonely.

LAST DINNER

Supper. We sit in an oval as Mom, forty-eight and looking pain-fully thin in a floral summer dress, orbits the dining room table laying out place settings that for one more day will number five of us. Her straw-colored hair is styled. Teeth capped. Sixty-four inches, one hundred seventeen pounds of icy Northeastern reserve. Thomas, my brother, is a junior in high school. He plays the guitar. He also plays football and, although I don't really pay attention to what he does on the field when we go to his games, his numbers jump out at me when I study the local paper: 16.0 sacks (national average 1.19), 11 interceptions (national average 1.16), total tackles 38 (national average 14). I find comfort in numbers. They're concrete. Finite. Honest. Not all confusing and jumbled like the world around me. Thomas is big and square, and I don't think he likes me. He gets mad at me a lot. He doesn't like that I don't say much and never look at him. He sometimes calls me "weird" behind my back. (I guess he doesn't know that my ears work a lot better than my mouth.)

As we begin eating, Becca makes her appearance. But she won't stay with us, even though Mom set up her plate and utensils just in case. She lives and works in New York. Finance or something like that. She's just here for the weekend. She'll grab a quick mouthful of food and then tear out to meet her friends at a club on the shore. It's Dad's last night, but this is how she copes, I guess. Becca's ten years older than me. We had another sister, between her and Thomas; that's why there's such a gap. But she died when she was just a baby. Fell asleep in her crib and never woke up again. My mom tried to tell me once what happened to her. I didn't ask. I didn't look at her when she described how she stepped in the nursery and saw her baby lying still, her face like a blueberry. When I was a little boy, I thought someone named "Sid" killed her. But now I know it was something called SIDS. Whatever it's called, it left my mom hollow inside. She had Thomas and then me. She does her job as a mother. But she still brings up little Annabel when we're alone sometimes. I think she wanted me to be a girl. I know she wanted me to be an Ord. Annabel, she said, was "normal." Why couldn't I be? "Why couldn't you just be normal like your sister would have been, Wes?"

But she's not saying those things now. She has other things on her mind. Dad has to leave in the middle of the night. There's a pall over the house. I can feel it. Sadness. Fear. Regret. Mom's like the core reactor that sets the mood of our home. This evening that mood is dark, and it frightens me. At dinner I want to scream. I'm not hungry. I just want to rock and moan and bang my plate. I don't want Dad to go away.

Thomas is also tense, and he's sharper than usual tonight. It's in the air. "Can we please just one time eat in peace?"

Dad glares at him. "Thomas. Your brother's upset. Can't you see that?"

Thomas recedes. Dad's the only one who intimidates him. "He's always upset," he says quietly, looking my way. I stare down at my carrots.

Becca passes through the kitchen on her way out the door for the night. She's very pretty. Brunette. Short hair, almost like a boy's. Athletic, with toned legs highlighted by a denim miniskirt. She ran track at Penn State. I imagine boys like her. She rubs my hair as she walks by and I throw my hands up to deflect it. "I don't know why I bother," she sighs.

"You know he hates that," says Thomas.

Mom says to my sister, "You're going out even though it's your father's last night home?"

She pauses at the door, her hand with slender fingers and brightly painted nails grips the doorknob tightly. She exhales, bows her head, and turns to face Dad. He looks up at her. "I can stay home if you want."

"No," he says. "It's okay. You have a life to live."

She walks over to him and throws her bare arms around him. Her eyes are swollen. I can tell she's been crying upstairs. "I'm gonna miss you, Daddy."

"You have a funny way of showing it," mumbles my brother while cutting into his steak.

"I know," says Dad. "I'll miss you too, baby girl."

"Skype us?" she says weakly as she disengages from him and heads once more for the exit.

He nods. "Sure, Becks. Have fun tonight."

I moan in protest. She looks at me and then lowers her head as she opens the door and disappears into the night, shutting it with a slam that sounds like a gunshot to my sensitive ears.

"That's messed up, man," Thomas says in protest as he ladles himself a heaping mound of mashed potatoes. His spoon clinks against the plate and makes me start. He ignores me. "Dad's going off to war and she goes out partying? Nice daughter."

"It's alright, Thomas," Dad says. "In a way it shows she cares."

Mom stares at him. "Peter, you can't be serious. If she wasn't over twenty-one, I swear."

"But she is."

I don't understand. *She is, she is, she is!* "She is!" I shout and slap my hand on the table with a loud *smack!*

"Jesus, Wes, shut up!" snaps Thomas.

"What did you say to him?" my father says through gritted teeth. His eyes are malevolent slits. The eyes of a company commander facing down a mutiny.

Thomas looks at him; fear radiates from him. "I'm sorry. I just wish he could control himself. That's all. I mean, well, shit, I don't get how you can be so coddling to him."

"Thomas," my mother injects. (She sometimes calls him Tommy but calls him Thomas whenever she's mad at him. That's how I know she's mad now). "That's your brother. And he's in this room."

"Is he?" he says. "Does he even know that Dad's going away? That he could get killed? Does he even care? Christ, does anyone in this madhouse care?"

My mother throws her napkin down and rockets to her feet. "I care! This man is my husband. How do you think I feel? Tomorrow I'll be left with an absentee daughter, and two sons, one who only thinks about his guitar, football, and girls, and another one who I don't think cares for anyone at all. Look at him!"

I can only hear all this as I rock in my chair with my eyes clamped shut, arms tightly folded to my chest.

The discussion continues. It's an old issue. "I swear I don't know why I married a military man."

"You're a sucker for a uniform," my dad answers as he aimlessly shuffles his peas on the plate with his fork. "That, and we fell in love."

My mom softens and sinks back into her chair. "Yes, we did, didn't we? But…I just didn't bargain for this."

Although she's referring to her husband's career of long absences and danger, I know what she really means. She didn't bargain for *me*.

"DON'T GO"

Nighttime is the worst. Ambient crackles and squeals assault me, like a radio that can't find the proper signal. The busy crickets *cree-cree* outside my window. The leaves rustle as the late summer breeze passes through them. Although I know it's too far away, based on the map placemat I always insist upon eating over, I swear I can hear the faint whispers of the ocean in my ears. But also in this blue world of the moonlight, as if sinking down in the abyss of a nautical canyon miles beneath the waves, comes the terror. I can't explain it really. Just a sense that all the world is atilt and I'm struggling to maintain my balance on a platform that some malevolent giant is determined to gradually pitch ever more steeply until I tumble into the void. I see shadows. Shadows of shadows. Haunting shapes stretch out across the darkened walls of my bedroom like threatening stains. I imagine the world in the blackness as an endless stream of static coming at me. A persistent pulse from a far-distant quasar. It hits me every night as I try to sleep with the restless mind of the Extra-Ord. My heart races and skips. My breath comes to me in staccato chuffs.

I don't want you to go. Don't leave me with them. You say they love me, but they don't understand....

"Hey, Wes." A soothing yet powerful hand caresses my soft cheek. "You having another tough dream?"

My eyes snap open. All is still dark, but soon the pale moonlight fills my view and lines the chiseled face of my dad gazing down on me. He wears his camouflage fatigues and heavy boots, twin bars of a captain on his collar, and an eagle, anchor, and globe emblem of the

Marines on his soft-billed cap. He looks like a different person when he's dressed to fight the bad people. More serious. Meaner. Maybe it's just the clothes. Still, I don't know how a man who picks sand crabs with his Ex son on the beach can also hurt people, which is really what he does if I understand his job right. I wonder, when I watch him without his noticing me, who is my real dad? I think sometimes he does too.

My room is like one of those Picasso paintings Antoinette at the special school shows me. His "blue period" she calls it. "Wes, do you know what 'blue' is?" Of course, I do. It's the color of Dad's dress uniform when he parades at the camp or attends weddings, funerals, and parties with Mom in her evening best. The color of the ocean and the sky and the canvas of my world.

I look up to him and then turn away. It almost burns to look at him in the dimness of the shadow world. *Don't go.*

"I have to shove off now." I frown. "I know. It's hard, Son. Someday you'll understand."

The word escapes my lips as I curl up in my sheets. His weight against the side of my bed. "No," I whisper.

"What did you say?" I can't tell if he smiles or frowns.

"No," I squeak again. I don't know where the word comes from. I'm like a drowning man who breeches the surface with my hand to let the world know I'm here. "No...no...*no!*" I scream.

Lights explode in the hallway. Hasty footfalls. Dad raises his thick brow and grins at me. His hand once again strokes my cheek as I cling to the sheet over my chin. "No," I say more softly now.

Mom appears in the lighted doorway. A bright yellow rectangle in the blue. "Wes? I thought I heard..." Her voice fades when Dad turns to face her while still seated on the edge of my bed.

"It's okay, Bug," he assures her calmly. "I'm just saying good-bye to my Ex-man here." He smiles at me as I retreat like a turtle under the shell of my covers. The warmth of my breath against the sheets makes me sweat. My dad calls my mom "Bug," and she seems to like it. It's a pet name that goes back to when they met. I don't know how it came about but I like that he calls her that now. It means things are okay between them. That the connection so often lacking between them is alight like a live wire tonight. I think she'll miss him too. I think she wishes it was me leaving in the middle of the night to catch a ride to the base and then the big grey transport plane to a faraway place called Iraq.

NEW DAY, FAR AWAY

In the morning he's gone.

The house feels empty. None of the subdued noise of a stirring household. Although it's breakfast time, I pick up no muffled chatter from the kitchen one floor below. No scraping of plates or the *shusssh* of the sink rinsing out a pan. It must not be a school day. I wander into my parents' bedroom. Blades of light stream through the windows to rest on a queen bed stripped of its blankets and sheets. A bare mattress. Mom likes to wash Dad's scent away when he goes off to war. She wants no reminders of the man who's left her behind to cope with the year to come. If he dies, she wants nothing left to trigger a memory. I breathe in the air. And I can still smell him. I want to smile but nothing comes. I stare at my feet and wriggle my toes in the soft carpet. "Someday you'll smile for me," Dad would always promise. I think, someday.

Every night I sleep in the same clothes. An Eli Manning T-shirt with holes worn in the elbow and flannel pajama pants that are creeping up my ankles as I grow. The shirt's getting tight around my chest and shoulders, but I can't let it go. Dad gave it to me. I descend the stairs at the same time every morning, 7:30 sharp. Sometimes I'll wait at the top step and peek into my room to read the digital clock on my nightstand until the glowing numbers turn: 7:28...7:29...7:30. Once downstairs, I start my day by grabbing my tablet off the bookshelf in the kitchen. I retreat into the den, curl up on the leather couch, and touch the icon with the motion picture camera. I swipe through the selection until I find my movie and tap my finger on the glass. *The Sound of Music.* Sometimes I'll hear Thomas say, "Christ, if I hear 'The Lonely Goatherd' one more time, I'm going down to Hobby Lobby with Dad's gun and blasting every puppet I find." Mom just sighs, moves a strand of hair out of her eye, and explains, "Your brother likes routine."

An hour later I find Mom sitting in the screened-in porch, a mug of tea in her hand. She studies two squirrels frolicking in the back-yard by the swing set. The animals flit and race and jerk their heads. I moan. I don't like quick movements. She turns to me. Forces a smile.

"Hey, kiddo. Your movie over?" I look out to the yard. "Let me guess," she says, "the Von Trapps made it out safe again." She thinks sarcasm doesn't register with me. It does. And it hurts. I like that movie.

I sit down next to her and study the yard. I avoid looking at the animals. She reaches out for my hand, but I retreat. It's not genuine to me. Her love feels dutiful. I know she wishes I was sent away. I've heard her talk with Dad about it when she thought I was sleeping. My ears really are like radar. "Who needs a cat around when we could just use you to listen for mice in the walls," Dad would laugh.

Mom looks at her hand as if it has a rash and then places it in her lap. She sits very straight. Boarding school posture. An only child. Her family has a lot of money. I don't know how. It's how we can live in a nice house near the shore. It belonged to her father, and he gave it to her as a wedding gift. "Well," he said, "if you marry a Goddamned gyrene, you'll need all the help you can get." He didn't want Mom to marry Dad. Something about him being "beneath her station," but I'm not sure what the train has to do with anything. I think she believes I'm her punishment for not listening to Grampa Frank. She sometimes says to Dad: "If I'd married someone else like my dad wanted, would I have had *him?*"

Her dad's money doesn't seem to matter to her this morning. She's sad. More than that. She looks mad. Mad at the world. I give her no comfort as her other children do. When Thomas and Becca walk into a room, her face lights up. When I do, it's as if someone broke a plate in the next room and she knows she has to sweep up the pieces.

"Next week you start school again," she says robotically. "You'll like that, won't you?" I say nothing. I like school. I like my friend Maria. She has the same name as Frau Von Trapp, but she doesn't look like her. She has black hair and skin that's always tan. Dark brown eyes, like two coffee beans. She talks a lot. "You must like something," Mom says. "This world can't be so blank to you."

I stare at the slate floor. Gray and crimson. Glued together by mortar the color of paste. They look to me like the skin of a dragon. A being that's swallowed me whole and I now wander its innards like a lost corpuscle. The world isn't blank to me. It's filled with static. Vibrations and erratic movements. From squirrels in the grass to screeching jet planes above me slicing against the blue ceiling and painting the sky with their crisscrossing cloud lines as if weaving a drifting web over the world...and me. *No, Mommy*, I want to say. The world is very much alive to me. It fills me with wonder, and with dread. Each day I climb down the stairs is like storming an enemy shore. I think of my walks with Dad along the beach. He tells me what the Marines did at faraway places long ago. Places with funny names like Guadalcanal and Peleliu, Iwo Jima and Okinawa, Chosin and Huế. I wonder if it was the same for them. I think Dad senses my fears. The kind of terror he must feel when he goes into the dangerous places of the land called Iraq for me. For all of us. "Those Marines. Those guys were 'Exes' like you," he says. "They were scared too, Son." He puts his hand on my shoulder and it doesn't burn. "But do you know what brave is? It's being really afraid to do something. I mean so damned scared that you want to crawl underneath your bedsheets and cry until it goes away. But then you pull yourself up and do it anyway. I have a hunch you go through that every day. And yet here you are by my side, aren't you, Wes? My boy. My brave little

Ex-man. You're my favorite Marine." He pretends to look around as if eavesdroppers are behind us. "Shh," he says in a whisper. "You're not supposed to call anyone who hasn't served a Marine. But that's only for the Ords. You're my exception. See? An Ex-ception. My Ex-man." Does he ever know I am laughing inside? Even as I look away.

"Oh, Wes," my mother says, staring into her tea. "I'd give Daddy's pension just to know what goes on inside that head of yours."

No, I think. No, you wouldn't.

MY FAVORITE THINGS

Each member of my family deals with Dad's absence in a different way. I find myself retreating deeper into my quiet vibration land. Mom tries to connect with me. I can feel it. But I just want to look away. I don't think she wants me here. She is happiest when she drops me off at the special school. Then she's free to sit out on the porch and I guess watch the squirrels while she drinks her tea in the morning, wine in the afternoon. She looks scared to me. I just make it worse.

Thomas has his own thing when not taking out his frustrations on petrified quarterbacks under the Friday night lights. I can hear it from all the way up in my bedroom, even though he's out in the garage. The loud crash of cymbals, the deep hum of the bass guitar, the screech of his electric Gibson SG. His band. I lie on the bed in my pajama bottoms and Eli T-shirt on a weekend night and I try to figure out what they're playing through the whining of the amp. Frequencies that assault my sensitive ears like a roaring tinnitus. I don't know what the songs are called. I just know I like one of them. The notes leap out at me and I feel compelled to exit my room and head for the garage. I know this song. Through the distorted ultra-gain crunch of Thomas's 100-watt Marshall, I recognize the chord pattern. I'm very good with patterns. I see them all around. And I hear them too. His solo howls over the backing track so familiar to me. D minor, B flat minor, G minor, C, F, B flat, A, D minor, G minor, A, and back to D minor again. In my mind I run through the transmission but whining amplifiers distort the words in my mind: *Raindrops...roses...whiskers on kittens.* Something's not right. It's the wrong key. Suddenly I'm distressed by this, but I don't know why. I usually don't. I know that I just...am. What's he doing? That's my song.

I look down and follow my feet as the music grows louder. A breezeway connects the detached garage that Thomas has commandeered and made into a music studio while Dad's gone. (Dad sold his shiny black pick-up truck a month ago and gave the money to Mom "just in case." That made her cry. But it made Thomas happy. It freed up space for him to expand into his own life.)

I pass through the crisp night air and open the side door to the garage. The noise hits me like a gust of wind. I can't help myself. I crouch and slam my palms to my ears and scream. "These are a few of my favorite *things!* These are a few of my favorite—"

"Holy shit, Tommy!" shouts the drummer, who immediately stops his pounding. *Things!* "I thought you said he was upstairs."

"Whoa!" adds the lanky bassist. "He okay, dude?"

Thomas turns my way and glares. I scream again. *"Things! Things! Favorite things! Strudel and things! When the dog bites and the bee stings! Things! Things!"* And again...and again. Even as I holler, a softer boy within me knows I shouldn't have come here.

"Dammit, Wes!" Thomas says. "Just once, man! Just fucking once!" He whips his guitar off his shoulder and drops it onto the stand. Then he blows past me through the breezeway and into the house where I hear him shouting. "Mom! *Mom!* Come and get your son please! He's going postal again! I don't need this shit! *Mom!*"

I remain crouched, like a baseball catcher, and my screams subside to a hum as I rock back and forth to calm myself. I expect Dad's strong hands to rest on my shoulder and make the pain disappear like a faith healer. But he's far away now. And bad people are trying to kill him and that makes me moan louder.

"Shit...he okay?" asks the drummer. He shows a look of pity which I get sometimes. But that at least means he's not mad. And that helps.

"Hell, I dunno. Seems kinda whacko to me." I can tell the bassist is a dim kid. If Dad heard him say that…

"Wes?" Mom's voice. Her hands. Icy hot on my shoulders and I shrug them off. "Come on. Let Tommy's band play. Okay? Let's go watch *The Sound of Music*." Mom looks over to Thomas. "Is that what you were playing?" She tries, I guess. But she just doesn't feel it.

"A backing track, yeah," he spits. "So what? It's a cool jam. Chicks love it."

"Oh, for heaven's sake! You know that's his movie. What did you expect?"

Thomas says to me: "I expect that you don't come in here ranting like that, Wes. That's what I expect. It's messed up on so many levels, man."

"Thomas," says Mom. "Boys. Please don't play that song when he's around. Be nice."

"To hell with nice, Mom. It's not fair." My brother's more assertive without Dad to put him in his place like he does one of his privates. I think Mom's a little afraid of him. So am I. He's a big guy. And he knows it.

"Tommy, man," the drummer says with a calming voice. "It's okay. We get it. Your bro's not all there."

Thomas ignores the conciliatory bandmate and glares at Mom. "This is the third time he's done this shit to me. I have a life too, you know."

"Yes, Thomas," she says coldly. "You do. And you're living it. Wes isn't so lucky. And what kind of life does this give *me!*"

The two musicians fidget. This is a conversation for another time, away from strange ears. Mom realizes this and without another word ushers me out of the garage to leave Thomas and his band to play in peace. But they don't play anymore. I hear the bassist's muffled voice through the door. "Let's call it. I'm tired anyway. If you guys want we can practice in my basement next week."

"Fuck it," says Thomas. "Sure, why not. I'm sick of that tune anyway."

Mom escorts me into the family room and sits me down on the couch. "I'll get your iPad. Don't move." As she leaves the room I want to ask her, *What did I do wrong?* The music hurt me, and I screamed. Isn't that what people do? I can't help it. How do I tell her I'm an actor on a stage where everyone but me has the script? I'm lost. Alone. I miss Dad.

Mom returns with my tablet. My movie's already running, and I see Maria Von Trapp twirling in the sunlit hills of Austria. And I'm okay again. At least for a little while.

I hope Dad's safe. I can't wait for him to come home. For a brief moment, she can read my thoughts. "Soon," Mom assures me. "Very soon now." Then the moment is gone.

NOT NORMAL

I'm not allowed to go to the regular middle school down the road. When the principal told him, that really got my dad angry and I think he even tried to force them to let me in. Sitting at the top of the stairs at 7:26 one morning, waiting for the next four minutes to pass before coming down, I heard Mom speaking in a low voice. It's funny how when you're an Ex like me, some people think that what's going on in your mind somehow makes you deaf. But my senses are razors. I just wish I could make more sense of all the information they throw at me every second of every day.

"Peter, there's nothing you can do about it. Just accept it."

"I may get a lawyer," Dad said to Mom quietly. (He knows my ears work, but not even he knows just how well.)

"Why bother?" she shot back. "It's already difficult enough to have any social life with him. Now you want to alienate us, and by 'us' I mean me and Thomas, from the town even more by suing the school?"

"I don't care what people think."

"Of course you don't. You don't need friends. You have the damned Corps. And you go a year at a time when you don't have to live here. Here among the very people who'd despise us for wasting their tax dollars in a lawsuit and then, even if we did win, the extra expense of one special ed teacher they'd need to bring on just for him. Not to mention diminishing the quality of their own kids' educations in the classroom with all the distractions of…" I can tell she paused to gauge whether I'm moving about one floor above her.

"Of what?" Dad said defensively.

"Oh, stop it, Pete. You know what I mean. He shouts. He bangs his head. He rarely talks in full sentences. He sometimes needs a tablet to communicate. He even gets violent sometimes. How on earth could he ever fit in in a regular classroom? Kids can be cruel. They'd just mock him. And you know what?"

"What, Joanne?"

"They'd have a point."

"They'd have a point mocking him?"

"No," she whispered grittily. "Don't you dare suggest I'd ever say such a thing. No, Peter. They'd be right that he belongs with kids like him."

There followed a silence that I read as my father looking away from her. Maybe staring out the window or something. His own conflicts between love and reason raging in him.

"He's got a real condition, Pete. He's not normal. No matter how much you wish him to be. Maybe that's why he hates me. Because I've always seen him for what he is. I accepted this years ago. I wish you would."

"I did." My father cleared his throat. "I have. It's just..." then his voice trailed off.

"I know."

But I didn't know. What I knew was that it was 7:30. Time to head downstairs and visit with the Von Trapps. I still don't know.

SPECIAL SCHOOL DAY

I know it's a school day because Dad—now Mom because Dad's off fighting the war—wakes me up before my usual time. I don't like getting out of bed before I'm ready and sometimes I slap my forehead or yelp in protest. It's the only way to rid me of the pressures I feel. Mom sometimes gets annoyed with me. She's never in a good mood when Dad's away. "Not today, Wesley, please. Give us a break today. Okay, kiddo?" She hauls me to my feet and hands me the laminated cards Dad made a while back to help me dress myself. "Don't go back to bed. It's a school day." I howl again. "Don't you want to see your friend Maria?" This calms me. Maria's in my inner group class of four. She talks a lot. She makes me laugh inside. I'm better now.

Mom disappears and calls to my brother who's getting dressed in his bedroom. I hear the *thump-thump* of Drake music through the door. "Tommy, can you make sure your brother keeps moving, please?"

"Okay, Mom," he says back, emerging in the hallway. "He got his dressing cards?"

The cards have pictures of different articles of clothing on them. They remind me what I need to put on when I start to think about other things and the noises around me clog my brain pipes like bristly hairballs. I match them up with the clothes Mom's hung neatly in my closet. Pants card to pants. Shirt card to shirt. Down the line to my undies.

"You got this, Wes?" Thomas leans against the door jamb watching over me, hands in his pockets. He wears a throwback Lawrence

Taylor jersey over his T-shirt and striped athletic pants. A weathered Giants cap with bill swiveled around the back. I cringe when I see him. He rolls his eyes. "Jesus. Don't worry. I'm one of the good guys, remember? You brush your teeth yet?" I sit on the bed and look down at my feet while pulling the blue socks over them, one then the other. I wriggle my toes. They feel so confined. I prefer bare feet. I like walking in the sand in them and feeling the wet chill on my skin. *I miss you, Dad—* "Come on, Squid, stay focused. Mom! Did he brush?" Thomas likes to call me "Squid." He said because trying to wrestle me down is like trying to pin down a slippery squid. Something like that. I can't decide if I like it. Because I can't decide if it's a term of affection or resentment. Probably both.

"After breakfast," she calls from the kitchen. "Send him down, please."

He steps into the room. "You heard the lady. Time for chow." He reaches for my arm unconsciously. I leap back while batting him away. *Don't touch me! I want Dad!*

He raises his hands in a gesture of neutrality. "Okay, man. Take it easy. All good, bro." He leans in and grits his teeth. "Don't drive Mom to drink, Wes. I swear to God…" I yelp, he backs away. Then he looks at the clock. 7:29. He gets it. "God, what a fucking life. I'm outta here."

At exactly 7:30 I make my way downstairs. I look for my iPad on the bookshelf but it's in the kitchen with Mom. She's laid it on the table next to a plate of bacon and eggs. "No Von Trapps today, Wes. It's a school day, remember?"

Now I do. That's right. It's why I'm already dressed. I sit down at the table. The tablet has several pictures on it. It's an app the school recommends for me while I eat. I grab the bacon and crunch. Then I tap on the picture of the same thing. "Bacon," it says like a girl robot. I sip orange juice and tap again. "Orange juice." Mom watches me. Pale arms folded. Her pretty, if cold, face shows indifference.

Exhaustion. She used to get excited when I did this. ("That's right, Wes! Bacon! Very good!") But now not so much. She just looks tired.

"I can't believe your father's been gone so long already," she says with a sigh. "Just nine months to go. As long as I carried you in me." She aims this at me but I'm not looking at her. She keeps talking as much to herself as me. "What do they say in the service? Count backwards? Like three months in. Not nine to go? Or did I just see that on a war movie once? What do you think, kiddo? Any idea what movie?" (It's *Platoon*. I remember the scene clearly. *"Count backwards... Think positive, dude."*) Mom smiles wanly. "No, I guess you couldn't tell me which one even if you wanted to." The robot voice chimes in as I tap and eat. Eat and tap. "Toast...Bacon...Toast... Orange Juice...Eggs...."

"Well, we know he can eat, anyway." Thomas enters the kitchen and rummages noisily through the refrigerator. He startles me, and I want to hit my head to let it out, but I stay calm.

"Aren't you eating breakfast?" Mom asks to his back.

"No time," he says. "I'll grab something from the machine at school. I got football practice tonight, so I'll be home late again. Bye, Mom. Later, Wes." Then he's gone. A few seconds later I hear a car's ignition, the crunch of tires as it pulls out of the drive, and its engine softens into a faint guttural echo as my brother disappears down the road.

Mom nods in acceptance. Her oldest boy. Her Ord boy, as her absentee husband might call him, is slowly slipping away. Shoulders wide. Voice deep. A shadow on his jaw. Soon he'll be gone like Rebecca. Like Pete. I sense her fears. She dreads a life with just me in the house. I moan as if in sync with her thoughts. She ignores my outburst and just turns to face the window over the sink. She briefly rests her forehead against it and stares out to the rusty blanket of autumn leaves that smothers the backyard. When she stands straight again there's a greasy oval print on the glass. She wipes it off with her sleeve and then turns to face me. I tap. "Breakfast over…Breakfast done… Breakfast…good-bye."

"Yeah, I get it," she says. "Good-bye." She looks at the clock. Relief. The bus will be here soon. "Come on, Wes. Let's brush those teeth before they fall out."

SPECIAL SCHOOL

The little yellow bus pulls up to the house at 8:45. Mom walks me to the opened door and ushers me up the steps into the vehicle. She tries to take me by the hand, but I refuse. *No touching.* "Right," she says. "How silly of me. Well…have a good day at school. Try to behave, okay?" The other kids are already on the bus since I'm the last stop. No one says anything as I climb aboard and take my usual seat, six in to the left, by the aisle. Some look down, or stare through the windows. Others rock and hum and flap their hands trying to shoo away thoughts of leaving home for the day.

We drive past the Franklin Middle School where both my sister and brother went when they were my age. I see the Ord kids with their backpacks and hoodies gazing down at cell phones making their bouncy ways up the sidewalk and into the huge sets of doors to the three-story stone building. Some of the kids wear shorts as if it's still summer. They must be cold. I'm all bundled up. A bunch of the students laugh and talk incessantly, some high-five each other in greeting. They move in packs. A few of them walk by themselves. Islands of solitude. Sad looks on their faces. I guess middle school can even be tough for some of the Ords. What would have happened to me in there? Still, I'd like to have followed in Becca's and Thomas's footsteps. "God's mapped out a different path for you, Wesley," Dad assured me when he broke the news I wouldn't be going to Franklin after all.

My school's a few miles farther away, near the town center. A one-story limb to the whitewashed Catholic church where we also try to attend mass every Sunday unless I'm really in a mood. Sometimes I just can't take being bombarded by all the singing, the smells of incense, the standing, sitting, standing, kneeling, standing, chanting. The wooden pews creak. People cough. Babies cry. Mom sometimes takes me out of the mass halfway through. We wait outside and listen to the muted sounds of the organ and choir while I bat my forehead and scream. Mom produces a cigarette from her bag and lights it up. "His will be done," she says, chuckling to herself. It's a defeated, resigned laugh.

My special school is private. They just rent the space from the parish. Every once in a while, I'll encounter one of the stern-faced nuns from the small convent across the tree-lined street, cloaked in their habits, like scowling penguins. I don't think they like our school very much. "They like the rent, though," Mom once snorted when Dad made the same observation.

I don't know about that. I'm not sure what rent means. But I know that I like the school. Antoinette's my primary care instructor. We're one-on-one here. She knows not to touch me. Although as I get older, I sometimes want to feel her skin against mine, but this idea just confuses me more and gets me real agitated, so I try to put those thoughts away. I like the way she smells, and she has flowing brown hair as if she's always in one of those shampoo commercials. I wish I could look into her eyes. They're big and blue. She's nice to me. She waits for me along with the other teachers at the bus drop-off. I step onto the curb and she approaches.

"There's my favorite man in my life! How are you today, Wes?"

I don't look at her as we head indoors. I follow her heels, counting the number of concrete squares that make up the walkway from the bus stop to the main doors of the school. *Clip-clop-clip-clop. One...two...three...four...*each step is like one and a half squares by Antoinette's stride, so I try to do the math. Seventeen strides. *Clip-clop.* Then we're inside. It should be twenty-four-point-six squares. I moan as I realize my number's off. It must be twenty-five. "Twenty-five! Twenty-five!" I shout. She just keeps walking. "That's right, Wes. Twenty-five squares." I hear the scrape of her ballpoint pen on the paper attached to the clipboard. She always carries a clipboard. I like the smell of her perfume. Her shirt's light blue. Like her eyes. "Blue shirt, blue eyes, blue sky," I say as we make our way with the rest of the kids into the hallway where we hang up our coats and lay down our heavy book bags.

"Oh, you like my blouse? I just bought it. That's sweet of you to notice, Wes." More scraping pen on paper.

The days here are good for me. Ordered. No change in the routine. It's difficult enough for me to just make sense of all I see and hear and smell without any surprises. I hang my coat on the same hook. I follow Antoinette into the same room for period one. We play the same games in the same common space with the netted trampoline, the stationary bikes, and the colorful mats over parquet. Seventy-seven scuffed wooden squares make up the floor. Then we go to a classroom and sit at a table. I use the tablet to identify objects Antoinette puts in front of me. "What's this?" she asks. The tablet translates: "bahloon." "Right! Balloon! Awesome!" Silly Antoinette, just because I hate to talk doesn't mean I don't know what everything is. I can hear my dad from within my brain's shadowlands. A distant recollection from when I was a little boy. Complaining to Mom: "Heck, I bet the kid can do calculus if given the chance. Instead they got him punching 'ball' and 'hat'? C'mon." He's right. I do like numbers. But what good is what's going on inside me if no one knows? Dad knows. Mom wants to know but is too frustrated to break through to me. Maybe someday. I don't think Thomas and Becca really care anymore. Antoinette cares. I look down at the table and slap it a few times to get the bugs out of me, but then she'll show me a peach and I'll glance up briefly at the glass square, see the word P-E-A-C-H, and tap it.

"Peach," it says. "Very good, Wes. What's this one?" All the while she scribbles on her clipboard.

Lunchtime. My usual ham and cheese, plain bread, mustard. Box of juice. Six Oreos. Antoinette sits across from me and picks at the salad she's packed in a plastic container. She usually starts to look tired by this time. Her smiles are less frequent. They fade quickly. It's a long day for her. She has to tell me to stop slapping my thigh twelve times. Don't hit my temple twice. After three screams that's enough. We need to behave, she says. Pen to clipboard. But sometimes I feel like I'm one of those exchange students Thomas talks about. There's a boy from Thailand who at first didn't speak and seemed lost. Bewildered. A counselor took him around. For a while he had no idea where to go, what to say, and I know people laughed at him. That's the way I feel everywhere. Almost all the time.

Sometimes the frustration is so great, the agitation so strong, I have to let it out. A scream, a slap to the head. People frown at me, but is this so strange? I know whenever Thomas has a game in the morning he plucks his eyebrows and bites his nails until they bleed. Becca would constantly twirl her hair at the dinner table the night before a big test.

"It's not such odd behavior," Antoinette often explains to my mother who seems lost with how to deal with me whenever Dad's off fighting the bad guys. "If he was a five-year-old engaging in such stress-relieving actions, no one would think twice about it."

"But he's fourteen," Mom says dully. Exhausted.

"I know, Missus Scott. I'm just trying to put it in some perspective for you. Wes has many gifts. I truly believe that. But social skills, to put it mildly, are not among them."

"Not yet, anyway," Mom says with forlorn hope.

"We'll see. Every child on the spectrum is different. There's only so much we can do for him," my teacher reminds her gently, bringing her back to the ground.

Mom shakes her head. "Do you know until he was eighteen months, he seemed perfectly normal? Then it's like he just shut down to the outside world. We still don't understand what happened to him."

"No one does. Autism Spectrum Disorder is still a mystery in many ways. Mainly because it's such a broad spectrum, as the name implies."

"Did we do anything? Maybe the vaccines?"

Antoinette shrugs. "I'm not a doctor nor a clinical researcher. All I can say is the literature I've read debunks this theory. It's just a combination of genetics and environment. But that's really all we know."

"You know, Miss…"

"Olensky."

Mom chuckles weakly. "Funny, I thought you're Italian. I can't even read you right, let alone my own son."

Antoinette folds her arms. "It's my married name. Garguilo's my maiden name. But we try to keep things on a first-name basis here. Familiarity puts the kids at ease. And it establishes trust."

"Oh." Mom beats back an urge to cry. "It's such a helpless feeling. Even if, God forbid, our son was sick, like with an infection, or a cancer, at least we'd understand it. At least we'd know what treatment options are out there and, sad to say in some cases, how it's going to end. But with ASD, we don't know how he got it, we don't know where it's going, and we don't know what will happen to him when we're gone."

"You're not alone, Missus Scott. My advice is just take it one day, one small triumph, at a time."

"I guess I really have no choice in the matter, do I?"

Antoinette smiles. "He's a good kid. Always try to remember that. There's a very interesting and beautiful person in there somewhere. We just have to try to find him together."

❧

We don't eat lunch by ourselves. The other kids and their teachers join us in the cafeteria that doubles as a playroom. The walls have letters and numbers on them. The numbers I get. There's a happy regularity to them. I like the numbers that are perfect. You can't cut them in two. One...two...three... five...seven...eleven...thirteen. They're honest. But the letters, even though there are only twenty-six, force me to step outside of my world. To "be creative" as my best friend Maria says. She likes to talk. She talks and talks and talks while her own teacher, Diane, scribbles on her own clipboard. Maria rocks constantly and her hands whip like flailing tentacles. She's all energy. Movement after movement. We don't look at each other but she chatters all the time. I hear Diane say once to another supervisor that Ria, as Diane calls her, is hypo-something. She doesn't feel much pain, so she has bandages on her and sometimes a cast. She sometimes bites her arm. Diane stops her whenever she does this and writes on her own clipboard. Some days Maria bangs her head against a wall pretty hard, making her forehead bleed even, and I scream. It's so loud. Diane pulls her away and whisks her to the bathroom to find the first aid kit. I get pretty upset. But Antoinette calms me down and explains it to me as I rock and stare down at my new shoes. "Sometimes she just wants to feel something, Wes. Anything at all." We all feel that way sometimes.

Today Maria's happy. "Hi Wes. Hello Wes. What's shakin'? What's cookin'? How's Trix? How's life? See any good movies lately? You like rainbows? Look at this pony. Is it gonna rain? You think we can play on the tramp? Bet ya can jump real high..." She comes at me like a machine gun. Then she fades for a second, as if to reload. I shake my head trying to collate all the different bits of data she hurls at me, but inside she makes me smile through the chaos. I'm lost but I know there's something good there. When Maria's around I don't have to say a thing. And she has pretty hands. Tan and smooth. Someday I may touch them. Maybe after Dad comes home. I miss Dad. But school's okay. I just wish I could be at the middle school with all the Ords. Sometimes life doesn't give you what you want, though. I learn that every time Dad goes away. I don't need Antoinette to tell me.

SKYPING

It must be a special day because we're all together at the dining room table. All of us except Dad. I'm confused why he's not here if it's Christmas. Carols are playing, and the house is decorated. "We have to keep up appearances," Mom says to Becca when she enters the house and compliments her on the tree. Thomas is here too. We sit at the table facing an opened laptop like it's a religious statue. Thomas fiddles with it while Becca scans her text messages and I rock back and forth to beat away the confusion. I know to the family, the music on the iPad player is soft. *"Hark the herald angels sing…Glory to the new-born king!"* To me the children's choir sounds like a stadium of voices all screeching in my ear. I start to moan, and Mom picks up my mood.

"Rebecca, turn off the music."

She looks up from her phone. "Why? I like it. It's Charlie Brown."

Mom grits her teeth and motions towards me as I rock and coo. "Why do you think?"

My sister exhales. "Fine." She disappears into the living room and the music stops.

Now the sound of the Peanuts gang is replaced in the void by the clickety-click of my brother's nails against the iBook's keyboard. But it's tolerable. "That boy's got some sensitive ears," he says while focusing on the commands he's giving to the lighted screen. "I bet if it was *Sound of Music* he wouldn't be so uptight."

"Please don't give him any ideas," Becca says as she returns from the kitchen and sits back down at the table. "What time is it over there, anyway?"

"Almost midnight," Mom says. "Half a world away."

I do the math in my head and come up with eight time zones. "Five thousand nine hundred miles," I blurt out.

"I'll have to Google that later," says Thomas. "On second thought, I'll take your word for it, Wes." My brother taps the touchpad and there's a ring, like a warbling dove. It's a phone. *Ring. Ring.* I look up from my shoes and press my arms tight to my side as I rock. Suddenly Dad's face appears on the screen!

I briefly look up and see the mottled image of Dad in his tanned camouflage fatigues and cap. He wiggles slightly as he adjusts the camera on his end. Then he's in the center of the screen. There's what looks like a hangar behind him. A Huey helicopter, I think. He smiles at his family from the far side of the world, well past the horizon line I ponder when he and I walk the beach.

"Hey guys," he says in his baritone voice. "How's my favorite squad holding up?"

"Daddy!" cries Becca. "My gosh, you look good."

"Yeah, Dad," says Thomas. "Nice duds. Can you get me one of them desert jackets?"

"I'll see what I can do, Tee. Becks, you staying out of mischief in Manhattan?"

She nods. "Only the bad kind."

"I'll take it."

"How are you, Peter?" Mom asks with a smokiness to her voice. This is how she sounds when she's about to cry. I've heard it several times since he left home. Usually when she thinks I'm not listening. But I'm always listening. I'm here.

"Oh, you know," he says. "Things are a grind. It's damned hot for one thing."

"Are you staying safe?"

He hesitates. "As safe as I can be. It's not an amusement park here, as you may have seen on the news." I know what he's saying. It's scary over there. He can get hurt there. This thought makes me moan as I peer at a chip in the wooden table.

"That my youngest Marine?"

Mom nudges me. "Say hello to your father, Wes." I moan again. "Say anything at all. Let him know you can hear him at least."

"Hi, Wesley," he says. His voice is softer now. "There's a lot of sand here. But no crabs, I'm afraid."

"No crabs," I say back.

"No crabs," he replies. I don't look at him, but I can tell he's smiling. I made him happy by saying that.

"Maybe in the marshes by the Tigris," he says. "But not in downtown Tikrit."

"Where the hell's that?" asks my brother.

"Go on Google Maps and find 'Nowhere.' Then type in for the address 'The Middle.' That's where I am."

"Oh, Peter," says Mom. "It must be difficult for you. We miss you very much, hon."

His voice whispers back, "I miss you too, Bug. I love you guys."

"We love you too," says Becca. Now she's on the verge of tears too. I groan and slap my head. My sister glares at me. "Stop it, Wes! He doesn't need to hear this now."

"And we do?" adds Thomas. He cringes. If Dad was here, he might smack him on the back of his head for saying such a thing. Dad always protects me when he's around. But he's not here. He's way over there. He doesn't say anything. No one does.

Dad seems different. Like a once-sharp blade that's been filed down to a nub by the world he's in. I can't explain it. I can only feel it. There's a darkness to him. He's a Marine again.

He and the family talk for a little bit more. Subjects include Thomas's football, Becca's job, Mom's loneliness, and the bills. They talk about my school. I don't pay attention. My thoughts rattle through my brain like maraca sands and I just can't make sense of why he has to go so far away. I don't care about bad guys on the other side of the planet. I want him home. Right in front of me. I want to walk the beach with him again. I want him to kiss me goodnight and, when I need to scream, to soothe me and let me know all will be okay. But he's just a blurry image on a laptop screen. I look up and catch him smiling at me. His hand reaches out until it fills the screen. I want to touch it. I want to feel his skin on mine. His calloused hands. His Marine hands. I raise my arm…but then he suddenly stands up and looks around him as if something's just distracted him. We see his waist now. There's a loud noise.

"Peter, what was that?" my mother says with a start. "What's happening?"

"Dad, is that thunder?" asks Thomas.

"In the desert?" snaps Becca impatiently. "Daddy, are you okay?"

He bends down so his face is in our view again and forces a smile. "Hey guys, I gotta run. I'm sure it's nothing. You all take care of your mother for me. Rebecca, try not to be a stranger to her, okay? And Thomas, be nice to your brother. He's the only one you have."

"Please be careful!" cries my mother.

"We love you, Daddy!" His daughter who was too busy to spend his last night at home suddenly feels the urge to call to him.

"Love you too!" Another rumble. It's not thunder.

My mother cries now. "Oh God, please don't let—"

"I have to go now!"

He abruptly reaches off-screen. The laptop goes black. And he's gone.

PEPPER SPRAY

I sit at the kitchen table with the low winter sun piercing through the bay window. The tablet laying on its distressed wooden surface chimes at me as I drink my box of fruit juice. "Bicycle." I search the pad for the drawing of the bike and the letters B-I-C-Y-C-L-E. I tap it. "Pear." I tap the P-E-A-R and sip. There's tension in the air. I don't know why. It's a bright day out. But the house feels dark. Somber. Mom is out of the house. If I heard her right, Dad is home! Becca's come from New York for one of her rare visits, so today must be important. Thomas sits across from me slurping cereal, and I feel him watching me. His glare burns my skin like a heat lamp.

"Thomas. What Thomas? What? Thomas. Thomas!" I blurt out.

"Nothing," he says.

"What? What? What?"

"Stop saying that. Jesus you're like a damned skipping record."

"Skip, skip," I say. I'm not sure why. I just like how it sounds.

He suddenly looks around as if to make sure we're alone. Then he leans in and grabs my wrist.

"No!" I shout. But he holds me tight in a lobster-claw grip. I think he's trying to hurt me.

His voice is low. Threatening. I'm scared. "Listen, Wes. I don't know if you can hear what I'm saying with all that shit in your brain. But if you can, then hear me good and loud. Mom's getting Dad from the base airport and bringing him home today. And I don't know what he's gonna be like. You understand?" *My arm! Let me go! No touch!* "Something bad happened that she hasn't told us yet. He got

• 36 •

hurt over there. A lot of the guys in his company were wasted. And I'm a little ticked off about it all right now. I mean I'm a live wire, in the red. So I don't need you screaming and hollering like some fucking werewolf when he walks through that door."

I stare at the tablet and try not to scream as his grip cuts off my circulation. Thomas is an angry boy. Always was. I try to shake my arm loose from his grip, but he won't let go of me! "Do...you... understand...me...Wes," he hisses. There's a silence. The pain in my arm swells. I can't take it. Then I explode!

I grab his hand and pull it to my mouth and bite down! I can taste the salt on his flesh, then the bitter wetness of his blood. "Jesus Christ!" he howls and rips his injured hand out of my grinding mouth. I wipe a maroon paste off my lips. He leaps to his feet and I follow for some reason. I'm not afraid of him. Not when I get like this. I can't control it any more than I can my own breathing. I'm in a rage now. "Don't touch!" I yell as I lunge for him.

He instinctively deploys his football reflexes—16.0 sacks, national average 1.19—to laterally evade my tackle and I crash into a cabinet and fall to the ground. I beat my head and moan and roll as a tidal wave of emotion drowns me. Then I'm on my feet. I feel strong and I want to strike out. *Who hurt Dad! Don't touch me!* In my wrath I hear Thomas calling desperately for me to stop. His own anger gone now, replaced by primordial fear for his life. "Becca!" he shouts while backing away from me as a careless hiker would a surprised grizzly bear. "He's going nuts! Get in here with that stuff! Hurry!" I make a move at him, but then a searing mist laces my face and my only thought now is to wipe it from my eyes before it burns into my sockets. I roar and collapse on the ground.

"He's fucking lost it!" I hear Thomas say.

Becca's breathless voice answers: "What'd you do to him?"

"What'd *I* do to *him*? He came at me!"

I furiously rub my burning eyes as all aggression in me drains away. Mucous gushes from my nose and I want to scream but can't. I sit up with my back to the cabinet under the sink and rock gently. I hear water flowing from the faucet above me and then feel a wet dishrag dabbing my eyes. The touch is gentle. Feminine.

"I'm sorry I had to do that, Wes," Becca says softly. "You can't attack people anymore. You're getting too big for that. You could really hurt someone."

"Don't touch!"

"I'm not touching you, okay? Just let me get the pepper spray out of your eyes." My vision starts to return, and I see soft shadow and light where there was just a fiery darkness before.

"Careful, Becca," warns Thomas through the haze. "He hits."

Her voice stays calm. "He won't hit me. Will you, Wes." She puts the dripping rag in my hand and lets me wipe away the repellant more vigorously. I hear her admonish my brother: "He has fingerprints on his wrist, Thomas. Did you do that?"

"I just…yeah."

"Why? Why would you do that? You know how he gets."

"I didn't want him to go apeshit when Dad comes home. He wasn't listening."

She pauses. "Sometimes I think you're just…" Her voice trails off. "Get out of here. I'll watch him."

"Dad'll be home any minute," he says. Then he looks up at the ceiling. I've never seen this look on my brother before. "Becca, I'm real scared."

She stands up and leans cross-armed against the countertop. My eyes work again, and I wipe my nose but stay seated on the floor. "I know. Me too. I don't even think Mom knows how bad he is. Or if she does, she hasn't told anyone." My sister looks down at me. "You think maybe he does? Maybe he has like a sixth sense about these things. Like a clairvoyant?"

Thomas snorts as he turns to leave. "I don't think he knows anything at all. Except what a bicycle looks like. And the Von Trapps. Nice fucking life."

She calls to his back, louder to be heard over my moaning. "You know, you could care about your brother more."

He turns. "I know, Becca. I've been hearing that every day of my life. From the time when he stopped talking and Mom and Dad finally admitted that he's never said a Goddamned complete sentence since. That's all I hear. 'Be kind to Wes. Care about Wes. We love Wes.' Yeah? Well, what about me?"

"What about you? You sound pretty selfish."

He laughs sarcastically. "Says the sister who ran away to New York and we only see at weddings and funerals."

"I'm here now, aren't I?" she says softly. I can tell that hurt.

"Who's to say it isn't a funeral?" Thomas says. And then he disappears into the living room. I hear NCAA football fire up on the TV. And I close my eyes and wonder. Whose funeral?

HOMECOMING

"P-L-E-A-S-E...G-O-D," I type into the tablet with one finger from each hand. "Let...Daddy...be...okay." I have it on silent mode so no one can hear it. Becca leans over to try and read it, but I block her view with my arms, like a hawk protecting its kill.

"What'cha writing, Wes?"

I tap it to save, unmute it, and then flip to the pictures app. I see one and type: "F-L-O-W-E-R." The robot voice recites the word.

"Yep." She smiles. "It's a flower. Very pretty." She puts her hand on my shoulder and I shrug it away violently. "Right," she says. "So sorry." My sister sits down next to me and runs her hand through her short hair. She stares out the bay window to the back yard. "I'm worried about Daddy. Aren't you?"

I say nothing. I tap again. "B-O-O-K."

"Yeah," she sighs. "That's a book, alright." She places her elbows on the table and rests her face in the palm of her hands. "Must be nice to live in your own world. You have no clue what's happening, do you? Lucky squirt." She looks at me. "Hey. Your eyes okay?" I moan. "I hated doing that. But you were getting too rough. You're getting bigger, Wes. You can hurt someone now. Even Thomas. You know that old expression? It's not the size of the man in the fight but the fight in the man? Well, that second guy. That's you now. It's scary, Wes." I tap out the word Q-U-I-L-T. I'm not looking at her. "Quilt. Sure. I guess it's not your fault." She rubs her eyes in exhaustion. Then she raises her head. "I hear the car." In the other room, the Ohio State-Iowa game goes soft.

"Hey guys," calls out Thomas from the living room. "They're here."

Becca rubs her temples with her fingertips and then peers out the far window. She can see the car pull up to the driveway. I hear a car door open and then close with a loud *chunk*. Becca watches the scene outside then closes her eyes. "Oh, God."

⟡

"Kids," Mom calls. "Your father's home."

My sister pushes her chair away from the table and stands slowly, as if she's lifting fifty pounds on her back. She exhales and seems to be bracing herself for something. I'm still sitting, trying not to look up at her, but our eyes meet briefly before I turn away. I see anxiety in her face. I rock and hum softly to open the pressure valve. She looks down at me and forces a smile. "Let's go, baby brother. Daddy's back. Just, well, go easy if you can. Okay?"

The football game in the living room goes quiet and I hear Mom talking to Thomas. "Where are Wes and Rebecca? I know your father would like to see you all at once. I'll go get him."

I'll go get him? I don't understand what she means by that. Why would she have to get him?

Becca walks towards the next room and then turns to face me. "Come on, Wes."

I don't want to get up. I rock harder. There's something bad in the air. Like the vaguely foul odor of a dead animal trapped behind Sheetrock. And I realize then that my dad was hurt by the bad guys. The one thing I feared. The thing that picked at my brain in the darkness. A tormenting blackbird visiting me in the night. "How bad? How bad?" I mutter.

Becca says calmly, "I don't know, Wes. I couldn't see much from the window." She steps over to offer me her hand. The same hand that just sprayed burning mist in my eyes. I shake my head. "Fine. I tried." She leaves the room for good.

•41•

I sit and moan and poke my finger on the tablet. S-C-A-R-E-D. Then I type some more.

In a few minutes, I hear the familiar voice. "There you guys are!"

"Daddy!"

"Hey…Dad."

Hugs and backslaps. "Oh, it's good to see you." His voice sounds different. Weak. That deep baritone replaced by something light. "Where's my Ex-man?" He tries to say this with enough force behind it to sound enthusiastic. But I can hear the exhaustion in his voice.

I shut down the tablet and stand. I start to walk slowly towards the living room. My eyes focus on the hardwood slats beneath my shuffling Nikes. *One…two…three…four.* I cross the saddle into the next room. The voices go silent and I force myself, with all my might, to raise my eyes and find my dad. I will only do this for him. I'm his Ex-man. His young Marine.

I see him now. Thomas and Becca stand at either side of him. Mom is behind him. Dad isn't standing up. He's sitting in a wheel-chair. As I scan him to try and figure out what's different, I spot the metal poles where his calves and ankles should be. A wooden cane lays across his lap, traversing the armrests like a roller coaster's safety bar. He wears a ruby-red sweat suit with the letters *USMC* in yellow across his chest. But my eyes dart back to his legs. *They're gone.* Just the metal poles peeking out between the pant legs and the bunched-up socks and sneakers. Where are they?

"No legs!" I cry. Thomas shoots me a searing look.

"I know, Son," Dad says calmly. The pain comes through his voice like a fog. "I know. But the rest of me's still here."

With a grimace he pushes himself up from the chair with his arms until he stands wobbly before me. Mom reaches for his bicep to stabilize him, but he waves her off. He grabs his cane and jams it to the ground. Just the effort of standing up on his fake legs has him popping sweat beads on his forehead…on which I see a new jagged scar. There's another scar on his cheek too. *What happened to him?*

"No legs," I moan again. "Legs! Legs! Le—"

"Shut up, Wes!" blurts Thomas as he fights off tears.

Dad turns to him and struggles to maintain his balance as he puts a hand on his older son's shoulder. "It's okay, Tee. It must be hard for him to understand."

"I don't understand it either," my mother says with a cracked voice. Dad ignores her and focuses on me. Then he takes an uneasy step forward. Even though he's thinner now, the cane totters under his weight. He's not used to walking on his metal limbs yet. This is a man who jogs three miles a day, and plays tennis, and leads his company on long marches through rugged mountains. Now he struggles to even take three steps towards his youngest boy. I look down and shuffle my feet as he approaches.

"Hello, Wesley," he says. "I can't wait for us to walk on the beach again." I slap my hand against my thigh, trying to exorcise the confusing signals humming in my spinning brain. The static is so loud in my ears I can barely hear him. The knob is on ten.

He puts his hand on my shoulder and I grimace, but I don't pull away. Mom looks on with a mixture of sadness and what? Envy perhaps? No, more like resentment. Only Dad can touch me. She doesn't get why. It pains her. She wants to hold her boy. But she can't. And that's how it is.

"Home," I say.

"Yes, Son. I'm home."

IMAGES

7:28...7:29...7:30. Time to head downstairs and watch *The Sound of Music*. I find my tablet in the kitchen drawer and make my way to the den. This morning I'm not alone. It's too cold to sit out on the porch so Mom rests on the leather couch, staring blankly at a TV screen that's shut off, its black square facing her from the other wall. She seems to be looking through it. As if something on the other side has answers, but she just can't find them.

Dad sleeps upstairs. He sleeps a lot in the weeks since he's been home. Every now and then, I'll hear him roll out of bed to use the bathroom. The clumsy *bumpety-bump* sound his cane makes as he pulls himself along on his new metal legs resonates in my ears. I hear it now, one floor above me. Mom glances up at the ceiling, and I see she's been crying and her eyes are red. She looks over to me standing against the wall, shifting my weight back and forth, back and forth like a metronome.

"Oh. Hello, Wes. Is it that time already?" Silence. "I guess you want to watch your movie?"

I slap my thigh with my free hand. "Von Trapp!" I say.

She closes her eyes. "Yeah, I know." I approach the couch and notice that her laptop sits on the coffee table. It's open and in sleep mode. I sit down next to her and lay my tablet on the leather cushion and make a move to tap a key on the iBook to bring it back to life.

"Please don't," she says. But I do it anyway.

Dad's face, younger, unscarred, suddenly emerges on the screen. I stare at his image. It's only real eyes, in the flesh, that compel me to turn away. This is just a picture. It's the man I know. The man who walks with me along the sandy shoreline. Not the man who spends most of his time in the bedroom alone.

"Will you ever listen to me?" Mom says. The weariness of life is in her voice.

I analyze the portrait of her husband as a freshly commissioned Marine officer in his dress blues and white visor cap. That's not the man upstairs. Something real bad happened to him over on the other side of the world and it's changed him. I sense it in the very air I breathe around him. Mom knows it too. I think she's trying to remember who Dad is. But she finds it hard to remember now as she too contemplates the shuffling sounds directly above us. A toilet flushes. More bumps. A muffled groan. Then silence again.

I begin to scroll through the other photos she's called up onto the screen. I see her hand come into view. She tries to stop me, but I shove her away with some force.

"Dammit, Wes!" she seethes. "Can't anyone ever touch you but... *him?*" Her rejected hand points to my dad on the screen. "I gave birth to you, for shit's sake. I carried you, fed you, gained forty pounds for you. I puked in the morning and fought off heartburn in the evening for you. Do you even know what I've given up in my life? Do you know anything at all? Do you even care?" I stare at Dad. Her quavering voice comes to me in waves. "Look at me. Just once look at me and not him." I reach for the tablet and I start to rock while cradling the iPad to my chest. I need to retreat to the hills of Austria. This is too much for me.

"Von Trapp," I mutter. "Von Trapp! Climb every mountain!" Mom's agitating me like she always does. I want to escape to the captain's mansion by the lake and sing with Maria, and Liesl, and Kurt. I don't want to be here, next to Mom. I want her to go away. She's making me sad because she's sad. I want my dad back, so I stare at his image…his intact, unwounded image. His smile that tells me I'm no Ord. That I'm his Marine.

"To hell with the Von Trapps!" my mother snorts. "This is real life. Do you know what that is? Do you understand what's happened to your father at all? Do you care? Are you even capable of feelings?" She takes a deep breath. "Look at me. Please. Look at me just once like you do him. He's not who he was, Wes." She starts to sob. "Nothing's as it was. Goddamn this life!"

While she leans back in the couch and wipes tears from her eyes, I ignore her and scroll through the images as the laptop fan whirs loudly in my ears. One of them in particular shows Marine Captain P. Scott and one of his platoons in full combat dress and helmets on patrol in some dusty, dun-colored street on the far side of the world. Snapped by a *Time* magazine combat photographer as they take a break amidst the rubble of a smoldering, war-ravaged town. They look so serious, nervously alert, like they know angry faces peer down at them from every window and rooftop. Their wary eyes bore through the camera lens and into me. Behind them, in the distance, plumes of black smoke rise from jagged desert hills. A gray smudge in the mustard-yellow sky looks to be a Huey helicopter swooping in low. I gaze into my dad's sallow eyes for a long time, and he stares back at me. What's he thinking here?

This picture was snapped just days before the bad thing happened. Before his world changed, and with it ours. No one tells me, but I heard Mom telling Thomas and Becca in the kitchen one night while I sat up on the top of the steps how it happened. She says he was attacked the night we Skyped with him. A truck driven by a bad guy crashed through the sentry post into Dad's compound and detonated a bomb that blew apart a barracks where he and his men were housed. More trucks with more bombs blew up all around him as he was trying to help his men, and he was buried for hours in rubble, his legs pinned and crushed by a falling wall. I have this vision of him lying helpless within the dark prison of his crumbled-concrete-and-twisted-rebar tomb. He listens in helpless despair to the pandemonium and shouts and thumping of helicopter blades…but no outside sounds are loud enough to drown out the shrieks of agony coming from his men either trapped in the debris nearby or lying in heaps in the early morning light above him. Sometimes I feel my own life is like Dad's trapped in that tomb. Just hints of light through the cracks. Time to think. Time to be scared. But then I can stand up and walk when the storm passes.

"Pain," I say. I tap the track pad on Mom's laptop more intently now. I want to see more.

"Wes, please don't," she says again. But I keep tapping. She tries to pull my arm away, but it burns, and I scream and cover my ears. She recedes. Then back to the screen. *Tap…tap…tap.*

A baby. Newborn. Cloth cap swaddled in a blanket. Little pink hands peek through the folds curled in little fists. Eyes closed. "Baby Annabel" written on the hospital label laid across her chest for the photo.

"Goddammit," Mom says through bared teeth. "How did that get in these?" She makes another move for my hand, violent and sharp, and I smack it away and howl. She rubs her hand and looks at me wide-eyed, too stunned to say anything more. Now my mother's afraid of me (I'm getting pretty big), but I quickly return to equilibrium and tap the misplaced photo away. I notice in the top corner of the desktop there's an image file labeled "Annabel" and I know it belongs there. How many images of the sister I never knew, the daughter Mom never got to raise, are in there? I know Mom wishes I was her and she was me. It's not my fault I am the way I am. It's not my fault I only have one sister. But Mom sometimes makes me feel like everything's my fault. I don't know. *Tap tap.*

Next image. I study a black-and-white photo downloaded from some military blog she came across. It's a wounded Marine being carried away from the bomb crater by three determined corpsmen, one hoisting him under each arm and the other shuffling backwards while holding the shattered man's thighs as his mangled lower legs loosely dangle over the blood-soaked ground. The wounded man in the photo is Dad. Across the top the caption reads: "Carnage In Iraq: Wave Of Suicide Bombers Hits The Marines." Dad survives the attack, but his legs are too mangled to save and they cut them both off at the knees. The surgery saves his life, but it takes more than his legs from him. He's not the man who left us. He screams in his sleep now. He rarely comes out of his room. I think something's broken inside him. I'm scared. I don't think he's going to be with us for very long.

Mom worries too. I can read it in her face. I see regret beneath the cold mask. I understand what lies beneath. She asks her dark apparition on the empty TV screen looking back at her, how could she marry a Marine? With all those other men who wanted her. I once heard Mom telling a friend over the phone that Rebecca had been "an accident." But I didn't know what she meant by that. My sister looks fine to me...when I see her, which isn't much. But as I get older, I think I'm starting to understand. My mother's trapped. Trapped by the life of a military wife, and now the wife of a hobbled man whose heart I think was left behind with his dead men in the rubble and sands of Iraq. Trapped by the reliance on her father's money to live the lifestyle we do along with his endless stream of *told-you-so*s. Trapped by the burdens of three children who drain her of resources, strength, spirit, life itself, for so little she feels she gets in return besides her oldest son's constant requests to borrow the car keys, her only daughter's promises to call from New York in a week...or sooner if she needs money for rent. And worst of all, she's trapped by her life tied to me. I'm the stone. The field pack she can never sluff off her shoulders. She once called me a word I didn't know and so I looked it up on my tablet. It hurt me deeply when I read the definition:

"Ubiquitous. U-bi-quit-ous. /yoō BIKwədəs/: (Adjective.) Always present. Or found everywhere."

That's it, isn't it? She can never get away from me. Ever. I will be old and gray and still with her as I am now. To Dad, I'm extraordinary. To Mom, I'm *ubiquitous.* Doesn't she love me? Is she capable of loving me?

There's something else I feel in her. Anger. She's mad at my dad for putting her in this situation. I was in my room yesterday. She didn't know because I was on my tablet quietly writing and was in a trance of sorts. I get like that sometimes when I really concentrate. So she was standing in the doorway to the master bedroom, peering in as her wounded husband slept. (He's still in a lot of pain so he takes a lot of pills to make it go away. They also make him drowsy. That and the bottle of something Thomas calls "Jack" on the nightstand.) I couldn't hear clearly, but it sounded like she was saying something to his sleeping form. "You had to go for another tour, didn't you. You selfish son of a bitch. Now what am I supposed to do, Pete? Tell me that, dear husband. Now what am I supposed to do?"

JUST TALK TO HIM

I'm on my way to school but this morning the sequence is different. I'm not on the bus. Instead I sit in the back seat of Mom's SUV. She's driving while Dad sits in the passenger seat next to her. He doesn't talk much anymore. He never smiles anymore. This morning's no different. He leans his head on the window and contemplates the returning greenery of fresh leaves and the spring sun, now higher in the sky than the day he returned to us. I hum and bark. I really want to be on the bus. It's what I do every day and I don't like this break in the routine. This whole ride-to-school thing seems off to me and I'm not sure how to process it. The strangest thing to me is the blue laminated slip of paper with the white wheelchair symbol dangling from the rear-view mirror. My dad hates it, but Mom insists we use it. It lets us park closer to wherever we need to go, making it easier on her disabled husband. *Disabled.* That's a word she uses when talking to Grampa Frank or one of her friends, but she never says it in front of him.

"Just talk to him, Pete," Mom says as she focuses her eyes on the road ahead. "Maybe he can help. It's what he does."

"There's no point," he replies.

"It can't hurt, though, can it?"

"Can he talk a pair of legs back onto me?" Dad says bitterly.

"No, he can't. But he can help you talk about your experiences. Get them out in the open instead of bottled up inside."

"What the hell does a shrink know about war?"

My mom tries to put a positive face on it, but I sense her patience eroding. "He came recommended by the VA. He's a vet too. You know, you're not the only one with problems, Captain. I mean, it's okay to feel this way. But, dammit, you've got to talk about this to someone who can help. Clearly I'm no consolation to you."

As my mom grows angrier and more animated, she forgets I'm in the back seat. Or maybe she just thinks I can't comprehend the gravity of the discussion in front of me. But I see it all too clearly. Dad's slipping. He's consumed by what happened to him over there. There's no way his lost legs, severe as it is, can be the sole root of it. It's not like him to go to pieces over something that's only happened to him. He's lost something far more than two limbs. I groan in anger at the bad guys who did this to him. I want him back!

"What can you tell me?" my dad says as he turns to face her. "That everything will be okay? That those men who died, well, what are you gonna do, sweetie. It happens in war."

Mom's face contorts. "Well, who the hell told you to stay in the Goddamned military! You have a family. And you'd already done two tours. Do you mean to tell me there was no way you could have sat this one out behind a desk? Where the only danger was burning your tongue on hot coffee! Why did you do this to me?"

Dad just looks at her. "Did this to you. Of course. I see the woman with two legs is still as selfish as ever. All the things your father gave you, but empathy somehow was never in the gift bag."

"That's not fair, Pete, and you know it. Look at you. Look at us. You've retreated from this family. From your friends. From the world. How many hours of TV up in that bedroom can you watch? Dammit, it's springtime. You need to get moving with your life. I want my husband to be more than a broken lump with a pension."

"What else can I do? The Corps was my life."

"What about me, Pete? What about Rebecca and Thomas. Aren't they your life too?"

I notice she doesn't mention me. To her, there's just the two Ords, then…

"You don't want me in your life, Joanne. Not now. Not like this. Hell, you hated me before. When I was a whole man."

"That's crazy talk," she says. But her reply is less sincere than she realizes. But Dad's mind is elsewhere. It's never been with us. He left it behind, far away.

"I can't be responsible for anyone anymore. I lost fifteen men in my company. Another twenty injured. Not to mention my legs. What good was I to them if I let them die?"

"You didn't kill them, Pete."

"I didn't protect them either." I think this is at the heart of why Dad's changed so much, but I'm not sure. All I know is his mood's gotten worse since he first came home. That was the only time I've seen him smile. I feel him slipping away, and the family I'm left with makes me sad. They never cared about me the way Dad did. But even he can't seem to feel anymore. What happened to him? How does a man break apart like this? I slap my head trying to make sense of it all, but I can't. The static is too loud. I scream out.

Suddenly I hear a sharp voice: "Wes, could you just be quiet! I can't take this today. Not today…." But it's not Mom doing the hollering. It's Dad. As the car pulls up to the school, not even Antoinette's smiling face waiting for me on the walkway can shake away the sadness I feel towards the man who no longer calls me his Ex. In fact, a man who no longer has any spark at all. I'm especially agitated this morning. There's gonna be a lot of pen to clipboard today. I sense something terrible in the offing. The sun still shines, but a wall of black and gray clouds is rolling in above the horizon. The last of the sun will soon be gone.

A DARKENED ROOM

I don't recognize the metallic sound. I've never heard it before. *Chi-chink*. It's coming from Dad's bedroom. The one he rarely leaves these days. Thomas sits sprawled across the couch watching NBA highlights. Mom tends to the garden out back. I'm left to my own devices, and since my visit with the Von Trapps for the day is over, I'm bored and restless, looking for something to do. I decide to go see Dad. Maybe he'll be nice to me again. He might even smile. I don't know. The stairs. *One...two...three....* All I know is...*four...five... six....* I get halfway up the steps and then stop dead in my tracks. What is that noise? I don't like it when new things I can't make sense of enter my busy world. *Chi-chink*. There it is again. Definitely coming from the master bedroom. Something unearthly behind the door. Something bad. I feel it.

I bang my hand hard on my thigh to clear my thoughts and then ascend the remaining steps. *Seven...eight...nine...ten...eleven... twelve.* I stand before the closed door and stare down at the knob. What's on the other side? Is Dad sleeping? In the middle of the day? What was that noise? The humming in my ears is overpowering and I want to shout out from the top of the stairway. But I control it. Antoinette tells me to think of the Austrian Alps when I get agitated. I pretend from the top step that I'm with the Von Trapps as they frolic on a grassy hilltop, framed by high mountains basted in sunlight. Sometimes it works. I try real hard to get a grip, as my brother might say to me. But I'm too tightly wound. I just know something bad's happening on the other side of this door. I watch my pasty hand push up against it. It slowly opens. When it does the hinges creak. It sounds like a firecracker up to my ears.

I step in and find my dad sitting on the desk chair facing his bed. I only see his back. I'm afraid to look up at his head. The balding patch is the clue it's him. That and his red-orange sweatshirt and pants. He doesn't turn to face me. Can he hear me? As I step up closer to him, I peer over his large shoulder and see the source of that awful metallic slinging noise. Shiny and black and sleek. A pistol. Why is he holding this?

"Hummmmm!" I say. It's all I can say, although I'm thinking so much more. But I'm too upset to piece together letters to form words at this moment.

He turns slowly to face me. The gun in one hand resting in his lap. I try to look away but something so sad in his eyes compels me to stay with them just for a brief second. I see the war in them. I see despair. Guilt. Misery over his lost legs. What I don't see anymore is my dad.

"Jesus," he says in a booming voice. "Can't a man have any private moments even in his own Goddamned bedroom!" I scream. His free arm lurches at me, while he grips the gun tightly in his other hand. "Stop it! Stop screaming! I can't take any more screams! Do you understand me? Do you Goddamned get it? I need to be alone!"

I'm really on fire now. I bang my hands against the Sheetrock with loud slaps and wail at the top of my lungs. Then I find myself on my knees with my hands up to my ears.

"I said stop it!" I feel a powerful hand wrench me up by my shirt collar and I'm face-to-face with the demon inside my dad. I smell an acrid aroma on his breath. Alcohol. He must just sit up here and drink. What's happened to him? "Wes, if you don't stop screaming I swear to Christ—"

"Dad?" A third voice. Deeper than mine, but higher than Dad's. Through the haze of my meltdown, I spy Thomas standing in the doorway, his face ashen at the sight of his father seated in the chair and clutching his flailing little brother with one powerful hand. And even more frightening, a pistol clenched in his other. Dad looks past me to his older son. "Dad," Thomas says again, this time more commanding. His hand is out, as if he's trying not to spook a bronco he's trying to rope. "Calm down, Captain." My dad's passion drains, and I feel his grip on my stretched-out collar loosen.

I fall to the floor and cup my hands over my ears. I want to be far away from here. I want my dad back. This man is not him. I want sand crabs again. I want to feel the cool of the ocean waves and the warmth of his smile. Instead there's nothing but the darkness of his new world, and the confused madness of my own at this moment. Thomas is the only voice of sanity here, and he moves in to defuse a situation above his grade level as best he can.

My brother steps into the room and tries to pat me on the back to comfort me before confronting our father but I shrug him away. He moves on. With my head to the floor and eyes clamped shut, I don't see the confrontation, I only hear it through the snow, as if it's a radio show on a garbled frequency. "Dad," he says with a dry mouth. "Come on and put that gun down, okay?" Silence. "Please…it can't be that bad."

"So bad…so bad…so bad," I moan.

"Shhh, Wes," my brother says, but without his usual reproach. I know why he's being nice to me. He's scared out of his wits at the man facing him with no legs and a gun in his hand. "Dad, here. Just hand me that gun. You don't want to be holding that right now."

"I'm okay, Tee," Dad says. But his voice is robotic. He's lying.

"Wes," says Thomas. "Why don't you go watch the Von Trapps, okay? Dad and I are just gonna talk a little. After he gives me his gun. Right, Captain?"

"Don't call me that. I'm not in the Corps anymore," Dad says.

"Come on now," Thomas replies, trying to be as casual as he can in a room with a legless man who's snapped and still holds a nine-millimeter Glock-19 in his hand. "You know the old line. Once a Marine, always a Marine. You know better than that."

I find I'm so upset I can't move from my ball on the floor. It's as if my muscles have frozen in their place. I can only listen and feel the vibes as Thomas moves past me, walking deliberately and slowly. He's afraid of Dad. Afraid he might shoot us both. He may be right. I've never been so scared. Not even in my dreams. Mom's right. There's something about reality that makes even the darkest nightmares pale in severity. This is real bad.

"Thomas, please don't come any closer. I think it best for everyone if you let me do this."

Thomas halts. "Do what, Dad?"

I hear the *chi-chink!* "No!" I scream.

"It's okay, Wes. Come on, Dad. That's a crazy idea."

Dad groans. "Maybe I *am* crazy."

Thomas's voice is kinder and gentler than I've ever heard it before. I've never understood how much he loves his father too until this moment. "You're not crazy, Dad. A crazy man wouldn't feel what you're feeling. I think at this moment, you're the sanest guy I ever met." A pause. "Everyone in this family loves you. Please don't throw that away. Put the gun down."

My father gives a wan smile as he looks over his shoulder. "It's a pistol."

Thomas inches closer. "Fine. Whatever you wanna call it. Just… please put it down."

Dad turns away. Then he raises the pistol to his temple and squeezes the trigger.

"No!" shouts Thomas as he lunges forward and tackles his father's legless body off the chair. The furniture rolls onto its side as the two big men tumble to the ground. I shout and scream. But through the cloud of my screams, I hear the *click!* of the weapon's misfire. That or maybe it's never been loaded.

"Get off of me, Goddamn it!" my dad bellows at his son, who easily pins him to the ground since there are no legs to buck him off. The gun spirals harmlessly to the floor and lands on the carpet with a soft thud just a foot away from my pounding hands.

"No way!" Thomas says with more defiance than I've ever heard from him before. "No fucking way! Not until I know you're alright!"

My dad cries out to the ceiling: "No, boy. I am not alright. I'm an officer in the Marine Corps who just got taken down by a damned teenager! Hell, what good am I to my family if I can't even defend myself? What good am I to anyone!"

"Pistol Pete! Pistol Pete!" I suddenly shout, remembering a name one of his friends on golf course calls him. I don't know why I say this, but it makes my brother furious.

"Shut the fuck up, Wes! Get outta here!" But I know Thomas can't shove me out of the bedroom into the hallway and stay on the ground pinning Dad to the floor at the same time.

"Pistol Pete! Pistol Pete!" I shout again, daring him to make a choice. Next thing I know, I'm standing up straight with Dad's gun in my hand. I don't point it at anyone. I just stare down at it with fascination. Black, shiny, sleek. So very unearthly. I hum as I rub my hand across the smooth metallic surface, as if polishing it with my fingertips.

"Wes?" I hear a shaky voice behind me. Feminine. It's Mom. "Pete? Tommy?" She rattles off each name like taking roll call. From the bedroom entrance she tries to absorb an incomprehensible scene. Her oldest son, who grows larger and more powerful by the day, is on his hands and knees, hyperventilating and straddling her legless husband who seems to have a vacant look to him. He's not all there, she realizes. Her eyes dart to her special-needs boy, smaller and frailer, grimacing and moaning as he clutches something matte black and blunt in his hand. He strokes it the way Gollum might the ring of power. She immediately processes the danger and her maternal instincts ignite.

"Wes!" she shouts at me, and I yelp and back away, clutching the weapon in my hand, its barrel waving at the ceiling. Her hand propels towards me and clamps down hard on my wrist and I cry out some more, struggling to get away, all the while the pistol gyrating like a conductor's baton, its opening occasionally passing dangerously across everyone's location.

"Get that thing away from him!" shouts Thomas. "He'll kill someone!"

"No, Wes!" Mom screams and tries to wrestle the gun from me by grabbing my wrist in both of hers like a rowing oar, but even though I'm not Thomas, I'm strong for my age, despite my wiry frame. Anger and adrenaline are powerful fuel for someone like me. I wrench my arm out of her grasp and Mom goes flying to the floor, landing next to her son and husband. "Please, Wes!" she shouts from the ground, tears streaming down her face as she stares up at me wide-eyed. "Please put the gun down!"

I ignore her begging and just gawk down at it. It feels like real power in my hands. I'm not sure why but I just know that at this moment, everyone here is at my mercy. That thought frightens me and I shout out at the top of my lungs and pound my temple with the clenched fist of my free hand while waving the gun with the other. "Pistol! Pistol!" I cry. "Pistol Pete! Pis—"

"*Wesley!*" I stop, and it feels like my mind goes into shut-down mode. I've never heard my father's deep voice so strong before. This is the voice he uses to command men in battle. Now he turns it on me, his favorite Marine. "Wesley Scott, I order you to put that sidearm down! Now!" I groan but stop my flailing. I look down at him peering up at me over Thomas's broad back. "I…said…*now!*"

I whimper and drop the gun as if it suddenly turns white-hot. "No yell! No yell!"

"Now, Tee," Dad says, turning his attention to the linebacker who has him pinned to the ground. "I want you to get off of me. Then help me up to the chair. Joanne, get that weapon away from Wes."

I crouch to the ground in a ball in the corner of the bedroom while I see Mom's trembling hand reach into my field of vision and pick up the pistol lying at my twitching feet. She straightens up and examines it coldly. Thomas says: "Come on, sir. Up onto the chair." Once he hoists Dad onto the chair, his legs ending in two stumps at the end of the cushion, he retreats to the far wall next to me and watches.

"Thank you, Tee," Dad says, as he looks up at his wife with a mixture of defiance and shame.

"Pete," she says weakly while holding up the gun. "How did our son, our *autistic* son, manage to get ahold of this?"

He sighs. "I had it out."

"Why?" she says with a quavering mouth and a squeaky voice. But I think she knows the answer.

Dad says nothing. Finally, Thomas tells her the truth. "He had it in his hand." He looks to Dad with a pained expression. "You tried to kill yourself. Didn't you?"

"My God, Pete," my mother blurts while slowly walking towards him. I can see she's still repulsed by his half-legs. She can't hide it. But she presses on, the gun clenched firmly in her spindly hand. "I didn't know it was so bad. It can't be. No! It cannot be this bad, Pete."

He rubs his hands down his face as if trying to wipe off a layer of his new self. They instinctively find the nubs of his mutilated limbs.

"It is."

"No," she insists. "I said it can't be, and so it can't."

"Mom, he just said—"

"Be quiet, Thomas! Both of you shut up! Wes! Quit that maddening howling right now. Right now, or I swear…" My mother, her mind tipping off the edge of sanity, actually aims the gun at my crumbled, rocking form.

"Mom!" says Thomas. "Have you lost your mind?" He steps over and knocks her arm so the barrel harmlessly faces the far wall.

"You better take it away from her, Tee," Dad says weakly. "Joanne, give it to him." She robotically hands the hot-potato gun off to her oldest son, who takes it reluctantly, and after flicking on the safety, he makes sure to hold it by the barrel to be safe.

"Take your brother and get the hell out of here," Mom barks to Thomas. "Your father and I need to talk."

"I think you need more than that," my brother says. "Let's go, Squid."

"Pistol Pete!" I shout while waving him away.

"Shut up, Wes. Please," says Thomas. "Let's get out of here."

My dad nods, back in control again. A shadow of authority in his voice. "Go with your brother, Wes." I stand up and briefly catch his eye before following my hulking brother out the door. "Don't worry. It's okay. I'll make everything okay."

THE BOARDWALK

Mom decides we should all as a family visit the shore and stroll the boardwalk. Not only is it the first really warm day of the year, but there's a military air show three towns over, and if it's anything like last year's, we can watch the old-time warplanes zoom overhead against a clear blue sky. Mom thinks this might lift Dad's sagging spirits since he's a military aviation buff, but I'm not so sure. He's dying inside. It's a decaying vibration I feel in him. A spinning top starting to wobble as gravity takes hold. I don't think anyone else can sense what I do. I guess that's one thing that makes me an Ex. Dad needs more than a trip to the ocean. He needs a time machine.

Brittany's a quaint beach town a few miles from our house. It's tucked up against dunes piled real high. Beyond them, the ocean's color subtly shifts like the fluid skin of a giant cuttlefish to match the changing shades of the sky. Today the water's bluest blue. Brittany's more of a summer town, but I have some friends from special school who live here all the time. Maria's one of them. I wonder if I'll see her today. I'd like that. On sunny days like today, the vendors try to sell you anything from temporary tattoos, to caricatures on the spot, to seashell trinkets, bracelets, kites, headscarves, and sunglasses. Brightly colored flags and streamers snap in the steady ocean breeze as cars and bicycles crawl their way through the narrow streets in the compact downtown.

Almost everyone who lives in the area seems to be on the boardwalk that stretches for a mile and a half, its path following the shoreline. At certain points on the elevated walkway, the beach is accessible by weathered steps leading to the white sand. In this intense heat, the seashore's jammed with sunbathers sprawled out on blankets and beach towels, with handy umbrellas opened up behind them to both mark their territory and provide refuge from the blazing sun. The water's still pretty cold this time of year, so only a few swimmers splash in the shallows or do serious freestyle beyond the breakers, keeping the lifeguards perched high on wooden towers alert with ropes and bright orange rescue floats at the ready.

After only a short time on the boardwalk, Dad has to use the bathroom at one of the concession houses that line the miles-long plank path over the dunes, and so Mom goes with him, wheeling him on his chair. He's lost a lot of weight and it's easier for her to just push him along, weaving through the mass of people in bathing suits, huffing joggers, some pushing three-wheeled strollers with kids before them, dog walkers, and bicyclists who come at them from all directions.

"The bathroom in the big field house is handicapped accessible," he says. "Can't believe I'm saying that."

"It is what it is, Pete," Mom sighs.

"For now," he says. His energy's sagged with his spirits. The man I once knew is long gone.

"Stay close to your brother," Mom commands my older sibs. "We'll be back in ten minutes."

"We've got him," Becca says to Mom's back as she hauls Dad away. "Isn't that right, Wes?" I guess. I don't feel like answering.

Once my parents are safely out of earshot, Thomas asks, "Exactly why are we here again?" He looks around as if he's afraid of being spotted on the boardwalk with his family. My brother's never been close with Becca. My sister looks detached in her dark glasses. And she's let her hair grow long, which I think is strange since Mom just yesterday cut my hair extra short for the summer. (Believe me, I wasn't happy about that and put up a fight. Thomas had to help hold me in place. "Damn, this squid's strong!" he huffed. "Just buzz him already!" Mom cuts it herself because she doesn't want to take me to the local barber anymore. She's afraid of what I might do to him, with all the scissors in arm's reach.) Becca's always been kind of a satellite of the Scott family. Whenever she's with us, she spends most of her time looking down at her phone, or just wishing she could be back in New York where she can be herself, whoever that person is. I don't really know. Maybe she doesn't either.

"It's good for Dad," she says. But I can tell she'd rather be far away. I sit on one of the benches and rock underneath the blistering sun. It's still technically spring which doesn't end until June 21, 10:58 a.m. Eastern Time, yet it already feels like deepest August. The heat doesn't really bother me like it does my brother. It feels good to me. Maybe I just like the fact that a bright day like this is the very absence of the darkness I fear.

"Fuck this global warming shit," exhales Thomas as he wipes sweat off his brow with his powerful forearm.

"It's only going to get worse unless we do something now about the—"

"Spare the lectures, sis. This isn't Washington Park, and I like big cars." My brother leans on the wooden rail overlooking the crowded beach, then looks back over at me. "Doesn't he sweat?"

"I don't know. You sweat enough for all of us."

"It's called a killer metab."

"Metab? Ugh. Are we really related?"

He shakes his head. "Easier to believe you and me, than us…and him."

Becca glares at him through her shades. "That's cruel, Thomas."

"It's true." He thinks I can't hear him. He always thinks that. He's always wrong. I just want to be one of them. Sometimes I hate being an Ex.

"You really should be nicer to him. He's family."

He snorts and shields his eyes from the glare as he canvasses the beach for girls. "Says the woman who cares so much she ran off to the big city the moment she turned eighteen."

"Stop saying that."

"Truth hurts, don't it?"

"It's called going to college. Remember? Fordham? Business major? That whole thing?"

"How's it you work at a bank? You're too, I dunno, 'earthy.'"

She chuckles. "Earthy? Even a liberal snowflake like me needs to eat."

He shoots her a knowing frown. "Save it for your Starbucks friends, Becks. You and I are both children of the Marine Corps. Even if you're not proud of it."

"Not proud!" I bark.

She snaps her head to me then back to Thomas. "That's not true."

"You never approved of him."

"I didn't like the position he put Mom in."

"It was her call to marry him."

Becca opens her arms as if to display herself on a runway. "I didn't give them much of a choice."

"There are no coat hangers in the house?"

"God, you're twisted." She looks around. "Whatever the reason, he should've taken honorable discharge when his term was up. But I guess that's who he is."

"You mean who he *was*," Thomas corrects her.

She nods while casting her eyes towards the concession building. "Yeah. I always feared something like…something like what happened to him would happen."

Thomas turns to lean back on the rail facing us both. "You can say it, Becks. He got his fuckin' legs blown off."

She instinctively moves over to me and puts her hand on my shoulder. I quickly recoil, and she grabs the backrest of the bench. "Not in front of him. Come on."

"What?" says Thomas, his teeth showing, glinting incisors in the sunlight. "You think he really gets what's going on here? You think he understands just how fucked in the head both Dad *and* Mom are because of his little mishap with the towel-heads?"

"You shouldn't call them that. Not all—"

"I'll call 'em whatever I want to call 'em. They tried to kill Dad. And I'll say what I want to say in front of bubble boy here." My brother struts across the planks and crouches down until he's in my face. "You lucky little shit. All the world's just one big musical to you."

I don't face him but look down at my sandaled feet and wave my hand in front of my eyes. I don't know why. I guess because Thomas is bugging me. I want to answer him but all I can say is, "Music. Music."

"Yeah," he sniffs. "Music all day long for you, huh?"

"Leave him alone," says my sister.

Thomas stands and once again faces the water. The beach is especially crowded today. The bathers remind me of a colony of sea lions in one of those nature shows Antoinette likes to put on for me during free time. But with all the colors of the rainbow in a tapestry of humanity added. The roar of the ocean waves provides an endless backtrack to it all.

"You know, sis," Thomas says as a sea breeze blows his wavy blonde hair across his eyes. "I sometimes envy him."

"You *envy* him?"

"Well, yeah. I mean, think about it. He'll never have to worry about the world outside his stupid school, those ridiculous labels Dad made for his clothes, just so he can dress himself, his iPad, the fucking Von Trapps. He'll never have to know how much of his father we lost. He'll never have to face the cold, cruel world."

"Who knows how cruel his world is," she says. They speak about me in front of me as if I'm a lab animal behind glass rather than their little brother. "I think you underestimate him."

Thomas grins at the notion. "That's because you don't live with him."

"I used to."

"And now you don't."

She steps over to Thomas and pats his back in a way I'd never let her pat mine. "I don't understand your anger towards him sometimes, little brother."

He runs a hand through his hair and then points out to sea. "You see that boat out there? The little white one almost to the horizon."

She looks out to the blue edge of the world. "The sailboat?"

"Yeah. Well, imagine that boat is all the attention I get at home."

"Okay."

"Now…the ocean. That's how much attention Wes gets. Every day. Morning, noon, night. It never ends. I see the look of relief on Mom's face when he finally stops howling and goes to sleep. It's like she's locked a wild dog back in its crate for the night. And it's only gonna get worse if he gets to be my size. Now with Dad a cripple…"

Becca breathes in deep. "It's not easy for you, is it? I admit I don't see much of it."

"Easier to just move away, right? He's not the only one I envy."

She nods. "Out of sight, out of mind." They both gaze at the ocean, while passersby on the boardwalk stare at me. It's hard to tell at a glance that I'm with the brother and sister facing away from me towards the beach. But they hear me. They've learned to gauge my groans and grunts like reading sonar.

Thomas goes on. "Do you know I'll be a senior next year, and I've still never visited one college campus? Not with Mom or Dad, anyway. I mean, Dad, yeah, I guess I gotta accept that. Even before being wounded. Him being away fighting and all. But Mom was home. What's her excuse?"

Becca motions towards me as I rock and hum on the bench. "Him, I suppose."

"Give the lady a prize."

"Is he really that difficult?"

Thomas laughs. "Um, you've had to put him down with pepper spray, haven't you? So you tell me."

Becca's eyes drift to her hand resting on the wooden rail. She examines a chip in her nail polish. "I hated doing that," she says in a voice barely audible over the ocean and the ambient noise of the beach crowd. "It must be so exhausting for Mom. Especially now with Dad the way he is."

"I'm sure it is." Thomas glances at me. "He takes all the air out of the room. And our lives. And that doesn't help me when I need to figure out where the hell I'm going to college in a year."

"What about Fordham?" she asks. "I know someone in admissions there. Dated him, in fact," she says with a devious grin. "He owes me some payback."

"Eww," says Thomas. "No east coast schools for me."

"Why not?"

He takes a deep breath of salty sea air and peers down the length of the boardwalk towards the woman pushing the legless man in the wheelchair coming our way among the steady stream of pedestrians out enjoying the sunshine. I can feel my brother looking over at me. "Fordham!" I shout to the plank beneath my feet.

He shakes his head and says to his sister. "Not far away enough."

AIR SHOW

I desperately want to scream. But I settle for my usual noises to open the pressure valve. My mom's and sister's voices come to me in muffled waves forcing their way through my palms clamped tight over my ringing, rattling ears. The airplanes are so loud! Each one that whooshes over the water past the beach sounds like a thunderclap and makes my whole body shake. The crowd on the sand below us or standing on the boardwalk or lining the pier points up and claps as the latest one, a fierce F-22 Raptor, roars past, sucking up vapors from the ocean below its flaming engines like a speeding vacuum cleaner. It sounds like something ripping the sky in half. I ball up against the railing to shield myself, but the sound penetrates through me like an X-ray.

"Dammit!" Mom says to Becca. "I didn't realize there'd be jets at this thing. Last year it was just those old prop planes."

"They've really got him going," Becca says as she crouches down next to me. She knows better than to try to rub my back or hair to comfort me. It'll just set me off more. The sun now feels like an oven coil above my back and shoulders and the chatter of people walking past are a dissonant chorus in my ears. ("Mommy, what's wrong with that boy?" "Keep moving...don't stare." "He havin' a seizure?" "Who takes a kid like that out?" "Yo, yo. Check out the retard.") The fighter jet does a loop for the enthralled crowd even though the actual show itself is farther up the shore, and the people cheer. The whining of the jet's engines, protesting its slow speed just above a stall to give everyone a good look, is a rusty nail against my ear drum. "Stop! Stop!" I shout.

"Shh, Wes," my sister says. "It's okay. Shh."

Mom stands over me. Her long, dark shadow engulfs mine. I look up, and out of the corner of my eye, I can see the embarrassment and frustration in her tired, sagging face. The weight of all her many troubles pressing her down. And I read her thoughts. *I hate my life.* She has one hand buried in her bag. Pepper spray. I try to fight the urge to jump up and run away.

"Pete," she says to her husband. "You don't need to deal with this. Becca and I've got him."

"He's okay," Dad says, trying to reassure me. He wheels up to me and touches me on the knee. I squeeze down hard on his now-frail hand. Then my own hand retreats to a fist jammed into my lap. Rocking, rocking. Make it stop.

"No," Mom replies sharply. "He's not okay. Not when he's like this. Tommy, take your dad someplace else."

Thomas frowns. "Where?"

"Anyplace but here. Please."

"Um, okay."

Dad doesn't protest. Instead he twists in his chair to face out to sea. He studies a long, wooden pier, reaching out far into the water like the robotic arm on a space shuttle. He seems fixated on it. As if he's just been given orders to secure the rickety structure at all costs. "What's the point anymore? Screw it," Dad says. "Take me out there, Tee." Thomas numbly obeys. He's too embarrassed by me to ask Dad why.

Then the jet fighter curves around again and my world explodes. And through the swirling, spinning, metallic shrieks of the engines slicing through the air above, I hear a faint voice. Dad's. He calls to me, just audible enough for me to hear him. "Don't worry, Wes. I'll make everything okay. You're always my favorite Marine."

ALL THE WATER IN THE WORLD

I try to imagine how the moment unfolds. My father, thin, wounded, unable to stand without his special metal legs. The sun glares out of the white haze sky and lays on everything like melted brass. The rubber wheels under his chair feel like they'll stick to the wooden planks. He's thirsty. Dehydrated even. Maybe he thinks about the men he left behind in Iraq. He misses them. He feels like he failed them. A glance down at the stubs that were once legs prompts a sense of an overwhelming uselessness. He's a man who can't take care of his family now that the only career he's ever known is gone. The jet fighter booms and he cringes at the sound. Familiar. It means air support needed. Pinned down and under fire. The intense heat awakens vivid memories of fighting in the desert, with the screaming planes and thumping helicopters overhead as rockets and bullets rain down on his men from every window and rooftop. He peers down into the glittering water off the edge of the jetty and sees in the dark green shallows the faces of his men. A company of ghosts. His legs start to tingle and itch, and he goes to scratch them, but his hand cruelly passes through nothing to the fabric of the chair his son dutifully pushes underneath him. Phantom pains to accompany his men's images. He feels that life is not worth living. Not this life of physical impotency and mental anguish. That shrink tried to help. But he wasn't there. No one in his family was there. They will never, ever understand. It's time to go. I don't think how it will affect me is even a remote concept to him at this point. I sure hope not. I like to think my Dad isn't a selfish man.

"Tee."

"Yeah, Dad."

"I'm parched. Can you get me a water?"

"From where?"

Dad points. "That stand down there."

Thomas squints in the sun and sees the blue and yellow umbrella poking above the bobbing heads of the pedestrians on the boardwalk.

"I'll take you. Let's go."

"No," says my father as he turns his head and stares down into the sloshing water as if scanning the surface for sharks. "I'll stay here. The breeze does me good."

Thomas removes his hands from the rear handles and locks the wheels. "You'll be okay?"

"I'm not helpless," my father snaps. No, he's not. He's in absolute control of what he's about to do.

"Sure, okay, Dad. Just stay put." Thomas cringes. He knows that's the wrong thing to say to a man who used to lead two hundred men into the teeth of battle. Like me, he misses the father he once knew but was left in the rubble of Tikrit.

Dad pulls out his wallet from the pocket of his rolled-up sweats and hands it to his son.

"I got money," Thomas says, waving him off. "How much can a water be? Two bucks?"

My father keeps his hand extended. "Take it."

Thomas grabs it dutifully. Thick leather and frayed. Weather-worn and tired like his dad. "You're the boss." Then he turns and walks down the length of the pier.

My father watches him go. Soon his oldest son, a big, strapping boy reminding him of the man he once was, disappears into the river of people crowding the boardwalk. He looks around for his wife, daughter, and youngest boy. His Ex-man. A brief pang of regret, but then the cloud of despair quickly smothers it. He'll make it alright. No one wants a cripple for a husband or a father. He faces the water, takes a deep breath of salt air, and unlocks the wheels to his chair. With one last glance up into the clear sky, he closes his eyes and rolls forward.

WHERE'S DAD?

The vice tightens around my temples. The ear-shattering noise. The glare. I shut out the suddenly torturous sunlight with closed eyes. I'm curled up and I rock and hum. My head pounds. That's when Thomas comes running over. "Has anyone seen Dad?"

Mom looks around. "What do you mean 'has anyone seen Dad?' I thought he was with you?"

"He was."

"Didn't I tell you to get him away from your brother?"

Thomas waves his arm. "Yeah, yeah, I know. I took him over to the end of the pier."

Mom follows the invisible line of his pointing finger. She lowers her magenta sunglasses to get a better glimpse of the edge of the wooden extension jutting far out over the sloshing surf. There's no one there. "Well, where the heck is he?" she says. Through my static I sense her anxiety building.

"Mom," my brother says with a hint of concern, "I don't know. He asked me to get him a water from that guy with the cart. When I came back to where we were, he was gone."

Becca looks up from trying to comfort me. "Well gosh, he couldn't have gone very far, right? Just go find him."

My mother goes still, my outbursts are suddenly unimportant. Becca looks at her and a silent alarm triggers in my sister. "Mom, what are you thinking?"

Mom looks around. She says to Becca: "Take Wes to the snack bar."

"But we just ate," she says quizzically.

Mom fires a stern look at her daughter. "Please, Rebecca. Just do it."

Becca realizes the snack bar's just a distraction. Something's terribly wrong. She gently taps my thigh to get my attention. I look up from the boardwalk. But I don't look at her. She's not Dad. I look out to the ocean and lock in on a swirling seagull while rocking soothingly with my arms folded up to my stomach.

"Wes?" she says over the acoustic shadow of the jet engines rolling through the sky and the chatter of passersby. "You want to get a pretzel?"

"Yesss," I tell her. I'm hungry.

"Okay, good. Come with me." She tries to take my hand, but I retreat as always. "Fine. Just stay close by me, then. You understand?"

"Yesss," I say again. I'm trying an affirmation that Antoinette suggested for me at my last one-on-one with her. ("Here, Wes. If I ask you something you like, just say 'yes' okay?") I like saying the word. "Yesss," I say again.

"Alrighty then," says Becca who's never heard such an encouraging sound from me. "Let's get something to eat."

I follow my sister who keeps looking over her shoulder, not at me but towards the pier where Mom follows a baffled Thomas to the end over the water. "He was right here!" my brother says, more insistent now.

"Please, no," Becca mutters as she leads me to the crowded concession stand that emits a weird aroma of sour vinegar and oily deep-fried potato skins.

"No! No! Pretzel!" I repeat to my waving hand as we take our place in line at the counter.

"Shh, Wes," she says. "You can have a pretzel. I didn't mean no to that."

"Yesss," I say. I really like that word now. I feel better when Becca hands me the soft pretzel with the chunks of salt glued to it and I tear a piece off and stuff it in my mouth. The jet plane still rumbles, but it's far away now, the noise receding from my humming ears like a thunderstorm rolling up the seashore. The seashore. Sand crabs. Maybe when Mom and Thomas find Dad we can go to the water's edge and dig for sand crabs in the brine again. I miss my time with Dad. I know he'll never walk on the beach again like he once did, but his metal legs will let him stand up at least. I want to find Dad. But where is he?

I follow Becca back to the area by the pier. We find my mom and my brother and as my eyes pass over theirs before I look away, I see a fear that turns my own brightening sky dark and ominous. Mom races over to the edge of the pier again. Her look of alarm is horrible.

I sit down on a bench and rip another piece of pretzel. Thomas approaches my sister who stands watch over me. "Please tell me you saw Dad over by the food stand."

She shakes her head. "No. Thomas, what's going on?"

"He's just disappeared. Vanished."

Becca says: "Well, what the hell? Weren't you just with him? How could you lose him?"

Thomas's face turns a shade of pink and not from the sun. "What am I, his fucking babysitter? You guys told me get him away from squid-boy here because he was having yet another one of his 'episodes.'" Although I'm looking down to the wooden planks, I can see his shadow hands air-quote that last word.

"Mom was getting the spray out," Becca snaps. "Dad doesn't need that."

"Yeah, and we do? Look, sis. I did what you asked and got him the hell outta there."

"Right," Becca says sharply. "We didn't say leave him alone."

"The guy wanted a drink of water, alright? I just left him for a second."

"That's all it takes," she said dourly.

"All it takes!" I shout.

"Shut up!" snaps Thomas. I shut up and wolf down more of my pretzel. Then to Becca. "All it takes for what?" Silence. Then realization. "Oh, no way, man. No fucking way. Not him."

Becca looks over to Mom by the edge of the pier. She frantically searches some more. But she doesn't look on the pier itself. She looks down at the dark water.

POLICEMEN

My soft pretzel's long gone. So is the tormenting jet fighter. It's moved on like a rolling artillery barrage to terrorize other boardwalks on other beaches. But my family hasn't moved from this spot. I stare down at the plastic flowers on Becca's sandals as they approach then recede then approach then recede again in cadence with my rocking. I can only listen to my mother's pleadings and Thomas protesting his innocence to my sister who stands quietly in front of me, minding me on the bench. When I do glance up, I see two policemen with black shorts and gray polo shirts with shiny badges on their belts. Young, tanned men on bicycles *(B-I-C-Y-C-L-E)* with muscular legs and crew cuts. Ray-Ban shades. I study the hissing and crackling on their radios clipped to their collars. My world in stereo. I also notice the shiny black stocks of holstered pistols, like the one Dad put to his temple not so long ago. We should have done more after that, I think to myself, though I can never find the words. The policemen lean their bikes up against the rail that lines the ocean side of the boardwalk and approach the frantic woman who waves them down.

"I swear he was right here, Becks," insists Thomas in a raspy whisper as if his life depends on her believing him.

"Well, he's not here now," she says. Her voice is wooden. Elsewhere. Thomas doesn't get that she couldn't care less what her brother has to say at this moment. All she cares about—besides making sure I don't have a meltdown with all the rising tension—is that her dad, her legless, emotionally disturbed dad, was last seen sitting in his wheelchair contemplating the deep, murky water at the end of the long pier before sending his Ord son to get him something she can't even remember now.

"Well shit," Thomas says. "It's not like he rolled into the water or anything."

Becca looks at him. "You sure about that?"

My brother goes silent. It's a thought too horrible to think about.

"Splash!" I say. I cringe, expecting Thomas to holler at me. Nothing. Only the sounds of the policemen trying to make sense of my mother.

"Ma'am. We need you to calm down, please. This is a public boardwalk."

"Calm down?" she says. "My husband's missing."

"How long?"

"A half hour." The policemen look at each other. "Are you sure he just didn't go to the bathroom or maybe he's on the beach—"

"He can't walk! He can't stand."

"Beg pardon?"

"He doesn't have any legs, you idiots! He's in a wheelchair. It'd be Goddamned tough to roll that thing down those steps and then over the sand, don't you think?"

The policemen are used to taking abuse and it doesn't faze them. "Please, ma'am. There's no need for that. We're trying to help you."

My mom gets hold of herself and takes a deep breath. "I'm sorry, officers. I know you're doing your jobs. It's just been so hard ever since he came back."

"Back from where?" asks the bigger one as the other pulls himself from the conversation and begins walking the length of the pier while looking over the side into the water.

"Iraq," she says. A sob escapes her throat. "He's a Marine. I mean, he was a Marine."

"I see." More sympathy in his voice now. "Is the wheelchair motorized?"

"No? Why?"

"It could give us an idea of how far he may have gone. Pushing a manual chair gets exhausting on these planks. I seen it before. That's a fifty-five-and-older apartment complex across the road there."

"Oh."

Thomas leaves Becca with me and approaches Mom and the young cop. He keeps eyeing the other one who's looking with real purpose over the edge of the pier. Everyone seems to be thinking the same thing now. I'm confused. Dad's gone. But he'll be back. It's the beach and we haven't gone looking for sand crabs yet.

"Please, God, no," my sister mutters softly. I wonder why she keeps saying that. Her voice cuts through the ambient chatter of seagulls and pedestrians on the walkway. Some people stop to lean back on the rail as if just taking a break from their strolls, but I know what they're doing. They're curious about what's happening with the crying woman and the two policemen in shorts and black sneakers. In fact, a small crowd's gathering, although they keep their distance. Some steal a quick glance my way, wondering where that moaning's coming from. I feel a need to scream at them to shoo them away. This is no business of theirs.

"Get out! Get out!"

"Shh!" says my sister, not with anger but sympathy. "I hear ya, kid. Just try to hold it together, okay?"

"Get out," I whisper.

"That's better. You tell 'em, little brother."

I'm starting to sense something terrible. And with it the buzzing in my ears swells. Thomas approaches Mom and offers what he can to the policeman, who still seems unsure if there's anything to worry about other than a man in a wheelchair who decided to go home alone. "He asked me to get him a water. Said he was thirsty. It's hot as balls out here."

The cop looks at him. He's bigger than Thomas, which I don't see too often. "Where'd you get the water?"

"Right over there," answers my brother while pointing to a cart about fifty yards down the boardwalk. "It's hard to see it through the crowd. The one with the Sabrett's umbrella."

"Got it. And you say when you came back…"

"He was gone."

I glance back down to Becca's flower sandals then force my gaze outward again. I zero in on the other policeman, smaller, stockier, red-headed, and follow him as he walks to the very end of the pier jutting far out over the frothing ocean. He abruptly stops and removes his sunglasses and stares hard down into the water. Into the splashing brine and floating kelp slapping up against the petrified wood pylons. He leans in to get a better look, squints, and then goes straight and rigid as if hit with an electric prod.

Through the static I hear, "Holy crap." Or maybe I just read his lips. At that distance I can't tell. But I know something has him really spooked. He abruptly turns and waves to his big partner who faces his direction with Mom's back to him. Thomas stands at an angle to them and he notices the smaller officer's insistent arm motions. He breaks from the conversation and trots towards the cop who isn't sure what to do now. The bigger one says "excuse me" to my confused mom and follows my brother. "Sir, wait. Stay where you are, please."

"Fuck that!" Thomas grunts and runs all the faster until he's intercepted by the smaller, red-headed policeman coming the other way.

"I need you to back up," the cop says as he grabs my brother and holds him firm, more from the force of his authority than strength, which Thomas has over him. The bigger cop catches up.

"Henry, what is it?" (The redhead must be named Henry.) "What's the matter?"

Officer Henry makes a head motion to the edge of the pier. The jetty looks so menacing to me. Like one of those planks on the pirate ship cartoons I watch with Maria at school. "Go there and tell me what you see."

"What?" says Thomas. "What do you see?"

"Sir, please," says Officer Henry. "I asked you to stay back."

By now Mom's with them and wringing her hands as if washing them in a basin. "What's happening? Thomas, what's going on?"

"I don't know, Mom."

"It could be nothing," says Officer Henry, although it's pretty obvious it could also be something pretty bad.

"What?" pleads my mother. "What could be nothing?"

"Ma'am, please just stay put a second. We'll be right back. Do not come out any further. Is that clear?"

"Why?" says my brother. "Come on, guys, what gives?"

Becca watches this whole scene unfold, her shaded eyes flitting back and forth from me to the scene on the pirate plank. "I don't like the look of this, Wes." She wants to leave me to join the small gathering some distance away. But she knows she can't leave me alone seated on a park bench on a crowded boardwalk. She's right. I really do want to run away at this point. There's just too much information bombarding me like one shotgun blast after another. I just want to leave. I don't even care where Dad is anymore. Well, almost....

The two policemen lean over the edge and scan the forest-green water about ten feet below them. Officer Henry points and the bigger one exhales and nods. "Yeah. I see it." He grabs his radio as if to make a call.

"What? What do you see?" Thomas's face is contorted by sheer panic now. I can hear his deep voice from here and suddenly he looks very menacing as the two policemen whip around to see this high school football star chugging towards them. They barely have time to react and they try to hold my brother back as he lunges to the far end of the pier.

"We need you to back up now!" Officer Henry says as he grabs my brother's bicep. But that just sends Thomas into full game-day mode. Forgetting that they're not opposing blockers but policemen, Thomas spins away from the smaller man's grasp and when the other tries to tackle him, the all-state defender knocks the bigger man to the ground with one powerful blow and steps over the stunned policeman who's now on all fours and struggling to raise himself back up off the wooden slats of the jetty. I think: *16.0 sacks (national average 1.19), 11 interceptions (national average 1.16), total tackles 38 (national average 14).* The big cop shakes his head as if to clear out a ringing in his ears, the kind I know all too well.

"Stay the fuck away from me!" my brother screams as he frantically paces back and forth along the edge of the pier looking down into the swirling waters and foam desperate to see what they see…all the while terrified of what he'll find.

Officer Henry's face is now as red as his hair. "You just assaulted a police officer, kid!" He's breathing hard and I'm afraid he's going to pull out his pistol and shoot my brother, but he checks his own temper and keeps his distance while helping his stunned partner to his feet. My brother doesn't even pay attention but keeps straining his eyes to make out anything in the cloudy water below.

Thomas suddenly freezes, and his mouth opens wide. "Mother fucker! Jesus, Dad, no!" he shouts. I force myself to watch as my brother dives headfirst off the pier, like one of those sea birds that suddenly wing over and slap into the water, and then surface with a struggling fish in their beak. He makes a big splash, and the two policemen watching him from the edge high above seem confused over what to do next. They flash each other a look as if to say: "I'm not going in there after him."

I rise to my feet to get a better view. Becca stands next to me. "Is he trying to paralyze himself?" she says. I can read the torment in her own mind. She desperately wants to run to Thomas. But she can't just leave me. She tries to pull me over towards my mother and the police-men by taking my hand, but I scream and slap it away and go rigid as a statue as I watch the drama unfolding in the water. "Wes, please!" she screams at me. "I think Tee sees Dad in the water!"

I just moan and fold my arms to my chest. My legs feel frozen in concrete now. Five Thomases couldn't move me. But only one Thomas matters right now, and his head suddenly pops up in the foaming, swirling surf among the pylons that hold up the very end of the pier. "Help!" he screams.

"Hey! Are you alright?" shouts Officer Henry.

"I need someone to help me get my dad! He's too heavy!" Then his head disappears again.

"Daddy!" Becca screams, and I shout and pound my head to clear out the horror in her voice. People turn to watch me. Again my sister contemplates just leaving me there, but she knows she can't. "Dammit, Wes!" she says in frustration while pacing wildly in front of me.

My mother's also screaming now and waving her arms. "Pete! Pete! Tommy, can you get him? Pete! No! What are you doing? No, Pete!"

The shrieks and splashes combined with my loud moans and Becca's shouts draw another batch of onlookers, and the two police-men briefly forget about my brother flailing in the water while patheti-cally trying to lift my father out of his wheelchair now resting beneath the waves. Controlling the swelling crowd becomes their main focus. The big policeman orders the people out of here: "We need everyone to step back, please. Step off this pier right now!"

My brother's head surfaces again, a sheen of watered-down blood covers his scalp and fingers. He looks defeated. *"God fucking dammit!"* he screams up to the clear sky. "Can't someone help me!" He grits his teeth and rubs his eyes furiously. *"Dad!"*

As his partner angrily moves the crowd off the pier and onto the boardwalk where they line up along the rail to watch the show, Officer Henry lowers his head and steps over to the edge above where Thomas treads water while cursing his father and the world. The policeman crouches like a baseball catcher and speaks down to my brother in a soothing voice, all anger gone. "I'm sorry, kid," he says. "I really am. I didn't want you to see this."

Then a lifeguard, who watches from his raised chair and runs into the water when Thomas jumps in, appears next to him in the surf with a bright orange float in tow. Two heads bobbing next to the pier above the body of a wounded warrior who'd had enough suffering. "Buddy, can you make it to shore?" he asks.

"Yeah," Thomas gurgles, spitting saltwater tainted with his own blood from his mouth. "Jesus, Dad. Why?"

"You got him, Mark?" Officer Henry shouts down to the lifeguard next to my brother. The would-be rescuer gives a thumbs-up. He and Thomas swim side-by-side away from the pylons and to the sand.

"Pete?" my mother says and tries to walk to where my brother and the lifeguard struggle to stay clear of the pylons as the tide tries to slam them into their splintered sides. The big cop gently intercepts her and says, "Ma'am, please move back. There's nothing any of you can do for him now. The lifeguard needs to get your son to shore before he tires and drowns out there."

"Is my husband okay?" she says in a weak voice. It's as if she doesn't hear a word the man says, or the meaning escapes her.

"Just, please…come with me. Let's get you all together and we'll go from there. Alright?"

Mom nods, and as the big police officer compassionately ushers her by the arm away from her drowned husband, and the exhausted son who tried to save him and now reluctantly swims to shore, he keys his radio mic and calls it in.

YELLOW TAPE

This section of the boardwalk is blocked off with long strands of yellow police tape. On the other side of the dunes, several trucks with flashing lights sit, waiting. I'm not sure what they're waiting for, but I know it has to do with the man in the wetsuit who leaps off the pier into the water. He jumps off right where Thomas, soaking wet, found Dad. Beyond the tape, a crowd gathers. Curiosity's such an Ord thing. I wonder too what's happening, but some of these people actually stop in the middle of their busy days just to catch a glimpse of whatever it is that's going down inside the enclosed scene. I rock on the bench, flanked by my siblings. Thomas also rocks, which I've never seen him do before. Becca wrings her hands mimicking her mother and keeps muttering, "No, please God, no." I look up to see Mom standing with arms tightly folded as if she's trying to squeeze herself in half talking nervously with the two short-pants policemen who have their notepads out. Her hands tremble. The smaller cop named Henry seems upset. I can feel his pity for Mom.

I make out bits of phrases. "...we have to do it this way...divers'll bring him up...I don't know why...can't make them go away, can only keep them back...it's a public beach...no ma'am, I don't know why..."

As I raise my head and fight through the humming in my brain, I see the black ball of the police diver's head pop up to the surface. He waves. While Officer Henry tries to hold my now-frantic mother back, the larger policeman crouching at the pier's edge stands up straight and nods, as if he's just been read a verdict. He turns to face

Mom and then us. Then he keys the handset on his mic clipped to his collar. "We need to extricate a fatality from the water. Tell them we're ready for them."

I close my eyes again. But even through the static, I can hear my mother's screams.

PERMANENCE

The knotted tie and tight collar chafe at my neck. I want to tear off this shirt. I feel as if I'm being strangled. I try to put up a fight about putting it on, but Thomas and Grampa Frank together hold me down and force the clothes on me. They're in no mood to argue. Becca tells them not to button the top.

"To hell with that!" growls my mother's father, who has the strength of a man who did plenty of backbreaking construction work onsite before becoming a millionaire contractor. "This is his father's funeral, and I don't care, retard or not, he *will* show some respect, Goddammit!"

Thomas looks at me with unnerving indifference to my agitation. "Fuckin' A right," he says.

Everyone's on edge. There's red-line tension in the house. A raw bitterness. It's so thick you can scoop it out of the air and swallow it. I think Thomas and Grampa have had seconds. I sense it and back off. I slip on the ill-fitting suitcoat and sit up, rocking on the edge of my bed. The men storm off while Becca stays behind to make sure I don't get undressed again. I'm so wired I want to explode. Where's Dad? What's happening today? What does "suicide" even mean? I grab my iPad off the end table and tap on my movies icon. There's only one. I find the scene I need. Becca sits next to me on the bed, but I ignore her and stare into the tablet. The Von Trapp family materializes before me and for a moment I forget the uncomfortable clothes that claw at me like a thousand fire ants. I'm in the bedroom with the Von Trapp children bouncing on the mattress while thunderclaps shake the walls and lightning flashes brighten the windows. But they're safe inside with Maria who smiles at them and sings about raindrops on roses, apple strudel, and packages tied up with strings.

My sister stays with me and watches the Austrian family shoo away their own fears. I can tell she's been crying. I see how pink and swollen her eyes are. But she looks pretty in the black dress and high heels. She reaches for my tie, and I slap away her hand.

"I'm just going to loosen it and undo your button, Wes. That's all."

"No," I say while staring into the iPad. "Dad will...Dad will... I'm his Ex-man!"

She takes a deep breath. "Oh, sweetie." Her voice quavers. "Daddy's gone."

"Be back!"

"No, Wes. Do you know where we're going today?"

"Funeral."

She nods and dabs her eyes with a balled, waterlogged Kleenex. "That's right. We're going to say good-bye to him."

I sing, "So long, farewell, Auf Wiedersehen, adieu!"

She stands. "Yes. Something like that." Then she stares into her trembling hands. "I wish I'd said good-bye to him that night. I wish I'd stayed home."

I briefly pull my eyes away from the Von Trapps' bedroom. I catch her look. "Yesss," I say. She slips out into the hallway and I hear her sobbing some more.

∽

In the plush office of the Elbert Funeral Home, Mister Elbert himself, the funeral director who also does the embalming, offers my rattled mother a tissue, which she takes robotically and dabs her wet eyes. The man recommends a closed casket for the viewing.

"Why's that?" asks Thomas.

He flashes a look to Mom and then back to my brother. "We... well," he clears his throat and tries again. "We did what we could. But the *manner* of his passing made it very hard to capture his visage properly." Mister Elbert lets that sink in.

"You mean the drowning distorted his features?" Thomas says impatiently. I flinch involuntarily when I hear him say it out loud. I slap my thigh.

Mom looks over to me. "Tommy, maybe you should take Wes outside."

"No. I want to hear what this stiff has to say."

"Thomas!" she snaps.

"Sir, please," says Elbert, with just a flash of anger that he quickly subdues. His pale face suddenly goes pink before returning to its almost translucent pallor. He's like an octopus in the nature shows I watch with Maria at school that change color real fast. "I realize this is difficult, but there's no reason for *ad hominem*."

Thomas calms down. "Sorry, man. Are you saying that he looks... different?"

"That's another way to put it, yes."

"May we see him anyway?" Becca asks with a weak voice.

"Very well," the undertaker says. We all stand, and he ushers us out of his carpeted office and into the viewing room. The perfumed aroma of fresh bouquets assails my nose. I want to sneeze.

He opens the lid and for some reason I force myself to look. The thing we see lying motionless in the coffin is a tragic rendition of my once-proud Marine father, just as the grim man warns us. Like a poorly executed casting at a cheap wax museum. My dad's face is bloated and pale, and no amount of make-up can alter his savaged appearance. His was a violent death. I wonder what he was thinking as he sank into the blackness of the cold water. Did he change his mind and struggle to swim, unable to without his legs until the salty brine filled his panicking lungs and the world went dark? Did he think of me at all?

"Oh!" my sister gasps. "It doesn't look anything like him!" My brother holds my mom close and nods to the uncomfortable mortician, who offers just a hint of told-you-so in his demeanor.

"Shut it! Shut it!" I suddenly blurt out. Then I start pounding my head trying to beat away the image as the noise all around me, the hissing of the vent, the classical music over the speakers, even the crunch of gravel from cars pulling in and out of the lot just outside the window rush through me like a train. Mom jumps back and lets out a startled squeal.

"Thomas, get him out of here now!"

This time my brother obeys her without protest. "Come on, Wes. Let's look at the fountain outside."

I push him away. "Shut it! Shut it! Fuck it! Shut it!"

"Madam, please!" cries Elbert.

Becca pins the small man to the wall with her eyes. "Shut up, old man! Can't you see he's upset? Come on, Wes. I'll go with you too. It's a pretty day out."

The sight of both siblings coming for me agitates me even more and I pound my fists on the smooth shiny wood of Dad's coffin.

"Missus Scott!" Elbert hisses. "Please, we have other mourners here. You need to control your son!"

Mom goes to say something but then realizes the man's right. She reaches into her bag and I look up just in time to feel the burning spray hit my face. My legs go rubbery and my palms slam up against my eyes which feel like a cactus has been jammed into them. I howl and collapse onto the carpet. When I open my lids, through the starbursts, I see Becca's high heels and Thomas's scuffed loafers on each side. They lift me up, and though I try to flail, I can't take my hands from my burning eyes for more than a second. I stand weakly, obediently, while still clutching my face.

"Oh my dear," squeaks Mister Elbert.

"Satisfied?" my mother says to him.

"Well, I didn't mean that you should assault—"

"Just close the fucking coffin!" Thomas shouts as he and Becca let me go and herd me out into the hall by blocking any other way for me to move. I see that now my sister carries the pepper spray and I scream and recede out the door, through the hallway, and out to the parking lot. Suddenly I feel the sun on my tear-soaked face, and the image of Dad's bloated face is burned away along with the pain in my eyes by the new sights and sounds all around me.

After we leave, Mom looks to Elbert, who nods impassively; this is a man whose profession demands he be immune, even cold, towards grief. "Closed it will be."

ℂ

At the funeral no one cares about my muffled protests. Not today. Not out here on the grass at the edge of the winding lane just on the other side of the iron gates. Beyond the service road is the highway. I can hear distant cars, their tires whining on the pavement that bakes under the hot sun. And I hear the sobs of my family. I've never cried. I can't. I just don't know how. So I rock all the harder.

The images are fleeting and fragmentary, as are those memories of Dad already fading into the noise and chaos of my busy mind. A cemetery on the outskirts of town with a wrought-iron gate and stone walls filled with tombstones, markers, and trees. A line of cars parked along a winding gravel lane. Several rows of folding chairs facing the coffin. People dressed in suits and ties, like me, sitting in them quietly. My family front and center. Becca and Mom in black dresses. They cry and cry. Thomas stares blankly ahead. Grampa Frank holds Mom's hand as the priest says his thing while standing next to the casket. I'm sandwiched between my siblings. In case I cause trouble. I wonder which one has the spray.

The soft, muffled droning of Father Dolan is carried away by the summer breeze whipping my hair. The priest's voice doesn't even reach the straining ears of those on the periphery of the dark-suited throng. "I know we as mourners will soon retreat away from Peter's family and back into our own lives. But let us be supportive not just today, but in the months to come. This man suffered for all of us. Not unlike someone else in whose name we pray. Let us try to be as good to these fine people (he means us, I guess) as the Apostles were to their own friend."

Thomas snorts under his breath so low that only Becca and I hear him. "So Dad was Jesus Christ now? He fucking killed himself. I thought that was a sin."

"Please, Thomas," says Becca through her sobs. "Not today."

"I know," the priest continues, "that resonating through this grim ritual is the deep bass note of mourning and reflection punctuated by a collective bafflement at how such a man's man, an officer who led Marines into the breach, could have ever had his journey come to such an end. All I can say to that is only God knows the mind. And the soul. We must leave it up to His all-knowing and perfect judgement, and trust that there is some meaning to this tragedy, as with all things in His divine wisdom."

I hear Thomas mumble again under his breath. "Bullshit."

I don't really pay attention to what the priest is saying, so I don't know why Thomas says that. Instead my line of sight briefly passes over the coffin that sits on a metal rack. I look at the hole in the ground next to it. An earthen rectangle several feet deep. Dad's in that shiny wooden box with the long handles. I keep expecting him to get up and out of it, like he's waking up from a long, dreamless sleep. A word keeps swimming around in my head. I'm not sure why. It's a word Antoinette has tried to explain to me because I said it once after watching a movie where it was used. (I think it was *Jaws*. I remember it being on a boat. I don't know for sure. Dad quickly turned the channel when he came into the room.) The word is "permanent." I think I surprised Antoinette by bringing it up and she tried to explain: "Permanent? It just means forever and ever and ever. It's not easy to explain, Wes. It tells you that this is the way things will always be. They'll never change." Every minute that goes by and Dad stays in that box, that word "permanent" seeps into my consciousness and fills me with the same terrors I see in my midnight dreams. Will I really never, ever, *ever* see him again? How long is forever and ever and ever? I moan at the thought.

"Ever…and ever…and ever," I crow.

"Shh!" both Thomas and Becca say in stereo.

After the priest stops talking, Grampa Frank slowly rises, pats my brother on the shoulder, and walks up to the coffin. He takes a deep breath and then turns to face the group. Men in uniform stand behind the people seated in the folding chairs. Marines in dress blues with white hats and gloves. Several carried Dad's coffin from the church to the hearse. Now they line the perimeter of the gathering like life-sized chess pieces. There's more people here than Mom expected. Antoinette is here. So is Diane, who teaches my friend Maria. I look for Maria but don't see her. I see a lot of primary care instructors from the special school. And I feel them watching me. Studying me. Antoinette doesn't have her clipboard, but I know she's filling it out in her mind. It's okay. I'm too confused to care. Too much is happening today. I want my tablet. But my lap is empty, so I pound my fists on my knees.

"Thomas, watch our brother," whispers Becca as Grampa Frank clears his throat.

"Don't do anything crazy, Wes," says Thomas in a voice barely audible over the chirping of the birds and the distant hum of the highway. "I swear to God I will end you if you go nuts today."

I don't want to be ended. So, I look down and study the reflections of the world on my shined leather shoes while trying not to shout.

My grandfather begins talking. As he speaks he looks directly at Mom. "How should one approach a man's wake and funeral when the death was at that same man's own hands? How are the mourners to feel? Should we be sad? Angry, perhaps? How about confused and befuddled? For me the answer is: 'all of the above.' I could say that he died nobly. That he gave his life for his country. But that would whitewash what happened. Peter was maimed in a place few have ever heard of. A hole in the wall of the world. He went to war a whole person. He came back a shell with no legs. A broken, sad man. And I'm pissed about that. But there'll be plenty of time for the 'whys' later, I reckon. Later." He pauses. His voice cracks. Then he coughs and continues. "Later for my daughter, when the sympathy cards and phone calls stop, despite what the good Father Dolan here says. The flowers go brown and wilt and are tossed in the trash. And all that's left are thoughts of what might have been. Broken promises and smashed dreams. Joanne, baby girl. You deserved a better hand than this. But still…my son-in-law did give me precious gifts in the form of my grandchildren. Becca, Thomas…" He hesitates. "Wes. And I suppose I'll always be grateful for what he's done in that regard. But it was a steep price to pay. I know my daughter loved him. I know she knew the risks of marrying a military man. Especially one who kept putting himself in harm's way when he had nothing left to prove. But his fellow Marines in the back know why Captain Peter Scott kept going back. He did it for them. And that's admirable in a way. Can't fault him for that. He could never sleep easy after a day at his desk back here when his fellow Marines were fighting over there. Yeah. I guess we can admire him for that. Even now as his family suffers for his devotion to something beyond them." His voice goes soft. Grampa Frank's angry at my dad. I can feel it. "Even as my daughter suffers. Left alone to handle a life barely manageable by the two of them. But this is how life goes. This is the here and now. Well, hell. I'm just rambling on now. Sorry. I'm not too good at something like this. Even if I should've been more prepared for this day that I knew would come…" He can't say anymore. He sits back down and stares up at the blue sky.

❧

Over two hundred visitors pay their respects to the man who finally finished the work the bad guys in Iraq started. Many of them are Thomas's high school friends. Some, like the guys in his band and on his football team, I know. They feel compelled to come and pat him on the back. (Ords like to touch each other a lot.)

But his friends aren't much help. For my brother, the reality of the moment slams into him like a shovel to the face as he stares down at the closed casket. He breaks down sobbing and storms away to be by himself under the shade of a maple tree. I watch him make a fist and swing and hit the tree as if it's the reason for his being here today, guilty of some crime I can't understand. He looks down at his cracked fourth knuckle and grimaces in pain. He'll spend the next three weeks with a splinted finger as a reminder.

I can only stare down at the blades of grass at my feet. A vivid green forest in miniature. A beetle crawls over my shined shoes like he's scaling a high wall. Six legs moving in tandem. Propelling him along. A land crab of sorts. I expect to see Dad's hand enter the frame and pick up the shiny black bug to show it to me. To gently place it in my hand so I can feel the tickle on my palm, the way we used to on the shore. The way things used to be. But the bug just moves on with whatever quest is before it. It slides down the other side of my shoe and back into the grass. Then it's gone.

PORCHES AND PLACE SETTINGS

In the immediate fog after Dad is gone, I ponder two signature images that I know will remain with me through the years. The first one is my mother sitting alone in the screened-in porch facing the woods behind the property. Sunset. The insects hum and skitter and a warm summer breeze whistles through the screens. She sits on the wicker chair, her legs crossed delicately, looking so very old to me. A drink in her hand even though it's early afternoon. White wine. It's her preferred sedative once the heavier prescriptions run out and the doctor, fearing addiction, grants her no more. She stares blankly as I enter the porch. Deep in thought. So very alone and lost. Widowed at forty-eight. Too old to reset her life, jam-packed with so many memories from her prime years. So many shared experiences with a dead husband. So many photo albums.

Is my mother crying? I don't know. Probably. I quietly enter the porch and, staring into my tablet, I sit down across from her. A crescendo of cicadas fills the air like a building electric charge.

"What are you looking at on there?" she asks weakly. Dutifully.

Her voice befits her frame which is fragile and weak. She's lost several pounds and her cotton white blouse hangs on her bony shoulders like a cloak over a statue. Dark circles like perverse blue grins hold her eyes on me even as I look away. "I'm so sorry, Wes," she sighs. "You're too young for something like this to happen. Even if you're oblivious to just what a crappy hand you've been dealt. To have to go so much further in life without your father. He was here just a month ago." She loses herself in an image of him, a phantom pain of her own, and then goes quiet.

I don't want to feel any pain, so I gaze into the doting eyes of Maria Von Trapp on the screen.

Mom considers me and wonders if I'm feeling the loss. The mother in her can't help it. I'm a part of her. An appendage whose every ache registers on her psyche.

"Are you okay, Wes?"

"Yesss," I say while Maria races past the nuns who wonder how to solve a problem like her.

"Well, there's nothing 'okay' about any of this. It's a cruel blow to a young man. Even a young man…like you." Her voice cracks and the balled Kleenex in her other hand rises to the corner of her eye. "You don't deserve this."

"And you do?" It's Thomas.

Mom looks up at him as he enters the room and sits next to me. He looks at the tablet and snorts. "*Sound of Music*. Shocking."

"No one does, Tommy. Not you. Not Rebecca. And especially not Wes." She pauses to collect her thoughts.

"Yeah. Especially not him," he says. "I mean I matter and all, but, well, it's him that really needs TLC."

"That's not what I meant."

"Sure it is. I'm used to it."

"Nobody deserves this. No one." She reaches over to take my brother's hand. "Not even your father."

"Dad!" I say. "Sand crabs!" Then I retreat back into the movie.

Thomas pulls his hand away as the flame inside his heart flickers then glows brighter. "Had me, then ya lost me," he says with an acerbic grimace. The way he looks at Mom prompts her to stare down and run her finger on the rim of her wineglass.

"He loved you all very much," she says quietly.

I break from the tablet to stare off into the woods. I can hear the rising sound of cicadas and it hurts my ears. But through the electric hum I hear Thomas clearly enough.

"I notice he's not here to tell us himself," he says.

Mom takes a sip and winces in an agony of regrets and what-ifs. "You can't know what he was dealing with, Thomas. None of us can."

"Mom," he suddenly says. "You were with the man for over twenty-five years. Why didn't you get him help? Especially after that day with the gun? How could you not know the asshole was suicidal?"

Her face contorts into a reproachful frown and some color returns to her cheeks. "Don't you dare call your father that!" she shouts, and a sharp crack suddenly registers in my ears. Mom looks with shock at the hand that just rose up from her lap and slapped her son, as if it belongs to someone else. Thomas rubs his burning cheek, sorting through a full deck of emotions, unsure which card to play. Rage. Concern. Resentment. Shame. In fact, I know that his first reaction whenever struck is to hit back harder at the offender and I spy his fist curl into a ball ready to unload as anger surges through him. But then I can see that his primordial inclinations drain, and reality takes hold again. He inhales a deep breath and lets the tension gripping his muscles loosen and then drain away. The reality of what almost happened sets in. He was this close to decking his own mother.

"I don't blame you for hitting me," he says calmly as he stands up and turns towards the house. "I blame him. For everything." The last thing my weeping mother hears from her seventeen-year-old son before he disappears into his room and the tunes start to play is this: "Fuck him anyway."

I think he means Dad. I think.

ॐ

Table settings.

Even when Dad's off to war, Mom always sets a place for him at the dinner table. "Your father's with us in spirit," she says. But ever since the funeral, she doesn't do that anymore. It really upsets me. I like four. Mom tries to calm me when I point to the empty space. "It's okay, Wes. Remember the song? 'Three Is a Magic Number'?"

But I like the number four.

I sit at the table and peck away on the tablet. Mom and Thomas are still eating, and they try to have a conversation, but the world is all confusion. The memory of Mom slapping him across the face is still fresh in his mind, I guess. And I think Mom's embarrassed. All I can think of between typing is that I wish Dad would wake up and come home. Through the waves of sound, I catch a moment of their conversation. Thomas tells Mom how hard it is. I think he says something that makes her sad because she puts down her fork and pats her eyes with the napkin. Then I realize what it is. He notes the missing table setting too.

"Like the missing man formation," he says, while pushing his peas around the plate with his fork.

"What do you mean, Tommy?" she says.

"Well, you know. Remember when Dad told us about that funeral for the Marine pilot he went to? The guy that crashed in the sea?"

"Yes."

"Yeah, well they had some planes fly over the burial. Like a salute or something. And he said they flew with one plane missing from the formation. The dead guy's plane." Then he motions to me. "I think Wes gets it too. As much as he can anything that's happening. Three. The magic number. Dad's the missing man at the table."

Mom fights back a tear. Her chest bounces and she takes a deep breath. "This must be so difficult for you."

Thomas nods and rests his cheek in his free hand while tapping the plate with his fork. He stares down at it. "Yeah. I guess the hardest part isn't so much the crying, and the confusion. Or those pitying looks from neighbors I want to throttle when they give me those eyes, you know?"

Mom smiles weakly. "I know." She looks over to me as I type furiously away, never looking up, but taking it all in over the static. "You expect those things as part of the grieving process. But…"

Thomas finishes her thought. "But no one tells you about the painfully prosaic aspects of life after the death of a parent."

Mom raises her eyebrows. "Prosaic? Someone's been doing more reading than they let on."

"It's from the SAT prep course. I think I'll use it in Scrabble." He cracks a smile but then it fades. "It's the little reminders of your emptiness that step up to smack you in the face. That empty space on the table really brings home the way things are now."

"I know, Tommy."

"I guess each person has their own private symbol. For me, and Wes maybe, it's the place settings. Just three." He counts with his fork. "One…two…three. I saw you before. I was watching you from the living room. You paused and stared down at the mat. Then I saw you fold it and put it back in the pantry. Three placemats. Three plates. Three glasses and three sets of silverware with three napkins. That's all we are now. Just the three of us."

"Becca!" I shout. Don't forget her. She could make it four. Nice and even.

Thomas and Mom both look at me. "Don't hold your breath, Squid," Thomas says grimly. "We'll be lucky to see her more than Christmas and Thanksgiving."

"I wish you wouldn't say that," Mom says with a hushed voice.

"How many times has she been out here since the funeral?" he asks bitterly.

"Two!" I shout. "Becca! Becca! Two! Two! Two!"

"You're the numbers geek," my brother says to me. "I'll take your word for it." Then he stands.

"You haven't finished your dinner," says Mom.

"I'm not that hungry." He turns to leave.

"Tommy, are you okay?"

He pauses at the door and takes a deep breath. I look up and he seems even bigger to me standing under the transom. He inhales and then says with his back to us both: "There are a hundred reasons to hate Dad after what he did. And believe me, I've taken them all out for a spin at one time or another over the month. But I think those fucking place settings are the worst."

Thomas spends long hours in his room alone. When he's not hitting a tackling dummy, he works out his frustrations playing his guitar. One day, I enter his room. It's fifteen steps from the door to his window. *One step… Two steps… Three steps.* The sun hits my face as I stare out into the backyard. Birds tweet, the late summer wind shushes through the leaves. His guitar sits on a stand next to the window, Gibson SG, black, strings gauge 10 through 46. My fingertips run along the strings, tracing them up the neck over the frets. I pluck one and it makes a metallic twang. His practice amp, a tiny black box with the word *Marshall* on it, is turned off. I pluck again. And again. And again. And—

"What do you want?"

I yelp and jump back. I'm so startled I pound my head with my palm to shake out all the energy that surges through my brain before it fries. Then I slide down into a ball and rock. Thomas sighs. He's used to my outbursts. "Jesus, take it easy. I thought you saw me."

Thomas lies on his bed, hands folded behind his head, eyes boring into the ceiling. He's just lying there. I haven't seen him all day. It's nice outside and my brother lies in bed staring up at nothing.

He sits up and pivots his legs around and slides off the mattress. He's in a pair of sweats and a Giants jersey. "You like this?" he says, sidling over to his guitar. He grabs it off the stand and crouches down to me. "It's okay. You can touch it. I'm not mad. You just sorta freaked me out."

I unbury my head in my folded arms on my knees and reach out to pluck it. The low E-string resonates through me. "Not bad," he says. "I wonder if you're like one of those retarded kids who can sit down at a piano after only hearing a tune like once and play it note-for-note." He looks at the window. "Why not. One more reason for you to get all the attention, I guess."

He sits down in a chair at the little desk he uses for schoolwork and Xbox and starts playing a tune that sounds sad. "That's called the blues, Wes. You hear it? It's a scale that builds on the pentatonic with an extra note that…" His voice trails off. "Why am I bothering." But I understand exactly what he means. The blues scale is the minor pentatonic with a flatted fifth.

"Flat the fifth…flat the fifth…flat the fifth," I say.

He looks at me as he plays. "Well, look at *you*." He keeps playing. "You know why they say most teenage white boys like me can't play the blues? Because we ain't fixin' to die yet. But I've seen death firsthand, Wes. What happened to Dad has really freaked me out, you know? I mean, fuck, man, I can't believe he's gone. I think I've paid my entrance fee to the Crossroads." His playing grows more intense. He bends the notes and strums hard. I don't know the song, but it goes from being sad to angry. "You know, in a way our daddy was murdered, Wes. I mean, no, he wasn't shot by a man down in Memphis over a crooked game of cards. It was worse. He killed himself. Yeah, he was messed up in the head, and fuck, man, those legs. I couldn't even look at 'em. But still. What the fuck, right?"

He leans down to press a button on his little amp and the light goes red and it starts to hum. Now his guitar is loud and growling.

Like some sleeping monster he poked awake and it's now looking for someone to tear apart. His voice rises, and I start to moan as the sound crashes into my ears. But he ignores me. He's talking to me, but not really. I think he's just talking to God, to life, to whatever is on the ceiling he was staring at when I walked in. I wish I hadn't now and I want to bolt. "They say 'the blues ain't about choice. When you stuck in a ditch, you stuck in a ditch. Ain't no way out.' Sometimes I think there's no way out for me. My Big Daddy's death was permanent. But somehow I gotta push through this finality."

"Permanent," I mutter. I know that word. The one Antoinette taught me. The one the fisherman in *Jaws* used.

In my brother's room, along with the obligatory posters of Lawrence Taylor and Eli Manning, photos of Eric Clapton and Jimi Hendrix torn from *Rolling Stone* and *Guitar* magazines are taped up in a collage that form a shrine to the musical alchemy that mixes together his pain and sorrow and conjures the blues. And I guess my brother draws strength from these images as a priest does when staring up at a crucifix. From his cocoon of introspection emerges a young man bent like a broken limb improperly set, the bones fused in a mangled unnatural pose that will eventually require re-breaking and re-healing. But he can play football and play the guitar. So he has that going for him. But enduring that summer is a steep price to pay for Thomas's musical rite of passage.

Solace eludes my brother. At night, when the guitar's stashed away and his calloused fingertips throb, he stares up at the ceiling, a restful sleep denied to him just as it must have been from Dad in those terrible days of torment before he made his final play.

My brother stops playing. Agitated now. More like the Thomas I know. "Quit your moaning. It's just a guitar."

"Von Trapp!" I shout. I want to hear something I like.

"Fuck *The Sound of Music*. Why do you like that stupid show so much? You think living in a big mansion with perfect kids is real life?

Hell no, man. What those fucking towelheads did to Dad in Iraq, and then what he did to himself here. That's life. That's the real fucking deal, bro. Even your singing la-la-land family lost everything in the end. Do you ever even get to that part? Do you understand that?"

I understand. I just don't care how my movie ends. I like that they're happy and love each other and sing. I wish Thomas could be happy. But I can see it. He has his own night terrors now. It's not the bad guys who killed Dad who come for Thomas in the darkness. He wages his nocturnal wars with fleeting images of a bloated, drowned man, a wailing mother, and the policemen trying in vain to hold him back from the edge of the pier.

"Sir, please step back!" But always it's too late. Too late to shield him from the image branded on his eyes forever. The sight of a dead Marine, his face the color of ash and swollen like a pillow, strands of kelp wrapped around his legless torso, being hauled out of the dark, salty brine like a prize catch.

He stops playing and rests his chin on the body of his guitar. The amp hums angrily and I want to leave. "Wes. Look at me." I can't. I look down at my wriggling fingers. "Fine. Don't, then. Stay in your world. It's probably better in there anyway." He sighs. "Do you sleep well at night? I bet you do, don't you? It's nice to be oblivious isn't it, Squid? Me, I can't sleep anymore. And when I do, it's that superficial kind, a restless mix of anxiety, frustration, and sadness. And I'm so fucking exhausted. I don't wake up any more refreshed than when I lay down to face my ceiling." He pauses. I can tell he's somewhere else, in his own world. And then: *"I don't know if I can handle this."*

I feel his eyes study me as I rock and shift my gaze from my fingers to count the Velcro straps on my sneakers.

"Can I tell you something? I'm even praying again. Like I used to at church. But I get nothing back." He waits to see if that registers with me. "You have no idea what I'm talking about, do you?"

Thomas doesn't know that I have a vision. It whips past me and then disappears back into the clutter. But I can still see it, dimly, in the periphery of my private chaos. I see him on a sweltering summer night when the shrill electric whine of the night bugs pierces the air like the shriek of an agitated teakettle. I imagine he even drops to his knees at his bedside, like the child he once was, in a feeble attempt to pray for relief from the anguish. But nothing comes back at him but a mocking darkness and a symphony of tiny creatures totally indifferent to his quest for answers.

ॐ

Then with the abrupt flip of the calendar leaf, August becomes September, and with the days perceptively shorter, the summer just slips away. Poof! A new school year with all its promise and peril is on me, whether I'm ready for it or not.

MEMORIES
IN THE ATTIC

Mom keeps all her mementoes of Dad stored in the attic. One day after school, I slip out of the living room and make my way up two flights of stairs into the dimly lit space hemmed in by slanted roof beams and lit by two dust-covered windows overlooking the backyard. I'm surrounded by stacks of boxes, an old bed frame, plastic containers filled with baby clothes from three cycles of raising kids...two Ords and one Ex. I sit alone in the cramped space that Thomas once said he'd like to clear out to make a bedroom, secluded from the rest of the house. An angry brother's sanctuary perched high in the rafters. But it isn't going to happen. Not now. Time creeps up on him like it did Becca, and he'll be moving out of the house soon. Then it will just be me...and Mom. No one else. Unless Dad somehow can wake up and join me. That would be nice. I miss him. But I don't think he's coming back. This idea tears at me, but I can't get out the words to tell anyone, so I can only pound on tables and moan out my frustrations. I wish I had another way. But I don't. I'm sorry about that. It's just who I am.

I scrounge around, searching for nothing in particular, when I come upon a cardboard box labeled **PETER** in scribbled black marker tucked away in a lonely corner where the slanting roof line meets the hardwood floor slats. Unlike the other containers neatly labeled with care like "Christmas Lights/Ornaments" or "Halloween" or "Children's Toys," this one looks hastily packed and thrown off to the side, as if my mom performed a distasteful errand she wanted to get over with as quickly as possible. Since the cardboard ends aren't taped but just folded together, I sit and rock on a creaking chair with the box at my feet, peering down into it like a magician does a top hat with a rabbit inside.

This is all we have of Dad now. Everything he was, jammed into a flimsy, three-cubic-foot box hidden in a dark corner of an unfinished attic along with the extra rolls of wallpaper and cans of touch-up paint. But through my static, I can remember more to Captain Peter Scott, USMC, than what's in this box. There is the mind that he protected from all the picklocks of his family and friends...except me, I think. He talked to me. Because he knew I listened. He knew that somewhere behind my slaps and kicks and moans was his son who cared about what he had to say. That I'm more than just the robot voice on a tablet pointing out "ball" and "screwdriver." He told me his dreams and aspirations, all taken away when he rolled his wheelchair over that pier. He relayed dreams to me of leaving the Marines and buying a house in the country where I could learn to ride horses. Where the Ords wouldn't bother me. He talked about Thomas's graduation, which he will never see. The future grandchildren he will never hold. A life he surrendered unlived. Leaving me in a world of Ords with no one to guide me but the people at the school. Although Mom tries. I just don't think she's made that way. Thomas is too angry to care. And Becca is too far away, where she wants to be. It's just me now. And suddenly this attic seems very dark and filled with the pops of steam pipes, the groans of expanding wood in the heat, the buzz of an angry fly, the caw of crows outside the window, the growl of a neighbor's lawn mower. Like shotgun blasts all around. I slap my palms to my ears and rock until the terror boils away, leaving me empty and sweaty and tired.

I calm down and reach into the box and dig out its contents. Dad's life unfolds before me one piece at a time. A news clipping from 1975 announcing the death of his own father, Harold, from cancer when Dad was just eleven. A graduation cap from his high school. A portrait of him as a freshly commissioned Marine officer in his dress blues and white visor cap...the same picture on his closed casket. Photos from Iraq. One of them in particular shows Captain P. Scott and his men on patrol in some dusty town. The people look very poor and scared. Some are veiled shapes like wraiths who show only their eyes. I wonder if they're Ords or Exes or maybe some other type of person Dad never told me about. The picture is taken by someone else as Dad and his men take a break in the rubble. It looks scary over there. Mean. These look like the same pictures I study on my tablet when Mom's not looking. Dad's men look into the camera with suspicious eyes that bore through me from deep within their sockets. I can look people in the eye in photographs. Just not in real life. I don't know why. And I wish I didn't meet these men's gazes. I see misery in them. What happened to Dad over there? Behind them in the distance, plumes of black smoke rise into the otherwise-clear sky. A black smudge looks like a helicopter swooping in low to do whatever damage it can to the unseen bad guys trying to hurt my dad. I study his worried face for a long time, and he stares back at me. What's he thinking here? What was I doing at the exact moment this was happening? Was I happily watching Liesl Von Trapp fall in love with Rolf? Was I having lunch with Maria at school? The date on the back tells me it's the last picture taken before the night he skyped us.

Digging deeper I find several news clippings of the bombing itself and an edition of *Time* magazine. I stare down at the cover. The same one on my tablet. A black-and-white photo of a wounded Marine being carried away from the bomb crater, a man hoisting him under each arm and the other shuffling backwards while holding the shattered man's booted feet so his legs are parallel to the blood-soaked ground. Across the top the caption reads: "Carnage In Iraq: Wave Of Suicide Bombers Hits The Marines." I find a framed photo of him sitting up in a sheeted bed wearing a hospital gown. A purple heart-shaped medal's pinned to his chest. A tube runs into his forearm. The lump of his body under the covers goes flat at the knees. As he sits up in his bed, he looks not at the camera but off into the distance, as if wary of the years ahead.

I lay the photos to one side and peruse my parents' bulky wedding album. My mother is so young, her face unlined, with light blonde hair. Grampa Frank walks her down the aisle. He looks mad. (He always looks mad. I don't think he likes me either. Not many people do. I wish I could be more Ord sometimes.) In another image frozen in time, my father proudly walks down the aisle in his uniform. The start of a tumultuous life that will bring these two some happy times but end badly...at least to the unsuspecting bride who smiles back at me. More photo albums and miscellany, from *Brookhaven Courier* news clippings of Becca's honor-roll status to announcements of Dad's promotion to captain. A carousel of memories beginning with baby Rebecca's first photo fresh from the womb, her head in a cap, eyes slits and her bunched-up little fists protruding from her swaddled blanket like a boxer's, and careening through almost three decades of one man's life to end with my parents standing on the Brookhaven football field before the Homecoming game of Thomas's sophomore year posing by his side. My brother's in a scarlet uniform and his helmet with a black horseshoe decal dangles from one taped-up hand. The numbers whir through my head...16.0 sacks (national average 1.19), 11 interceptions (national average 1.16), total tackles 38 (national average 14). He's grown taller than Dad by the time this is taken. In the image, my mother looks happy enough. My father in khaki uniform bears that same distant expression he manifests in the hospital bed. Like he knows he has to go back to the bad place. I never realize it until just now. But I can see it clearly in his eyes. He's not all there. I

grunt aloud at the thought that he has barely two years to live here…
and at my mother's tragic oblivion.

At the bottom of the box, I find the signature book from Elbert's
Funeral Home. I open it and am surprised by just how many sig-
natures are scribbled on the list. I flip through several pages' worth.
Many of them I recognized as Thomas's classmates.

Suddenly the book resting on my knees flies out of my hand. I
yelp and leap to my feet. "Book!" I howl and slam my fists against
my forehead.

Mom clutches the funeral book to her chest like it's a baby and
shouts back: "He's gone! Don't you understand that? How do I make
you see—Stop it, Wesley!"

I yell, "Stop it! Stop it!"

Through my shouts I hear: "Didn't you hear me calling? I was
worried sick about you!"

I fall to my knees on the floor and slam my palms with loud slaps
against the dusty hardwood slats. "Dad! Dad! Dad!" Mom goes to
touch my head and I slap her hand away. "Dad!" I shout again. "Dad!
Sand crabs! I'm his Ex-man! Dad! Dad!"

Then I go silent and stare down at the darkness within a crack
between the wood and hear her exhale and regain control. "Oh,
sweetheart. There is no 'Dad' anymore." She reaches out to hold me
and I leap up and back against the rafter. Her hands are like fire to me.
"Why can't you just let me touch you? What have I done that makes
you hate me so much?"

My eyes briefly meet hers before darting back to my feet. Like
a brief glance at the sun. She holds out the book. "Do you know
what this is?"

"B-O-O-K," I say, remembering something from somewhere in
the past with Antoinette at a table.

"Yes. It's a book of all the friends who came to say good-bye to
your dad. They know he's gone, Wes. You need to understand the

same thing and say good-bye to him." She lays it gently back into the box and closes the cardboard flaps. "You and Tommy both."

I just stand there. I'm sorry, Mom, but I just can't face you. You don't love me the way Dad does. The ringing in my ears blocks some of what she says. What does she mean about Thomas?

She moves the box back to its lonely space in the corner. "This is where your father lives now," she says quietly. "Someday you'll understand. And then maybe you'll let me in."

SKIMMING STONES

As with every day since Dad was put in the ground to sleep, I count three place settings at the table. *One...two...three.* The third spot, the one at the head of the table now where Dad used to sit, is for Thomas. As I run my fingers over the tablet lying flat on the tablecloth, my brother keeps asking Mom about something called "insurance." I don't know what this means, but I think it has to do with a lot of money, and I can tell the subject makes Mom agitated.

"I tried," she says in a pensive voice. "But that last policy was taken out too soon before he died."

"Who took it out?" asks Thomas. "Doesn't the Marine Corps give you something?"

"Some. But this was extra," she says. "Grampa Frank's been paying for it."

Thomas lets out a sarcastic laugh. "Wonderful. Your own father was betting that your husband would die so he could collect?"

"Thomas! No, it was nothing like that."

"He hated the fact you married a soldier."

"Marine!" I shout. I remember Dad never likes being called a soldier. That's Army, he always says.

Thomas looks at me. I catch his eye and can tell he's analyzing me. *How much do you really know?* his look says to me. "Okay. Marine."

Mom tosses down her napkin and shoots to her feet. "Your grandfather loved Pete. But he's not stupid. Good Lord, Tommy, what do you think your dad did for a living? He was a combat soldier—Marine. Whatever! I don't care anymore now. All I know is he's gone!" She pauses. "If it makes you feel better, the insurance company denied the claim. Try as he might, Grampa had no luck getting around the suicide clause. The policy's worthless. Are you happy? Six hundred thousand dollars. Life-changing money."

"You mean blood money," he says quietly while staring into his string beans.

"It must be nice to be young and so full of moral certitude. That 'blood money' could've bought you a trip to any college you could get into." She turns to face the window and folds her arms. "Captain Peter Scott…the gift that keeps on giving."

It's a daunting prospect and I can tell my brother is severely unsettled by it all.

ও

"I don't know how we're going to get by," Thomas confides to me as we take a walk down to nearby Schreiner Lake on a mild and pleasant Saturday afternoon. Mom asks him to give her a break from me. She has another headache and we leave her laying down on the couch, a wet towel over her eyes. Mom gets these pains in her forehead a lot lately. (I hear her telling Becca over the phone: "The doctor says they're just tension headaches, ever since the Paxil ran out. No, she won't refill it. Bitch.") The shadows are already lengthening even though it's just a little before six. The days are getting shorter. The summer's coming to an end…but it won't go quietly. "Do you get what's going on at all?" Thomas says to me. "Sometimes I wonder about you. I really do. Just how dumb are you, little brother?"

I crouch down and fish through the pebbles that line the shore. Smooth and soft to the touch. I can feel him looking down on me. My brother's eyes boring through my back like two drill bits. I hear a plunk as he tosses his own rock into the water, and I glance up to see the concentric circles ringing out over the surface. I find it unsettling how one event can so irritate the tranquility of the lake, its impact rippling out far and wide.

"Why couldn't she see what was happening?" he asks, more angry than perplexed. "It's such bullshit." I watch his powerful arm whip another flat disc of a stone out over the water. It pelts the surface and I count as it skips *one…two…three, four, five, six* times before gravity sucks it under.

"Bullshit…Bullshit…Bullshit," I blurt out, though I'm not sure what it means.

"I shoulda been there for him." He peers across the lake to the low line of trees on the far shore. A scattering of houses dots the waterline, just visible among the old growth forest.

"Yesss!" I say, again unsure why. Maybe I remember how the family receded from Dad when he came back from the bad place half a man. Maybe I'm thinking for all of us. In my vibration land, sometimes the truth reveals itself like one of those 3-D pin art toys. Thomas doesn't like my agreeing with him.

"What the hell's that supposed to mean?" A flash of darkness shows on his face. His defensiveness is electric. "Fuck it," he says. "You and Mom were the ones with him all the time. And dear sister was hiding with her pink pussy hat friends in New York." He defiantly glares at the sky. At God. "I don't feel any guilt at all."

I'm too busy now crouching and fishing through the rocks to notice his approach until his shadow falls over me like a sinister eclipse.

"And what were you doing during all this?" he says, standing over me. "Hiding in your room watching that stupid Von Trapp movie?"

I don't like what he's saying to me, so I stay in my squat while holding my palms over my ears. "Raindrops on roses! Whiskers on kittens!"

My brother shakes his head. "Jesus. No wonder he offed himself." He crouches down with me, as if we're two friends contemplating a mutual find on a fossil dig. "Did you sense it? Couldn't you tell? I know there's someone in there, Wes. Remember the gun? Didn't you know that your own father was getting ready to kill himself? God, he must have been so fucking miserable." He pauses. "I guess if I had a kid like you, I'd be a little messed up too."

Although I should be angry, all his mean words do is make me feel low. Is he trying to blame *me*? Did I do something wrong to Dad? I hum softly trying to work it out.

"Oh, stop it," Thomas says to me.

I need to unleash. I want to hit him, but I know he carries the pepper spray. So I jump up—I can tell he's startled by my sudden movement…good—and I let a rock sail gracefully across the lid of the water…*plip…plip…plip, plip, plip, plunk.*

He follows the stone's skimming path, leaving a long trail of widening circles like troubled thoughts in its wake. "Damn. Too bad you're not normal. You'd make a helluva pitcher. Shit, you're even a lefty. I never noticed that before." He stands and breathes in the humid air as the sun goes down. "I guess it was just one of those things."

"Just one of those things," I say.

"Yeah. Just one of those things. Come on, Squid. Mom's got dinner waiting." We leave the rocky beach and head for home in the fading twilight. The first crickets stir in the shoulder-high grass and floating coontail that hugs the briny edge of a narrow inlet that eventually leads to the sea. "I mean, Dad seemed fine to me, you know? Like that gun thing was the test and he passed it. He talked about Iraq some and drank a little more than usual. Stayed in bed a lot. But I just figured his physical therapy was wearing him down. I guess none of us knew." But then his placid mood slips back into that darker place. He's wrestling with something inside. "But how could Mom not know something was up?" he demands. "She shared the man's bed, for shit's sake. Well," he says with a final barb, "you're not all there. You're not capable of thinking beyond your stupid iPad. But maybe if Mom didn't care so much about herself, or you, our dad may still be alive."

I have nothing to say to that. We walk the rest of the way home in grim silence.

❧

Tonight Thomas barely touches his food.

Not even his chiseled good looks can hide his emotional exhaustion. At age seventeen he comes off as older. Not mature, just aged. He looks, in his own words, "tired and wired." Our conversation by the lake seeps through the noise and keeps playing in my mind. Did I do something wrong with Dad? Is Thomas right? Am I a bad son? After dinner he disappears into his room and an hour later comes downstairs showered and groomed and steps into the kitchen. He's dressed in a collared shirt, stylish jeans, and leather low-rider boots.

"My, don't you look handsome," Mom says while loading the dishwasher. I'm still seated at the table tapping away on the iPad. I hear Thomas grab something from the refrigerator and pop it open. A beer Mom keeps cold for visitors. I've never seen him drink before. Mom looks at him but says nothing. She senses something frayed and buzzing in him too.

"You're not taking my car if you have that," she says.

"Trevor's supposed to pick me up. But he's late, of course. We're just going to Jackson's party."

"Is Jackson the one with the big house on Lambert's Mill Road?" Mom asks.

"Yeah. His old man's loaded."

"Are there going to be any adults there?"

"No clue," he says. "It's not my house." He pauses. "There a problem with that?"

"No," she says quietly. "I just thought maybe we'd go to the country club for dinner. Get us all out of the house."

"I'm already getting out."

"You know what I mean."

Thomas takes a swig and wipes his mouth with his sleeve. He belches. "I didn't even know we still belonged. I thought it was Dad's membership?"

My mother's face shows disappointment. "Until the end of the year," she sighs. The country club membership is something she can no longer afford. I can sense she's bothered by Thomas's manner. He doesn't seem right tonight. The conversation at the beach flies through my head like bits of scattered recordings.

"I won't be gone long," he promises as if he's read her mind.

"Oh, don't be silly," Mom says, masking her concerns. "Go have fun."

"I'll try," he smiles thinly. I notice he's already drained the beer and crushed the can in his hand. He looks over to me at the table and leans in closer to see what I'm typing. I shut down the screen and return to the picture workbook. "Swing set?" he says with a smirk. I tap it and the next image comes up. "Sailboat." He pats me on the shoulder and I swipe his hand away while staying focused on the tablet. "So easy being you, isn't it?" The beer's hitting him already. He begins obnoxiously reciting John Cougar Mellencamp. "Hold on to sixteen, Squid. Hold on as long as you can."

"Fourteen," I reminded him.

"Right. Guess you still got time then." His phone chimes and he reads a text which I figure is from Trevor, his ride. "Another hour? Fuck that."

"Tommy!" Mom says. "Must you use that word?"

"Fuck that!" I say.

He shakes his head. "Sorry. I forgot we have a parrot in the house. I won't be late." With that, he just grabs the car keys from the drawer and waltzes out the door.

My mother's eyes follow him, but she doesn't protest his defiance. She leans up against a counter. "Does your brother seem okay to you?" she asks me, not expecting me to answer. She does it herself: "Are any of us?"

One word on my screen is "Rome." I tap on it and it brings me to a play called Julius Caesar. I tap again and find a line from the play. "*The evil that men do lives after them. The good is oft interred with their bones.*" I don't really know what that means but I think it matters when it comes to Dad. I can just barely make out the rumble of Mom's Buick, which Tom commandeers against Mom's wishes for the night, pulling down the drive and peeling out onto the street. Soon it's quiet outside again but for the remaining crickets that valiantly hang on to their last vestiges of life until the first frosts hit. Even though the skies are clear, a storm is brewing. Hurricane Thomas will make landfall at midnight.

HURRICANE THOMAS

"How could you let it happen! Huh? Get up, Goddammit!" These sounds in the haze. Like a dream at first. A familiar voice but distorted, like a cassette tape run at slower speed, giving it a more guttural, demonic quality. I hear a loud *thump!* And that's what snaps me out of my fading REM sleep and causes me to bolt upright in my bed.

"Stop it, Tommy!" I hear a squeal of protest. "You're scaring me!" A slamming door down the hallway. My mother's room. A furious slapping like an open palm on thin wood, then a more insistent pounding, a balled fist.

"How could you let him do it!" Is that Thomas?

More screams from my mom behind her bedroom door.

"Tommy, please go away! *Please!*" More pounding. The very house shakes with each hammer blow.

I spring out of bed and race around the corner to encounter Tom's dark silhouette at the far end of the hall. He's facing the closed door to Mom's bedroom and leaning up against it pounding and thumping like a raiding enemy. He has fifty pounds on me. And it's mostly muscle. He spends a lot of time burning off his excess stress-fueled energy in the gym, as befits his type-A personality, and he strikes me at that moment as an imposing monster in the shadows. He keeps screaming at the door while slamming away. "How couldn't you see! What the hell kind of wife lets her husband kill himself!" He's wearing square-toed boots and the flattened tip of his right foot slams against the bottom of the door, causing an audible crack of splintering wood. I howl and cover my ears. "No! No! *No!*"

"Tommy! What's *wrong* with you?" My mother's voice rings from inside the room again, this time with more desperate urgency, and fear. Fear of her own son whose temper explodes when mixed with alcohol like shaken nitroglycerin.

"Stop! Stop! Stop! Stop!" I scream as I storm down the hall to confront my enraged brother. One whiff tells me all I need to know. An odor cocktail of stale beer, whiskey, and perspiration exudes from his skin like waves of heat. When he turns to face me, his eyes are on fire and his upper lip curls in a feral snarl. Something in me snaps. My ears hum and the images come at me like strobes. I scream and lurch forward, heaving him off the door, which is right by the stairway. I shove him too hard in my adrenaline rush, and in his drunken disorientation, he falls away to the side and topples down the top of the stairs leading to the first floor. His hand flails in a forlorn attempt to grasp the handrail but misses its mark by a good six inches, and he goes cascading backwards down the steps to end up as a writhing ball of limbs and girth on the ground floor at the base of the stairwell. It all looks so surreal to me in the dark, his bulky form one story down and to my left, my mother still screaming from behind a locked bedroom door for her oldest son to please leave her be!

I try to clear my head to take it all in, still in my tight-fitting Eli Manning T-shirt and torn flannel pajama pants, but there's just too much coming at me and my ears ring. I want to explode. I've never seen Thomas like this before. Never seen such rage. And it's aimed squarely at the most innocent person in the house. My brother lies in a heap at the bottom of the stairs and I curl up in a ball by the locked door to Mom's room. I sing "Raindrops and roses and whiskers..." My voice fades.

"Wes?" The whimpering from the bedroom softens and I hear Mom's slippers shuffling across the polished hardwood. "Wesley? Is your brother gone?" she asks with her face up against the other side of the door. I look down to my left. He's moving. So I haven't hurt him too badly.

"Accident," I say. A nursery rhyme I learned at special school somersaults through my exploding mind. "Ashes, ashes…we all fall down…."

"Oh my Dear Lord!" The door whips open and there stands my mother, all five-four, and reduced one hundred five pounds of her, in her nightgown, her dirty blonde hair undone and falling around the slope of her freckled shoulders. Her hands furiously cling to something. It takes me a second to register what it is, so strange is the image. It's Dad's pistol. "Where's Tommy?" she asks. "Did he fall? What did you do to him? Is he hurt?" Questions come at me like the ripping of a machine gun. My mother's beside herself with confused terror mixed with the maternal urge that, even in the face of violence at the hands of her own child, trumps all others. But that gun. How scared had she been?

"Him," I say gently, the words unable to form coherently, which frustrates me all the more. I slam my palm against the drywall. "Him…" I try again. "Hurt…you!" I slowly reach my hand out to her. She thinks I'm reaching for her but then shows disappointment when I point. "Gun."

Her eyes go wide in a strange, bewildered panic. She looks down at the weapon in her hands. "I was afraid," she stammers with a hint of shame. "Your brother. I don't know what's gotten into him. He came home, and I was sleeping, and next thing I knew, he was just screaming craziness at me." She looks up at me, still clutching the pistol in her frail hand. "He said I let your father die. That I was a bad wife. And a bad mother to all of you. He said…" She broke down into sobs. "Oh, why am I bothering! You have no idea what any of this is all about! Just go back to your room and sing with the damned Von Trapps!"

"Whiskers on kittens," I say. She looks at me with surprise. "Not your fault." I whisper these soothing reassurances while I gingerly reach out to take the gun from her quavering hand. "Shhhh," I say again to her softly. "Him hurt you. Tee," I moan. "Angry. Mean to you." My voice trails off.

"No, Wes," she says, more in control now. "You can't have this. You've already hurt your brother."

"Hurt! Hurt you! Thomas!" I scream.

"He's not himself," she says. She moves to the top of the stairs. "He's just upset over your father. I swear…if you hurt him, I'm sending you away."

She's more upset with what I did to him than what he just did to her. I hear excuses for a brother who's just terrorized her to the point where she actually went for Dad's gun tucked away in their closet on a shelf behind a rack of clothes. I can't think clearly, or I'd be wondering what Thomas would have done to her had he kicked in the door. Or what would Mom have done with that deadly weapon in her hands and the hulking form of an intoxicated, wild-eyed man coming at her in the dark, even if it was her own son? I do think one of them would have died, considering what Thomas does next to me.

She stares at the gun in her hand. "This has to be a bizarre nightmare." I moan in frustration. "It's okay, Wes," she says, fighting back tears. Her skeletal frame looks so frail. She's just a bag of bones. And Thomas is so big. "He's angry and drunk and who knows what else."

"Why?" I ask.

"Don't you even know?" That's all she says before collapsing to the floor. She's fainted.

Through the darkness I hear a groan at the bottom of the steps. Thomas is stirring.

"How do you solve a problem like Thomas?" I sing to myself as I do something I've never done before. I crouch down and touch my mother. I feel something stir in me. Love? Hatred of bullies? Instinct?

I don't know. I hoist her up, the pistol still clutched in her hand. I carry Mom to her bed, the one shared for three decades with Dad (who I don't think is coming back) and lay her down to sleep. I notice a glass of water and a prescription bottle of some sort on the night table. Her eyes are closed, and the tears dry. I take the gun from her hand and study it. With my free hand, I cover her with her blanket. I can still smell Dad's cologne in the weave. She's never had it washed since that day on the pier. She usually washes his scent away whenever he goes off to fight bad guys. But not now. I pick up the bottle and try to read the label. Alprazolam, whatever that is. I place it back down on the table.

Before turning off the light and leaving her to resume her troubled sleep, I examine the pistol. There's no clip in it. I've seen enough movies to know that no clip means no bullet. Why, after all, should she know how to load a pistol, or what to do with the nineteen-round box magazine Dad keeps in his drawer? Dad says, "If you do the extra step of finding the mag and slapping it in the grip, and then go through the motion of aiming it at someone, that means you're ready to kill."

Mom isn't ready to kill. But there's a reason I say she may have hurt her son in spite of herself. Dad says every gun is loaded.

For some reason I don't return the gun to its space in Mom's closet behind the hanging blouses and dress belts. I'm clinging to it, I suppose. It's a piece of Dad and I'm not ready to let go just yet. It feels dangerous and I'm frightened by it. But I grip it tightly. My adrenaline rush subsides and now the reality of what I've awakened to comes over me. My older brother's come at his own mother, still grieving, still lost in her own mournful reality, and in his alcohol-driven rage, accuses her of letting his father go away. He's probably felt so powerless. Thomas is a boy who needs to feel in control of his life. Handsome to a fault. Football star.

The sign Dad hung in my room is still there. Mom went to take it down and I screamed and screamed. I was so mad at her I thought she'd use the pepper spray. It just says, "Press On." But I think Thomas is even more upset than I am about Dad leaving.

Becca says that Thomas also has two gears like the ones for me. Park and a hundred miles per hour. I'm getting a glimpse of the darker side of his high gear and it terrifies me. I mumble to myself. "Sixteen point oh sacks, national average one point one nine. Eleven interceptions, national average one point one six. Total tackles thirty-eight, national average fourteen. Sixteen point oh sacks, national average one point one nine. Eleven interceptions, national average one point one six. Total tackles thirty-eight, national average fourteen!" But the awful scene of him storming at his own mother is just a prelude. The main event comes when I slip quietly out of Mom's room and close the door behind me. I stand at the top of the steps holding the pistol, and as my eyes adjust, I can see that Thomas is no longer lying prone at the bottom of the stairs. But where is he?

Still in my tight pajamas and torn Eli Manning shirt, I make my way slowly down the risers. I'm being cautious not out of fear so much as not wanting to slip on some unseen article of clothing or piece of paper at my feet and tumble to the bottom as my brother had. Counting the steps soothes me. One…two…three…four…five…all the way down. I want to call out to him as he had to be in the dark house. At the foot of the stairs, I stand silent in the darkened foyer which serves as the main entrance to the big house, although we always enter through the side door from the breezeway connecting the house to the garage. I strain my eyes and ears but detect no movement. Where's Thomas? I want to call to him, but I can't get the words out. So I hum and moan instead.

More relaxed now from counting, I casually step through the darkened hall. Zigzagging shadows cast by the silvery light of a full moon framed by the large bay window painted eerie shapes on the walls. My ears ring and buzz but I shake out the noise. It's always worse when I'm scared. The darkness scares me. The gun scares me. Thomas scares me. I want Dad.

"Edelweiss. Edelweiss," I hum in a whisper. My hands shake. The gun shakes. The shiny black barrel reflects in the moonlight. "Clean and bright."

No sign of my brother. I look down to see that I'm pounding the pistol so hard on my thigh I feel a bruise forming and it hurts. (My special school friend Maria wouldn't feel a thing, I bet). I push through a swinging door to the family room expecting to find him sitting on the couch, which is where he often lounges in front of the TV when taking a study break or when a game's on. He's not here. Maybe he's climbed back up the stairs and stumbled into his room while I was in the master with Mom and the gun. He's probably sleeping off whatever laboratory serum courses through his veins. He'll have an apology to make for being so mean. He's also going to be nursing a lot of bruises from me pushing him down the stairs. "Hurt Thomas," I mutter. "Raindrops on roses…"

Without realizing it I find myself holding the pistol in both hands now as I search the dark house. I resemble someone rooting out a burglar rather than trying to find his own drunken brother. I creep into the kitchen where dishes from the dinner Thomas mindlessly sat through just six hours earlier sit stacked in a grimy pile. Silhouetted tree branches outside scrape against the high windows in the autumn breeze.

I gurgle to let off more steam and stare down at my bare feet, barely visible in the darkness that seems to ring with noise from the crickets outside to creaking, popping floorboards. I hear nothing.

"Rolf," I offer to the shadows. It's the only boy's name that I can get out. For some reason I can't say Thomas.

"Don't call me 'Rolf,' you freak," I hear a voice growl from somewhere outside my head. "This isn't a fucking movie, and you're not a fucking Von Trapp. And I sure as hell ain't no blonde Nazi."

"Rolf! Rolf! Rolf!" I scream. "Raindrops on—" *Wham!*

One second I'm standing in the darkened kitchen with Dad's gun held in my hands, the next I'm on the floor, leaning up against the trash compactor holding my head and howling. I find myself swimming up through a disoriented fog and frantically trying to scramble to my feet only to be slammed down to the floor once more by another very powerful hammer blow to the back of the head. On my knees I crane my neck and look up to see Thomas looming over me. He screams, "Motherfucker! I fucking hate all the noise! Can't you shut up! Can't you ever shut up!" Another blow, and I wail some more. "I never got to know Dad because you took so much of his time! And now he's gone. Forever. Do you get that? You selfish fucking freak!" *Wham!* I try to understand him and why he's so angry at me now, but I only register the grunting and shrieking and high-pitched screams as if fury in its rawest form's been released from him like a foul vapor. His fists raise and in the shadows they appear to me as high-swinging boulders on the end of sinewy muscular pendulum arms. The boulders descend, and I see white flashes and hear the hollow chucking sound as knuckles connect to my skull, rattling my ears and sending the world spinning. My older brother doesn't just hit me this night. He *unloads* on me. As if in a nightmare, every time I try to stand up a dark force pounds down at me again and again and again. "Throw me down the stairs!" A blow to the head. "The fuck you doin' besides wanting more and more when he was going insane!" Another fist to the scalp. "Self-absorbed asshole!"

Now I'm the one doing the begging.

"Stop! Stop! Bad brother! Stop! Hurts!" I squeal while defensively crouched in a ball down onto the kitchen floor with my hands over my head like bombs are exploding all around me. But the jackhammering continues. I keep my head down absorbing them, one then another, and another, until he tires out and steps back, panting like someone who's just run a footrace. He gawks down at his bleeding hands as if noticing them for the first time.

Suddenly all's quiet in the kitchen again as Thomas withdraws into the living room. I pull one of my hands down from protectively cupping the back of my head and find it wet and sticky. Spread out on the kitchen floor just two feet below me, I spy a small puddle, which in the moonlit space looks the brown color of motor oil. But I know that if the lights are flicked on it will show deep red. I'm bleeding heavily and my head swims. I see two of everything. I try again to stagger to my feet but I'm too dizzy, so I collapse back onto my back with my blood-soaked hands reaching up into the air, groping for nothing in particular. Through the fog a frightening thought runs through my head, jolting me into awareness. My hands are empty. Where's the gun?

A few minutes pass in silence but for the humming of static in my brain. I gather my wits about me and try yet again to hoist myself to my feet. This time I make it, and although it takes my brain a delayed second to follow where my eyes go, the wooziness starts to pass. I want to throw up. I can feel a large welt forming on the back of my head, which I think is good because one time when I banged my head against a wall in frustration and Dad stopped me, I heard him say to Mom, "Well, it's better to bruise out than in when it's the head." Dad still not home. Thomas beating me. Mom hiding in her room. My strange life so out of control like a planet spinning off into the void. For some reason it's not the Von Trapps but one of Thomas's rock albums that drifts through my head as I cautiously step back into the foyer and stand on wobbly legs at the bottom of the steps. A dark, ominous song about flames being long gone, but pain lingering on. I place a trembling hand on the newel post for balance and crane my aching neck to gaze up the flight of the stairs. The top may as well be the top of a mountain. A bloody handprint smears the finial. My blood. Then I see him.

Glaring down at me, like some silhouetted monster, is my brother…with the shiny black pistol in his hand. He says nothing. He's leaning up against our mother's bedroom door, which fortunately I didn't unlock when I closed it behind me. It's as if her room's under siege. Hopefully she's still asleep.

"What…want?" I groan with exhaustion. I'm too weak to continue looking up at him; a wave of vertigo hits me and I feel sick to my stomach. I turn and collapse, sitting on the third step, my back to my brother who's just beaten me senseless for the crime of protecting our mother from his rage. For the crime of being me. Of being an Ex. A brother who now stands one floor over me holding a gun in his drunken hand.

I cup my face into my palms and for the first time since Dad's buried, I cry aloud. The tears burst out of me in a frustrated expression of confusion and hopelessness. All of my own pent-up frustrations finally breaching the surface. I want to go to the beach with Dad and look for sand crabs in the surf. Why did he leave me?

"Mom?" Thomas then says, tapping on the door rather than kicking it this time. I don't turn. I just listen from below, sitting with my back to the stairway counting my bare toes.

"No," I mutter, still facing away from him. "Bad brother…"

In response what I hear is the distinctive *cha-chink!* of the handgun's chamber being loaded and locked. The same sound it made when Dad loaded it in his room. It fills me with terror. My eyes snap open. Even though it has no magazine, the sound of a gun bolt being pulled back when the weapon's in the hands of a violently drunk animal just one…two…three…four…five…six…seven…eight… nine …ten…risers above me is not a good thing. Especially when my blood-soaked Eli Manning T-shirt can attest to the mindset of the seventeen-year-old holding the gun. This prompts me to muster my depleted strength and pull myself by the newel post up to my feet, fighting through the lingering dizziness. I don't connect to Mom the way I do with Dad. I guess this bugs her. She's so very cold and unhappy all the time. But she's still my mother. But for my mom being on the other side of that thin interior door, I'd run from the house as fast as I can. Instead I meekly climb the steps towards my brother.

As I struggle up the stairs, I glance down at my feet to get my bearings, and in the dim light of my night vision, I notice dark spots on the carpeted risers. Like drips from a dangled paintbrush. At first I think it's my blood, but these stains are dry and faded. They are, in fact, months old. They release in me a smothered memory. When my mother came home from the police station, she was acting very weird to me. She brewed a pot of coffee. Then she poured herself a cup, climbed these same stairs, and went to her room where she sat on the bed, sipping her coffee and just staring out the window into the darkness. She must have spilled some climbing the steps. Our reality come home to me in the strangest place. When Becca once asked her exactly why she did this, Mom could never explain. "It was just one of those things we do when our mind's been blasted into shock," she said. The stains at my feet are for me a testament to the pain my mother's been enduring at the hands of her husband. At the hands of her angry son and distant daughter. And at the hands of me more than anyone. Thomas's mood will fade. My "special needs," as she calls them, will remain. I so wish it wasn't true. I so wish Dad was here to make all this right. Maybe he'll come back. And now her enraged son torments her anew. Climbing out of my fog, a desire to protect my mom propels my legs upwards.

"No gun!" I shout defiantly up at him. In the time it takes me to hurl that empty demand at him, I'm at his level in the hallway, looking up to account for his superior height. He finally flips on a hall light to give a first clear view of our tormentor. He looks mean. Like a wounded mountain lion. His eyes are slits. But somewhere deep within me, somewhere past the noise, I know he's still my brother. Something tells me he can't kill me. I hope not, anyway.

He shifts the gun to his left hand. His right's balled into a now-familiar fist at his side. He makes a move and I flinch as the fist comes towards my face this time. This blow's going to hurt and I close my eyes waiting for the explosion of pain and crunching bone. But it never comes. Instead I open them to see his knuckle suspended in the air, just six inches from the bridge of my nose. He sneers and unfolds his fist like a blooming flower to reveal a single unfired bullet resting in his palm. It's shiny gold with the tip a darker rust-tinted cone. It looks so miniscule and harmless. How something this size can do so much damage to a person is hard for me to fathom. But I know that anything can be deadly if thrown with enough speed. I sometimes hurl rocks through our garage windows when I'm angry and there's no one with pepper spray to stop me, and I always marvel at how even a tiny stone can make the glass rain down. At how enough force can overcome any resistance. Just like how even a brother can morph into a wild animal when given the right cocktail of booze and boiling anger.

He offers me a good look at the live round. "It was still in the chamber," he says. He stoops down and slides the bullet under the doorway into Mom's room. She's awake. I can hear sobs coming from the other side. Thomas speaks to the door: "That was meant for you, Mom. He was thinking about taking you with him. Do you know that?" My brother leans back against the wall and sucks in a deep, calming breath. He reeks of beer and sweat. Then he turns and with a final burst of frustrated rage plants his fist right into the wall. He's fortunate that he only hits Sheetrock. If he lands on a stud every bone in his hand will be shattered. The memory of him assaulting that innocent tree after Dad's funeral races through my mind.

I just stand there in the hall, this time in a rare silence, staring at him, my saturated palm glued to my bleeding scalp trying to stem the flow. We hear movement in the bedroom. The lock unhitches and then the door creaks open. Mom stands before us in her nightgown. The bullet's in her open hand and she stares down at it the way her most disappointing Ex child does an especially fascinating seashell picked up off the sand. Something's changed in her. She's no longer a helpless and frail middle-aged woman hiding behind a door from her oldest child's violence. She stands tall and straight, like a witness in the stand facing down her accuser with a defiance that can only come from knowing something the prosecution doesn't. Her steely gaze seems to exorcise Thomas's devil with the force of a powerful incantation, and where just a moment before there'd been fury in his eyes, now there's shame as he lowers them to fix on the tips of his scuffed boots. Banished is the monster that flailed away at a widowed mother and her defenseless son. He is now, at seventeen, a contrite child being scolded by a parent who's reclaimed her rightful authority.

"Drop that gun this instant. Have you gone mad?" My brother looks down at the sleek weapon. Like it's only now appeared in his hand. "Thomas!" she says. I hear the gun fall to the hardwood floor with a loud slap that makes me flinch. "How dare you come at me like that and try to blame me for what happened," she says with a firm tone. "And your brother. Look what you've done. You animal. You drunken, arrogant animal! His life's hard enough without a bully brother."

She glances over to me and pity fills her eyes. Drying blood traces maroon lines down my face and neck.

Thomas looks at me. Really looks at me. "Jesus, Squid," he says with the most normal tone, like watching a sack on the football field (16.0 sacks, national average 1.19). "You look like Carrie at the prom. Did I do that?"

"Bad! Mean Thomas!" I shout at the floor through wriggling fingers.

He looks to Mom then me again.

"Oh shit, man. Please don't be mad."

"Mad?!" Mom shouts. "He's bleeding! He might need a doctor. You may have really hurt him! I hate you. I hate your father! I hate all of you. I could have had a great life. Instead I'm stuck here a widow with two psychotic sons, a daughter who's checked out of this family, and the only thanks I get are the bills I have to pay! God damn all of you!"

She hates Thomas at this moment, and me, I guess. But no such vengeful spite burns in me. Not for my own brother, even as my ears still ring from his pounding. I'm too spent. Too in shock. I have no more screams to give to the night. I feel woozy and my stomach wretches. Half of me still expects to snap upright in sweat-soaked bed sheets, relieved that a queerly terrible dream about Dad dying and Thomas working me over like Rocky Balboa is over, already fading into that place where nightmares go to hide in my memories. But I understand enough to know that this is reality come to call and I'm wide awake. Thomas is more of an Ex in his own way than I ever realized before.

"Oh, Wesley," Mom cries. "As if you haven't been through enough."

I shake my spinning head while holding my hand over the laceration on my scalp that still seeps blood through my matted hair. "Hurt me," I say weakly. Thomas sure can land a punch.

Mom looks me over without touching me. The way I am if she lays a hand on me, I'll explode. "I don't think he needs an ambulance." Mom turns to face her ashamed son and fixes him with a glare that can scare off the tides. I've never seen her this angry. I've never seen her show any emotion at all other than regret.

"This wasn't meant for me," she says through gritting teeth and she hurls the bullet at my brother who flinches as it strikes him square in the face. "It was meant for him. Do you understand?" She points at the pistol lying indifferently on the floor. "I found him one day in the den sitting at his desk with that *thing* pointed up against the bottom of his jaw."

"So did I," Thomas says with a voice so quiet I can barely hear it. "I mean…so did we. Wes and me. Sitting in his chair in his room."

"I was there too, remember? But this time was before that," Mom says.

"When?" asks Thomas.

"Sometime before summer." Mom covers her face with her hands. "He looked so lost, the poor man. I slowly talked him out of it. I took the gun away from him. I should have thrown it out after that."

"Why didn't you?"

Mom takes a deep breath. "I think I was afraid. But I left it empty. He must have had extra bullets somewhere and reloaded it. Just one though. Like…he was saving it for him."

"Why didn't you tell me?"

"I guess I didn't want to believe it. Even after that second time we all found him." Mom sobs. "I know. Even then I thought he couldn't actually ever do something like that. You just don't think they'll really do it. Never. We're supposed to think it's just a cry for help. Isn't that what they say in *Doctor Phil?*" Her voice fades to a hush whisper. "Even so, I wanted to take him to a doctor, not just a shrink. I told him they had drugs to help his moods. But he said no. He promised me he was okay and that he didn't know what he'd been thinking. His mood seemed to brighten after that day we all found him. After you left the room, he even cracked a joke about almost adding a whole new meaning to the term 'scatterbrains' or something just as ludicrous."

"What?" my brother replied, the embarrassment and self-loathing heavy in his voice. I also raise my head upon hearing this. Just how messed up was Dad in his last days? Did thoughts of his family ever even cross his mind when he had the barrel poised to fire a round through his head?

"That's right," she says. "So I did stop him…twice. But I couldn't watch him all the time." She pauses. "Are you satisfied, Tommy? Are you satisfied that I did what I could? How about you, Wesley? What would you boys have had me do? Commit him against his will? Call the loony truck and have the men in white suits take him away in a straitjacket? Ruin his reputation? I may as well have pulled the trigger myself!"

"Mom," Thomas says, coming to her with his arms outstretched. She defiantly waves him off. She needs no hugs from the child who's just forced her descent into her own private hell down yet another ring, this time into the level of violence and accusation.

"No," she says defiantly. The anger dripping from her lips. "Don't come near me. What you did tonight is inexcusable."

"I've had a few," he offers feebly in his defense as he keeps his distance. "I'm so sorry. You too, Wes."

"Bad brother!" I snort, examining my blood-caked hand. It looks like a clay-red glove. At least the bleeding's stopped.

"That's enough!" Mom snaps. "Wes, are you sure you're alright? Can you understand me? Stop moaning!" I go silent and nod. "Good God, look at you. Thomas, look at what you've done to your own brother. I want you away from us. I want you in bed and don't come out until whatever's in your system runs its course. And if you ever drink or do drugs while under my roof again, you'll never be welcome here! I don't care how old you are or whether you think you're some hot-shot football player or musician or whatever you do. Take a look at what you really are." She points to me all banged up as if I'm a visual aid. "Is this how you deal with life? You think your father's passing is the only terrible thing that will ever happen to you? I thought I raised you better than this. I thought I raised a *man*."

"Maybe so," he says as he retreats into the bathroom to wash his sweating face. I can tell he's thinking of Dad with that gun resting against his chest with the barrel aimed up at his throat. "But you sure as hell didn't marry one."

Mom just stands in numbed silence as my brother's words hang in the air like a foul odor. He shuts the bathroom door behind him and Mom looks at me. "I'd help you clean yourself up, but we know you won't let me touch you." She goes into her own master bathroom and comes out with a wet towel. It's ruby red. So the blood won't leave a stain. She thrusts it into my hand, and I shout in protest. She ignores me and goes back into her bedroom and shuts the door. As I stand alone in the dim hallway, streaks of red running down my face and a wet towel in my hand, I hear my mom crying louder this time. I guess she misses Dad. So do I.

Eventually I go to the sink in the main bathroom in the hall and look into the mirror. A lost, blood-caked apparition stares back at me. My ears are humming like there's a freight train in my head. I run the water over my trembling hands and wash the blood off my face and into the sink. I look down in horrid fascination at the brown soup spiraling into the drain in a filthy whirlpool and I wonder what happened tonight.

BLIND FAITH

The next morning I stay in my bedroom. Unlike the other bedrooms—Mom's, Becca's (when she visits), and Thomas's, plus a guest room—my door has no lock. I guess they all don't want me to be alone with no way to reach me. I don't get that. I'm fine when I'm alone in my room…at least during the day when the sun pours through my window facing the front yard and driveway. Considering the strange ways that Thomas and Dad have been acting, how come I'm the one who can't have any privacy? Oh well. I guess they have their reasons. I don't care. I wouldn't lock my door anyway. I don't need it like Mom does. I don't have someone coming at me with a gun. Just his fists. My head still hurts, and I feel kind of woozy. But I think I'll be alright. Thomas sure can hit, though.

My brother has football practice every Saturday morning: 16.0 sacks (national average 1.19), 11 interceptions (national average 1.16), total tackles 38 (national average 14). It's raining pretty hard out but they practice anyway. Considering what happened last night, the gloom is comically fitting. Although my door has no lock, my brother knows the rules when coming to see me and the door's shut. Knock first. Wait for me to answer, or make a noise like a moan, or say "yesss." If you just walk in and surprise me, I might get so startled I'll throw something at you. I hurled a whole Lego house at Becca once. She ducked her head just as it flew past her ear. It shattered against the wall behind her and exploded in a cloud of red, blue, and yellow plastic bricks falling onto the floor. The noise was so loud it made me scream and I really lost it. I went after her and out came the pepper spray and then the burning and the apologies. Why am I like this? Why do things send me instantly from what Becca calls "park to a hundred miles an hour"? Dad knows. If he ever wakes up, I'll ask him.

So Thomas knocks gently. Cautiously. Ashamedly. A single knuckle on wood. The same knuckle that lacerated my scalp and made the blood flow. But I'm not thinking too hard about that. The rain sounds like a group of elves all tapping their fingers on the roof, along the outside walls, the window. *Tap...tap...tap.* I'm busy staring out the window, studying the raindrops as they run down the glass. It makes the image of the driveway and lawn all wiggly. Like I'm looking out to a strange, distorted world of bent lines and crooked shapes. Only the trees, already twisted and contorted, appear normal to me. I can't seem to focus. I see pairs of things. Thomas really hurt me. And he knows it.

He tries to talk to me before he leaves for the football field where he can take out his frustrations on other kids, big Ord kids like him, and be praised for it. I just pray that he goes away. Although praying doesn't seem to do me much good. Sometimes I wonder about God. Dad always talks about Him like He's always walking along side us. There to catch me when I fall. But I fall a lot, and unless Dad's around, there's never a hand to intercept me and gently lay me down. Just the slap onto the hard concrete surface of the Ex world. But Dad believes. And so do I, then. "Look out to the horizon, Wes. Look at that wide-open sky. Think how deep that ocean goes. Miles and miles down. Into the blackness where only the lights of the funny fish glow. Look up and see how high that plane's flying. Think of all the stars at night. God's bigger than all of it." *"Big!"* I say. He smiles. "Bigger than everything you'll ever see. And yet He loves every one of us. Ex kids most of all." I want to ask Dad why, if God loves me so much, would he make me so different? But then again, why would he take away Dad's legs when he tries to stop bad people from hurting good people? Some things I may never understand. A lot of things really.

I hear the rain pelting the roof as my attention stays with the outside world. The cascade of falling leaves knocked free from their branches by the drops of rainwater flutters past my window. They float gingerly to the ground and many land in flowing rivulets of run-off that carry them like empty canoes to the more gushing flows of the gutters outside our property...and then off to the ocean and the faraway places I'll never see. Thomas's knocking grows more insistent. He follows up with the frustrated jiggling of the knob. He knows it doesn't lock, but he doesn't try to open the door. I guess he doesn't want me chucking my lamp at him. I turn away from the rain and gaze at my closed door. This is the same position Mom was in just last night, but this time the force in the hall is penitent rather than in a frothing rage. "Come on, Wes," he pleads in exasperation. "I know you can hear me. We need to talk, man. Or whatever we can do to make this right. Please."

I slide over to my bed and recline on the ruffled sheets to stare up at the ceiling. By now I know every crack and fold in the Sheetrock overhead. A blank canvas upon which I've painted many a thought and mood as I've grown more conscious of myself. My latest mental fresco is a wish that Thomas would go away. There's still dried blood on my pillowcase. My scalp wound must've briefly opened in the night as I tossed and turned. Plus my eyes remain just out of sync. I just want to watch the Von Trapps. It's way too soon to make amends. Thomas wants to scour and put back into the cupboard a frying pan that still simmers from the heat of a flame just lowered beneath it. My confusion towards my brother will take time for me to process.

The rapping on the door ceases and Thomas finally retreats in defeat down the hall. His rankled voice is more muffled and distant, drowned out by the buzzing speakers pumping in my head amplifying the rain shower's *ssshhhhh* as it swells all around me, as if my walls have melted away and I'm one with the outside. "...he won't come out..." Muffled talk. "Can't be late for practice...."

There's another tapping on the door. More delicate this time. Mom gives it a try. "Wes?" I say nothing. Instead I tap on my tablet and when it lights up, there's Maria's dreamy eyes watching Captain Von Trapp as he strums his guitar and croons about edelweiss. "Wesley, honey, don't you want to at least hear your brother's apology before he leaves?" She's barely audible now. Liesl has joined in. Georg smiles at his daughter, the way Dad used to smile at me. *You look happy to meet me....* My iPad fills my world now.... "At least please tell me you're okay. Wesley, I demand to know that you're not hurt and that your head is healing. I have to come in."

"No!" I shout. *...Blossom of snow may you bloom and grow...*

"I'm sorry, Wes. I need to know you're okay." *Edelweiss... Edelweiss...bless my homeland forever...* "Don't throw anything. Please, I can't take that right now."

I sigh and heave my aching body off the bed. After pausing the movie and laying the tablet on the mattress, I pick up the pillow. Holding the case by the corners I shake it violently towards the ground until the bare cushion slides out and plops to the floor. I step over to my door and open it enough for Mom to see my face. She looks back at me relieved. Her eyes are red and swollen from a long night of intermittent sobbing. I glance past her and see a fresh splattering of white paste on the wall where Thomas's fist made the hole. Mom has flecks of white on her face and hands. She's already started repairing the damage to her home. Repairing the damage to her youngest child, her Ex child, will take more time.

"He just wants to say he's sorry," she says in her role as peace envoy.

I shake my head emotionlessly. "Sorry."

"No, Wes. He's sorry. You have nothing to be sorry about."

"No! Hurts!" I'm glancing down at my bare feet and rocking as I say this.

"What hurts? Are you hurt?" She kneels down to try and catch my eyes resting on the floor, but I look away. Her hands have white paste on them. The same color as her bony fingers. She's so frail. Translucent skin.

"Thomas," I say. Not sure why, as is often the case.

"Yes. He's sorry."

"No."

"Please, baby," she says. "If I can forgive him, you can."

"No. Thomas no." I hand her the bloodstained pillowcase. Then I retreat back into my room filled with the sound of the pouring rain and shut the door again. I stand in the middle of my room, unsure what to do next. Then people talking erupts from the iPad. *"Fraulein. I want to thank you. I don't really know my children. I want you—I ask you—to stay."* Stay, I think. I want Dad to stay.

I pull up a chair to once again face the window. It's a bird's-eye view of our car in the driveway parked among the forming puddles. Thomas's form darts for it, hunched up against the rain that's starting to come down in sheets. He's in his burgundy football pants with thigh and knee pads, cleats, and T-shirt. He carries his helmet, shoulder pads, water bottle, and practice jersey in one hand while fumbling with the keys in the other. The car door rips open and he hastily tosses his equipment over to the passenger seat. He's anxious to get out of the rain, but he pauses before sliding behind the wheel. My brother turns and gazes up at my window. I stare back at him like a captain on the top deck observing a flogging. He throws me a pained look that conveys everything from remorse to embarrassment to pity. My expression stays the same. I'm in "park." He waves furtively and then slips into the seat and shuts the door with a *thunk* that breaks through the white noise of the rain. I'd hate to have to play ball in this downpour. Maybe for him it'll wash away the stain he must feel. I don't know.

As he drives off, I pick up the tablet. I accidentally hit iTunes, which Thomas programmed on the iPad before Dad gave it to me the day he saw me type a sentence on it. The funny thing is the words I typed were the refrain to the last song Thomas had playing on it. So it pops up now and picks up where it left off many years ago. "Can't Find My Way Home." As my mind blocks out the rain to home in on the finger-picking guitar and its haunting D/C, D/Bb, D/C chord progression, I follow my brother's car as its image framed by the red dots of tail lights, like mean eyes looking back at me, ripples and dances through drops of rain running down the glass until it disappears down the drive, leaving parallel tire tracks of mud in its wake. I rock and hum the melody as the singer calls me to come down off my throne and leave my body alone; somebody must change. Somebody, I guess. But I know I can never change. I'll be this way, a drifting probe in the deep space of my mind, for all my days. I'll be on that throne for a long while, waiting for Dad to come home. Dad who I know can't find his way home. Whenever I feel like climbing down and chasing after Thomas's long-gone car to tell him it's okay, that I'm not mad, just confused by what he did, my double vision, throbbing head, and itchy scalp give me ample reason to remain up there, at least for a little while longer.

I tap the button and the music stops. I'm in Austria again, and the world feels safer now.

IN MY ROOM

I don't go to school for four days after Thomas's rage. For the first few mornings, watching the Von Trapps on my tablet gives me a searing headache, but I have no way to really tell anyone. So I just keep the iPad up on the shelf which I can tell makes Mom pretty nervous. Maybe she's come to rely on my routine without even realizing it. Maybe Ords need structure too. And when it's not there, they get all bent out of sorts. (Maybe that's what's wrong with Thomas.) Mom can tell I'm not feeling my best. But I want her to know I'm getting better. My eyes have found each other again, so I no longer see two of everything. Maybe today I'll try to visit my Austrian friends. Any place where it's not so mean as here.

Mom tries. She really does. And I find myself not so scared of her. I guess compared to my brother, she's an angel now. She looks me over as I stare at my wriggling fingers to check on my bruises and lumpy head. "Jesus Christ," she murmurs as she hands me an ibuprofen. She does this every four hours to help bring down the swelling. But I won't take it until exactly four hours have passed—that's two hundred forty minutes, which is fourteen thousand four hundred seconds. I don't understand why she gets so impatient with me for waiting. The bottle says every four hours and I find comfort in the precision of keeping schedule. It gives me a sense of security, like climbing down from swaying tree branches to hop onto solid ground. She just doesn't see it the way Dad does. Or maybe she doesn't care that it's just the way I am, and I guess the way I'll always be. Does anyone care about me? Am I that difficult to live with? Did I maybe deserve to be beaten down as punishment for who I am? That doesn't seem right to me. I know it's something else. I have to believe this. Otherwise, if my own family hates me, then who besides Dad can I turn to when the night shadows come? I miss him. I really wish he'd wake up.

Mom exhales in frustration when she spies me eying the clock. "Oh, just swallow it now, Wes. Can you do that for me? We need that swelling to go down, and I want to make sure you take this. And I've got things to do." Then she looks up at the ceiling. "You happy, Pete? Is this what you had in mind for me when you proposed?" I get excited. Is she talking to Dad? Is he up on the ceiling looking down on me like a protective Spiderman? I briefly glance up. But it's only Sheetrock. I hum and rock and look back down at the terracotta pill resting in the skin folds of my pasty white palm. She keeps talking. "I'd wring your brother's fat neck if I could. This is the last thing any of us need. Another maniac in this house." I wait and watch the clock. The last pill was at 3:58 so I wait until the glowing numbers turn from 7:56 to 7:57 to 7:58. I pop it in my mouth and force it down with a swig of water from the paper cup Mom hands me. When I look up, she's gone.

I stay up in my room a lot. To my surprise Becca shows up, visiting from New York. I stare out my bedroom window and catch a glimpse of a car I've never seen before pull into the driveway. It says "Uber" on the window but I don't know what the German word for "above" has to do with giving my sister a ride. Thomas plays basketball by himself, and as it grows dark under the setting sun, the bright floodlights above the garage door take over. He bounces his ball a few times then jumps and arcs it into the air. It lands dead center in the netted rim a good fifteen feet away. He jogs over to the hoop stand and scoops up the ball with the grace of an athlete. He dribbles. The ringing thwaps of his slamming the rubber ball on the pavement again and again and again concuss my ears. But I'm too enthralled by the motion of the orange sphere, like a happy sun, to turn away.

I track its movements and try to figure out the optimal trajectory to the net. Thomas is naturally gifted at this game, as he is with all things physical…including pummeling his kid brother.

Becca steps out of the car with her small travel bag slung over her bony shoulder. She watches Thomas sink another basket as the car pulls away. "Nice shot," she says coldly.

"That's a three." He turns to face her and spins the ball that balances on his index finger like a whirring globe. Then he catches it. "Nothin' but net."

There's an awkward silence between them and I feel like I'm watching a private dress rehearsal for a stage play.

"Is it Christmas?" Thomas says.

"What?"

"No," he says. "Too warm still. And it's not Thanksgiving because there's no Lions game on." He puts his hand to his mouth in a mocking gesture of shock and concern. "Oh no. Did someone die, then?"

She hoists the flower-patterned bag up further on her shoulder and folds her arms defensively.

"Shut up, Tee."

"Wait!" he says, continuing his act with raised finger. "Stay here while I grab my phone. I want to get a picture of you visiting for no special reason so I can post it on Instagram with my shots of Bigfoot and the Loch Ness Monster."

I can see by her tense pose, my sister's not amused. In fact, her face freezes in a scowl. "You have got to be kidding. You're lecturing me on family?" She steps forward until her face is only a foot from her brother who towers over her by several inches. Her teeth show like a growling dog's and she tries to speak under her breath, but still no one gets just how sharp my sensitive ears have become. "You know damned well why I'm here. Mom called me hysterical over the weekend." She pauses to let that sink in. Thomas stops dribbling and cradles the ball to his hip. "Well?" she says. "Was she exaggerating, or did you really do what she says you did to Wes? And her?"

He lowers his head and sighs. "Yeah. Sort of. I mean. Okay, yeah."

"Holy shit, Tee! You really chased your own mother around while waving Dad's gun? And please don't tell me that you actually beat up our own brother. Our *autistic* brother?"

He looks around as if he's afraid someone else will hear this very unpleasant, and true, accusation. In the growing twilight, no one sees me peering out the window. "Well…look, I don't know what you want me to say."

She shakes her head. "Wow. You know, I always suspected you're an asshole. But never really wanted to believe it. I guess I have no choice now, do I?" She turns away from him and walks to the side door. "Mom in there?"

"Becks," he says. "I don't know what came over me. I mean I was out of my mind drunk."

"Spare me."

She's far enough away now that he has to call out to her back. "I apologized to Mom."

My sister stops but doesn't turn around. Instead she looks up at the darkening sky. "And Wes?"

"I tried. He won't let me in."

Becca sighs. "That's the way he is."

"I mean his room," says Thomas. "I think he's really upset. Or at least as upset as someone like him can be."

"As would I be."

Thomas's voice goes softer. "I really feel awful about it. I don't know. It's like all the anger and frustration came out. It's been tough, you know? With Dad gone. And let's be real, it's not like it was ever really easy around here. Not with Wes."

Becca lets out a chuckle of disbelief. As if she'd hoped Mom was just exaggerating when she called and begged her to take a few days off to come and stay with her. She really needed to see her daughter. And, much to her credit, my sister came through. And now I've never seen her so…mad? That's not really the right word. Bitter maybe? Guilty? I don't know.

She pivots to face him, and her knuckles are white as she grips the strap of her bag extra tight, like she's imagining that's her brother's neck.

"I wonder," she says while aiming a glare at Thomas, who seems to have shrunk a few inches, "who's the real freak in this house?"

ᔣ

Later on I sit at the top of the steps and can hear from the kitchen Mom talking to Becca in a nervous staccato. She's a frayed rope.

"He still has that shiner. I can't send him to school like that."

"I can't believe Thomas did such a thing."

"I know."

"Aren't they going to wonder where he is?" Becca says. "This isn't some public school with a few thousand kids we're talking about."

"I told them he's sick."

"Sick? Just sick? Did you get specific at all?"

"No."

"They buy it?"

"Who the hell cares? I pay *them*, dammit!" Mom blurts.

"Dial it back, Mom. I'm just asking a question."

I hear some fumbling through a cabinet then the *shussssh* of water from the tap followed by a metallic ring. Then the *schlup… schlup…schlup* of percolating coffee. A warm hazelnut aroma soon fills the house.

"I know. I'm just beside myself over all this."

"You have every right to be."

"I suppose. And to answer your question, all I know is Antoinette's already called to see if everything's okay…twice."

"Who's Antoinette?"

·146·

Mom pauses. I can tell she's a little surprised by the question. "Wes's primary care instructor? The brunette? Wow, you really are checked out, aren't you?"

This stings, as does my sister's reply. "Hey. Only one person's checked out of this family. And he's over at the cemetery."

Another pause. "That was a mean thing to say, Rebecca."

Becca's tone softens. "I'm sorry, Mom. That was wrong. This whole situation. It just…hey, don't cry on me now. I'm here, aren't I?"

"Yes, you are. Thank you. It's times like this when I wonder just what kind of girl Annabel would've been. She'd be twenty-one now. Why'd I leave her in that crib alone?"

I can sense my sister's concern in the air. "Oh, Mom. You can't think like that. You did nothing wrong. It just wasn't meant to be."

My mother lets out a frustrated laugh. "And this life was? Oh, well. Woman plans, God laughs. One thing I do know for sure."

"What's that, Mom?"

"She'd have had a wonderful big sister." The chair scrapes against the floor as Mom stands. "How do you take it?"

"Black. Like my—"

"Yes, like your men, I know. Funny girl."

"Oh, just deal with it," she laughs. "He may become your son-in-law."

"My, my. We getting serious?"

"Well, I'm not playing the field anymore."

"Oh really?" A tittering girl-to-girl laugh. "And what's his name again?"

"Bryce. You remember? He's the IT man at Goldman I met in Amagansett over the summer. Works in Jersey City? Has a place on the Hudson?"

"Goldman Sachs? My dear daughter, I order you to marry that young man! Do you hear me? If you don't, I will."

That joke disintegrates into a chill silence. Mom means to be funny. To break the tension. But it just reminds her that she doesn't have a husband anymore. He's asleep. And he may never wake up. Mom clears her throat. "When can I meet him?"

"Soon. Mmm. You always made the best coffee."

"Thanks. It's hazelnut. Your favorite, if memory serves."

Silence. Then:

"So…Mom. What happened here the other day?"

FRIDAY

I match my cards to the clothes while Becca watches over me. "Come on, baby brother," she says, glancing at her watch. "The bus'll be here soon. I bet you're excited to get back to school, huh?"

"Yesss," I say as I sit on the edge of my bed and slip my red socks over my feet.

I can feel her not so much watching me as studying me. Like I've just been unknowingly slipped an experimental drug and she's waiting to see how I'll react to it. The other night while I listened to them from the stairs, Mom told my sister everything that happened with Thomas, and she went from being angry to concerned.

"Any idea how this is affecting Wes?" Becca asked.

"Oh, who knows. When your son rarely talks, it's not easy to have a heart-to-heart with him. He seems fine. Although he hasn't watched his movie in a day or two, which concerns me. I read that could be a sign of a concussion."

"Maybe you should take him to a doctor, Mom."

"I just can't," she said with a pained voice. "Not the way he looks."

"But there could be something wrong—"

"Rebecca!" Mom snapped. "Don't...push me. Please. I'm hanging by one nail here. I think a visit from child services right now might put me over the edge. I really do."

A brief silence as my sister took a sip of her coffee. The tick-tock of the grandfather clock in the living room slammed back and forth in my skull as I tried to focus. "Okay, Mom. I guess it could do more harm than good. But you do have to get him back to school. Back to the structure he needs. I can take off until Friday to help you. But then I gotta head back. We have a big presentation at the end of the month."

"I know," said Mom. "But going back Friday? Just one day before the weekend? That may confuse him."

"Mom," Becca replied with just a drop of impatience in her tone. "Get him back to school. The longer he's out, the more questions they'll ask and the harder it'll be to ease him back into the routine."

So I guess today must be Friday because Becca's still here and I'm getting ready for school. The sun's back out and the birds chirp outside my window so I'm in better spirits. The swelling in my head's gone. All that remains as any evidence of what happened last weekend is a little inverted crescent of a bruise under my right eye.

"You got everything you need?" Becca says to me as I hop off the bed and walk over to the New York Giants wall calendar. I count the dates, one…two…three…four…five…six— "Wes, come on. It's time to go to school now. Mom says you can brush your own teeth? That's great. Let's go to the bathroom and you can show me." I look for my tablet but it's not on my end table. It's missing. What happened to it? I feel an electric surge through my system.

"Von Trapp!" I shout.

"What about them?"

"Von Trapp! Von Trapp!"

"Wes, I'm sorry, I don't know what you're asking."

Where is it? "Von Trapp!" I scream, and out of frustration whip a book across the room.

"Jesus!" Becca steps back. When I stand straight, I'm taller than she is now. "Mom! He keeps screaming 'Von Trapp'? What the hell's he want?"

"He wants this." Becca turns to see Thomas, even bigger than me, standing by the door holding out the tablet in his hand. He steps into my room. At first I'm both startled and scared of him and I leap back onto the bed. "Hit!" I scream. Thomas bows his head.

"Does he do this every morning?" she asks Thomas.

"No," he answers flatly. Something's faded in him since that night he beat me. He casually walks past her and lays the iPad like an offering back on the end table. I go quiet and grab it. Someone's already pulled up the movie I like. I think it was Thomas, trying to make amends in his small way. Whoever it was, it was nice of them. I cradle the tablet in my arms and walk past them towards the bathroom. "He had this next to his bed last night. Mom moved it back to the shelf it's always on. But his routine's all messed up. I guess he was looking for it where he left it. He freaks out easily."

As I lay the tablet down on the hamper in the bathroom, I stare into the mirror. So this is me. This is what the world sees when I step outside the door to face the raging seas. I feel under my nose. There's hair there. Fine, yellow. A sprouting on my chin too. A soft pink blemish on my forehead. I'm changing. What's happening?

My sister's voice echoes down the hall. "Should I go into the bathroom with him?"

"I guess, yeah. Mom usually helps him by putting the toothpaste on the brush. Just don't touch him. You can hold the brush but that's it. Don't you remember? You did it for him when he was young."

"I remember," Becca says. "I guess I thought things might have changed."

I imagine my brother smiling at the notion. "Nothing ever changes with him."

As they talk I gaze into the mirror. I have light brown eyes. The color of sandstone. They're the only eyes I can bear to look into. I've changed. I think Dad's being gone has changed me. I know my body's changed. The nature shows we watch show how baby down turns to feathers, puppy fur to thick coat, caterpillar to butterfly. Wes the boy to Wes the young man? Will I be like Thomas one day? Will I be so big? So mean at times? And then so kind when he wants to be? I still love him. He's right. Some things about me never change after all.

Becca enters the bathroom. "Hey, Tee. He ever pour his own toothpaste and brush his teeth before?"

"Nope."

"Well, he's doing it now."

Thomas steps in through the door to stand behind me. My siblings watch with satisfaction as I *brush-brush-drink-spit...brush-brush-drink-spit. Up-down-side-to-side. Up-down-side-to-side.* White foam fills my mouth like I have rabies.

"He loaded up his brush himself?"

"Yep."

"Well I'll be a pisser on jumper cables," laughs my brother.

"Mom!" shouts Becca. "You should come up here!"

"Damn," says Thomas. "Nicely done, Squid."

I know.

BACK TO SCHOOL

Antoinette smiles as she waits for me to step off the bus. "There's my favorite man in my life! How are you today, Wes?" Then she adds: "Long time no see."

She looks me over as I walk towards her. I don't look up, but she notices the bruise right away. "Oh my, what happened here?" she says, pointing to my eye. I cringe and say nothing but focus harder on my wriggling fingers. I don't want to talk about it. She instantly scribbles something on the clipboard.

I count the number of concrete squares on the walkway like I always do. *One...two...three...four...* Antoinette wears sneakers today so the *clip-clop-clip-clop* of thick heels is replaced with a soft *shuff-shuff-shuff* of rubber soles. I find the sound soothing. I enjoy our little walk over the twenty-five squares. "Twenty-five! Twenty-five!" I shout.

She keeps walking. But she watches me closer than usual. "That's right, Wes. Twenty-five squares." I hear the scrape of her ballpoint pen on the paper attached to the clipboard. She wears a different perfume today. Or maybe it's just the natural smell of her skin. Her shirt's white with frills and stitched flowers.

"White shirt, white skin, white clouds," I say as we make our way with the rest of the kids into the hallway where we hang up our coats and lay down our heavy bookbags.

"Oh, you like my blouse? I only wear it when it's sunny out. I think it's a happy shirt. Don't you? Say, I love your stripes." She means the horizontal blue and red stripes on my Barcelona soccer T-shirt.

Thomas bought it for me this week. It's pretty cool. She keeps glancing at my eye. More scraping pen on paper. It's good to be back. Back with my same coat hook, my same room with the same toys and books and games. The same people. Even the same black-and-white nuns I spy passing by the window on their way to the convent.

Antoinette and I walk to the playroom for our daily word games. I see Maria approaching from the opposite direction down the hall with Diane and she smiles. "Hi Wes. Hello Wes. What's shakin'? What's cookin'? How's Trix? How's life? See any good movies lately?" I don't look up at her. "Hey that's a black eye!" she shouts. "Look at you! What happened! You got a black eye! You been fighting kangaroos? I saw someone boxing one once. I think it was Australia. You ever been to Aus—"

She reaches for my eye and I slap her hand away! Then I crouch down and cover my head like the building's about to cave in on me. I scream and rock. I can tell that Antionette and Diane exchange concerned looks. I bet a lot of ink will flow on their clipboards.

Maria's my friend but I don't want anyone touching me. And especially my eye. The Thomas eye. My lashing out upsets her and she shouts and bangs her head with her cupped hand. It makes a *pop-pop* sound. "Don't hit me, Wes! Now I'll get a bruise I bet. Doesn't hurt, doesn't hurt. Diane, he hit me!"

"Okay, Maria Conchita," says Diane, gently grabbing her offended hand and pulling her away from me. "Don't you want to go to the store with me?"

"Oh yeah! Store! Shopping! Get the cart! Get the cart! Bye Wes. Hope the eye feels better. You like banjos? I heard a man play one the other day! Pluck pluck…" Her voice fades as she and Diane disappear around the corner, leaving only me and Antoinette in the hall.

She crouches down to me. "Hey…Wes? You alright?" I moan and rock. I need to get the bugs out. "How'd you get hurt like that? Can you tell me?" I say nothing. "Can you show me? Make a game of it?"

But I have nothing to say. She presses, looking around to make sure no one hears us. "Did someone do this to you?"

"Yessss."

"Another boy?"

"Mmmmmm."

"A neighbor?"

"Mmmmmm."

I can feel her mood darkening. "Someone in your family?"

I look down at my fingers. They wriggle like the legs of a disturbed sand crab. I miss Dad. "Yessss," I say.

Her voice goes hoarse. "Did your mother do this to you?"

"Hmmmmm."

"Brother? Sister?"

I don't want to talk anymore. I want to play with the speaking tablet. I want to type B-A-L-L-O-O-N so Antoinette will be happy again. I want her to stop asking questions.

"Wes? Can you tell me? Was it your brother? I know he's been having some trouble at school this year." I don't know how she knows this. "It's alright. No one's in trouble."

"Trouble," I say. "Raindrops on roses. Rolf, blow the whistle! Trouble! Trouble!"

"Alright," she relents. "Maybe later...okay?"

"Later okay."

✌

I'm pretty tired at school. Antoinette keeps asking me questions about my eye. I ignore her. It's better just to look at my feet or tap T-U-G-B-O-A-T on the tablet and hum and moan. This way the memories of those fists coming down stay away. I can't escape the scratchy scratch of her pen to clipboard. It sounds especially grating to me. Maybe because I know she's writing bad things about me or my family. I'm not sleeping and I think my body needs a rest. I'm irritable and even the woodpecker outside our window perched on the oak tree at the end of the playground sounds like a jackhammer. At lunch Maria chats my ear off, and for some reason it bothers me today. I throw a cookie at her and she thinks it's a game—"Swing and a miss! You like baseball? I saw a baseball game once. Yankees win!"

I retreat into the comfort of numbers. Baseball's all about numbers. Thomas takes me to see the high school team play some nights when Mom needs a break. I think they play this weekend. Baseball. Yankees. My favorite player is Derek Jeter. I say: "Derek Jeter…Yankees…1995–2014…11,195 at bats, 1,923 runs…3,465 hits…310 batting average. Number two!"

Maria's dark eyes go wide with excitement. "Wes talks! Wes talks! Two what? Two what? I have a book about twos. Two cars, two spoons, Sally Two-Trees! Two of this, two of that. A pair for me and a pair for you. I like pears. Do you like pears?"

"Yesss."

And so our day goes. Our Ex world within the world. The Ord world is out there somewhere. Scary. Yet I'm curious to see it. I may go for a walk one day and explore. Dad likes to read me a book about an Australian native going on a "walkabout." That sounds like it's for me. Maybe later.

By the end of the day, I'm tired and glad I'm going home. When the bus pulls up to the driveway, Becca's waiting. Usually it's Mom. This agitates me a little, but I try to moan it away.

"Hey, Wes. How was school?" she asks. I don't look at her. For some reason I'm feeling a yearning that's been growing in me. I want someone else. I want…

"Mom," I say.

ANTOINETTE'S PHONE CALL

I follow Becca into the house and we find Mom sitting down hunched over at the kitchen table and a bunch of papers with numbers on them and words like "AT&T" and "mortgage." Mom leans on the tabletop with both elbows on the surface, head down. One hand holds the phone to her ear while the other runs through her disheveled hair. Whoever's on the phone with her has her really upset.

"I told you people, he was sick." A woman's voice is on the other end. Familiar to me. Becca stands by the door watching in silence. She can't hear the voice clearly, but I can. It's Antoinette.

"I understand that, Missus Scott. I'm not denying what you're saying."

"Then what are you saying?"

"He seemed healthy to me."

"Hence the term, 'got better.'"

Antoinette pauses. "Missus Scott. Are you going to pretend that your son doesn't have a black eye?"

Mom sighs. "He's a boy. Boys play rough."

"Did another boy do that to him?"

"No. I mean yes. His brother. They were roughhousing, and I guess it got a little out of control. Do you have children, Missus Olensky?"

"Please, call me Antoinette."

Mom nods. "Do you have children, Antoinette?"

"Not yet. We're trying. But what matters at this moment is not my family tree but the fact that Wes missed four days of school and then came back to us with signs of abuse."

"Abuse! How dare you—"

Antoinette quickly shifts gears. "I apologize. That was too severe a term. Let's just keep it as a black eye."

"Let's." Becca looks at Mom with a mixture of apprehension and confusion. She mouths, "What the hell?" and Mom gives her a knowing look.

Antoinette, for her part, keeps her cool. "I'm not accusing anyone of anything. But you know that based on what I saw today, I may have no choice but to file a report to the Department of Education Child Protection Services."

Mom shakes her head and cranes her neck up to the ceiling. She looks like she hasn't slept in weeks. "Why would you need to do that over something so simple as a fourteen-year-old boy with a shiner? What's next? A scraped knee? I don't bubble-wrap my kids, for Christ's sake."

"Wes is special, Missus Scott. You know that. Children on the autism spectrum don't 'roughhouse.' Especially not a child so sensitive as Wes. I can't imagine any behavior more out of character with his profile than that."

Mom exhales. "You don't live with him."

"No, but I do work with him for seven hours a day, five days a week. And I've worked with literally hundreds of developmentally challenged children for over a decade. And, Missus Scott, I can say that unless he has a second personality that only manifests itself at home, I frankly don't believe your explanation."

My mom goes silent. I think Becca can hear Antoinette too because she shakes her head and mouths, "Fucking asshole, Tee."

"Well. I couldn't care less what you think, *Missus Olensky*. I know what happens in my own house, damn you! In fact, I have a good mind to report you to your superiors."

Antoinette remains unfazed. "That's certainly your prerogative. But just know they're already aware I'm in touch with you. In fact, I'm violating usual protocol by doing this."

Mom takes a deep breath. "What do you mean?"

"Well, I'd hoped to arrange a private meeting with you. Off the school premises. In an unofficial capacity."

"I don't follow," says Mom, shrugging at her daughter across the room.

Antoinette collects her thoughts. "Do you know my father was a fireman?"

"What?"

"That's right. FDNY." Mom says nothing. "He was killed in the North Tower on nine-eleven."

I can't see because I'm too engrossed in my wriggling fingers while I listen, but I hear the chair scrape against the kitchen floor. Mom sits back. I have no idea what they're talking about. A tower what? Like my Lego towers? The Tower of London? And what do the square root of 81 and 121 have to do with anything? It must mean something to Mom. And Becca too because she steps over to the table and sits down.

"I'm very sorry to hear that. I didn't know."

"Thank you."

"But at the risk of seeming insensitive, what does this have to do with our discussion?"

"Wes's older brother is seventeen, I believe?"

"Yes."

"I was sixteen that day. The day my dad was killed. I had to struggle through the next two years of high school trying to be strong for my mom, a big sister to my twin brothers, they're four years younger than me, while trying to process all the anger, the confusion, the questions...even guilt, if you can believe it."

"Guilt?"

"Sure. My daddy was working that day to put food on his family's table and a roof over our heads. I know it seems a stretch, but you do feel these things."

Mom's voice softens. Maternal instincts are kicking in. "I can't imagine how hard it must have been for you."

"It was tough. It still hurts. And I'm sure it always will. But what I'm getting at, is that I can understand how hard it is for your son. Your other son, Thomas. Both deaths were tragic. Both at the hands of others."

Mom coughs. "At the hands of others? Antoinette, surely you know how my husband died. No one killed him."

"He wasn't himself. Whoever he was that day killed him. Can you honestly say the man who did that was the same man you knew? Mental illness is mysterious and cruel. I've studied it for years. And all I can tell you is that we know more about what the brain does and how than why. But I'm getting off-track."

"You were talking about Thomas."

"Right. I'm not going to say he did anything to Wes. Nor am I going to say I don't condemn it in the harshest way I can…if he did do something. But I will offer this, and this may sound cruel, but I hope you consider the source and forgive me. I honestly don't know if I could have coped with an autistic sibling during that time." Silence. Antoinette continues, "The emotional strain on him must be unbearable. Not to mention he has college to consider, SATs, sports; I hear he even plays music. What I mean is your son's plate is full. Probably overflowing. And I'm not saying anything like this happened, mind you. We're just talking. But if…if he was the one who gave Wes his bruise, I feel like there's an alternative to getting Child Services involved."

Mom runs her hand down her face and glances up at Becca. It's as if they don't even know I'm in the room. I feel like taking a walk. "I'm all ears," she says.

MISTER O.

Ever since he punched me, Thomas tries to spend more time with me. I can sense his mood and I feel sadness and regret. He really does love me, I guess, and Antoinette's right. It's not easy living with a brother like me. Sometimes I really wish I was an Ord like him. I think we'd have a better life together. Thomas knows I like numbers, so one crisp Saturday, he takes me again to see the bigger kids play baseball at the diamond in the park-like grounds behind the big Ord high school. He knows some of the players and high fives them when we briefly visit the dugout before the game starts. They sit like carrier pigeons behind chain-link fence cages, waiting for their turn to step up to the plate and swing away. I don't know how far it is on this field from pitching rubber to home plate but in the majors it's sixty feet six inches. Seven hundred twenty-six inches.

One of the players approaches my brother. He sports red pin-stripes and a fire-engine red helmet. I bet Antoinette's dad rode in a truck that color down to the North Tower (whatever that was).

"Yo, Tee."

"Sup, Jonny. You on third today?"

"We'll see. Rotator cuff's giving me hell again. I don't wanna risk the scholarship for a game that don't mean nothing." Jonny, number nine, punches his fist into his glove as he talks, and it reminds me of my brother's own fists coming down at me. I look away and moan. Jonny takes notice.

"So this is little brother?"

"In the flesh."

"What happened to his eye?"

Thomas fidgets. "He fell. No big deal. Right, Wes?"

I hum and moan and try to guess the number of baseballs in the canvas bag in the corner of the dugout. Boys sit on the benches chatting or stand out on the grass swinging bats with donut-shaped weights on them. There's a few people in the bleachers. Mostly parents. All come to watch their Ord kids doing an Ord thing on an Ord day. I wish I could be more like these boys. I don't know how they can even see the ball coming at them let alone hit it so far. I never could catch either.

"Damn, he's gotten big. I haven't seen him since the homecoming game sophomore year with your old man." The moment Jonny says that he regrets it. "Shit, sorry, bro."

"It's alright. I'm used to it."

"So what brings a football goon out to watch a real sport?"

Thomas shrugs. "The kid likes numbers."

"Jonny Schiff," I say. "Number nine. Last junior year, ten home runs, three-oh-five ERA, twenty-six RBIs, seventeen scored runs."

Jonny doesn't say anything for a second. I can feel him looking at me as I move on to counting the number of bats in the rack. "Fuckin' A, man. That's scary. You should take him to Vegas. You know, like *Rain Man*."

Thomas just says, "It's nothing like *Rain Man*."

"I guess not. Will we see you at Frankel's on Saturday? I hear his parents are letting him have a kegger and paying for everyone's Uber."

Thomas shrugs: "We'll see. I don't do so hot when I drink these days."

"Come on, bro," Jonny says. "Come out with us. I think it'll do you some good."

"We'll see."

The coach claps his hands and jogs towards the dugout. He wears the same uniform as the teenaged boys. "Alright, bring it in!"

Jonny turns his head. "That's my cue. Glad you came out, Tee."
He looks over to me. "You too, Wes. Let's hope I get those numbers
in your head a little higher today."

I watch the pitcher warming up. He winds up and hurls the little
ball to the catcher squatted in his crouch and covered in protective
gear from shin guards to facemask. I don't even see it. All I hear is
the ball making a loud *pop!* as it smacks into the catcher's leather
glove. Each one sounds like a cannon shot ringing in my ear, and I
cringe. Thomas notices my agitation which I express in a soft hum.
He reaches in a plastic bag and pulls out a soda and sandwich.

"Hungry?"

"Yesss," I say, forgetting about the banging of the ball.

"I made it for you. It's not hot dogs and a beer at Yankee Stadium,"
he says, "but I think you'll like it. I know you like ham and cheese."

"Yesss."

The players take the field, each at their respective positions. For a
few minutes, they toss a ball back and forth and boy do they talk a lot.
It looks like fun. Then an older man in dark blue with his own mask
and chest protector shouts, "Play ball!" and everyone gets real serious.
I rock as I eat my sandwich and wash it down with the soda. Thomas
shouts encouragement. "Let's go, Red!" He claps. My brother looks
relaxed. Sports seem to soothe him.

I clap with my sandwich in hand. "Red...red...red..."

I feel Thomas' eyes. Warm and loving today. "That's it, little
brother. Root, root, root for the home team."

"Root...root...root."

He laughs.

The pitcher twists, lifts his leg, and whips the ball like his arm's
a slingshot, and the batter watches it smack into the catcher's mitt.
"Ball," says the man in blue. But it sounds more like, "Hup."

"Hup!" I say.

I'm too engrossed in the game, counting the at-bats, balls, and strikes in my head, occasionally glancing up at the green scoreboard, to notice an older man sidling up next to Thomas. I just hear his voice.

"Your mother told me I could find you here."

Thomas looks over to him. "Mister O.?" Mister Olensky sips a can of seltzer water. "I didn't know you come to these things."

"It's a nice day for a ballgame. Plus my wife's painting the bathroom and I can't take the fumes. But that's not why I'm here." He looks over to me. "Hello, Wes. You having fun?"

"Root...root...root," I say again as I stare down into my half-eaten sandwich.

"So...then why are you here?" Thomas says defensively.

"How are you doing, Tom?" Balding with a broom-like auburn mustache, Stan Olensky is a guidance counselor at the high school.

"I'm alright, I guess. Why do you ask? Something wrong?"

Mister O. shrugs. "A man can still care without there being a problem."

Thomas sighs. "You came here to see me for the hell of it?"

"Yes, I did, Tom."

"Well, you're doing what you get paid for, I guess."

"This isn't overtime. I genuinely care for your and your brother's well-being. You know my wife is his teacher at Compass School?"

Thomas shakes his head. "No shit? Small world."

"But I wouldn't want to paint it."

"Funny."

"I try."

"So, this is like a Scott tag team? I imagine, in your guys' profession, Wes and I are juicy laboratory specimens."

Mister O. takes a swig from his can while keeping his eyes on the game. "What do you mean by that, Tom?"

My brother chuckles nervously. I can feel his discomfort. "Come on, man. You're a guidance counselor and we're, well, us. You're thinking not only did their dad die, he *killed himself.* What's going on inside this young man's brain? But I have little to tell you. It's way too soon."

"It's been months."

"So? I guess this is impossible to explain to anyone who hasn't walked my mile. All I can tell you is this. I'm fine," he says, leaning back in the bleacher and extending his legs out. "Goddamn, I've spent a lot of time assuring people that I'm fine." He looks over to his unexpected visitor and shields his eyes from the glare of the autumn sun. "Other than that, I'm not really sure what you want from me."

My brother's forwardness catches Mister O. off-guard, though he tries to not let on. He leans forward and folds his hands over his knees, looking out over the ball field. "Well, then," he clears his throat. "Good." Another pause. "I'm obviously aware of what happened to your family this summer." Thomas nods indifferently. "With your dad, I mean," he adds, as if my brother doesn't know what he's referring to. He grants the counselor another nod. "And I just want you to know that if you ever need to talk about anything, feel free to knock on my door."

"Okay." They look at each other. And then Mister O. glances over to me as I rock.

"Well?"

"Well?"

"Do you?"

Thomas frowns. "Do I what?"

"Do you want to talk about anything?" There's a slight irritation in his voice. As if my brother should know what he's hinting about.

"What do you want me to talk about?" says Thomas. "What it 'feels' like to see your dad fished out of the water in his wheelchair? How it is to know that at the very moment I was getting him a drink, he was rolling over that pier on purpose? That I should've been there?

Are you trying to tear at a scab on my heart while I'm out here trying to bond with my brother?"

"Sorry," he says, embarrassed. "I just want—"

"You want to know how I like hoisting around like a forty-pound field pack the knowledge that at that very moment I was bitching to a vendor that two bucks was a rip-off for a bottle of water, my dad was drowning? Or maybe you'd like some juicy details. Like what I saw when I jumped in the water to try and save him and damned near snapped my neck against the bottom? Should I tell you about his eyes? They were wide open…but lifeless. You know what I mean? Like fogged glass. Oh, and his mouth was open too. Nothing like frozen in that last scream, huh? I wonder if he changed his mind…but it was too late. *I know I was too late.* Should I tell you how I almost ripped out my fingernails trying to pull him out of the chair, tearing away through the tangled seaweed and cloud of my own blood as I was being slammed up against the wooden posts by the waves that kept crashing and yanking me away from him. You getting all this?"

"Getting all this!" I say. Then back to the game.

My brother pauses and catches himself. He stares blankly off into left field. Far beyond the wall and tree line behind it and all the way back to that faraway boardwalk and the edge of the pier. "I was the first to see him. Like that. Dead, I mean. I still see it." Thomas tries to chuckle. "Damn, that water was scary. I coulda killed myself. Two Scotts in one day. Imagine that."

"Tom," the counselor says softly. "I didn't know you saw him like that."

"How could you? I've never told anyone before. But the fun continues long after the body's put down in the ground. Maybe I should tell you how it feels to see your mom a broken widow in her late forties? Or how about what it's like to be on the receiving end of all those uncomfortable looks I'm getting in the halls? How about what it's like to go through all this with…my brother. The way he is."

"I'd like to know," he says.

"Well, you can't know. And I sure as hell hope you never can. I don't care what books on child shrinky-dinks you've read. Let's be real. I don't know you and until you deal with the same thing, you'll never ever in a gazillion years know what it is to be me."

The man eyes my brother coolly and I can sense his acute mind grappling for the right thing to say. "Tom. There are several kids in this school who've lost a parent. I know you know them. Have you tried reaching out to them for support?"

Thomas gives him a rather snide reply: "Any of their folks commit suicide, Mister O.?" I've sort of learned what "suicide" means and it makes me uncomfortable to hear the word.

"*No!*" I shout.

Two dads with beer guts and intense expressions lean on the fence lining the base line to get closer to the game and shout instructions to their frazzled kids on the field. They turn to stare up at me with irritated scowls.

Thomas reaches in his pocket. That's where he keeps the pepper spray. "Don't upset my brother. Please. You really don't want to see that." I see what Thomas is doing and fight the static extra hard until I calm down. Once my brother's sure I'm under control he finishes his thought. "Well? Any of their parents do...what my father did?"

"No," Mister O. says in a subdued tone. He lowers his eyes, feeling foolish.

I know a little about the kids he's referring to. Thomas used to talk about them. There's Matty Williams, whose father coached Thomas's little league baseball team when he was eight. I have vague memories of him. Warm smile, like Mister O.'s, and bright red hair. He was attacked by his heart one day. Then there are the twins, Sandra and Jess Forsythe, whose young mother was found at the bottom of her basement stairs. She'd taken a wrong step while carrying down a load of laundry and that was that. I wonder what these kids see as their placemats. What unremarkable piece of their old lives do they cling to in the dark?

"Mister O. You know my situation's different," says Thomas. "It was, I'll say it, a taboo way for a parent to die. One moral rung above murder-suicide. Just lose the first part. *'Scott's dad drowned himself, man!'* I see that in their eyes in the halls. And I'm sure, super-counselor, you do too."

I watch a player dash from first to second when it's not his turn. They call it "stealing a base" but he doesn't take it with him.

"Are you angry at your dad, Tom?"

My brother rolls his eyes. "What am I, some reality TV show to you?" Then he dials it back some. "No disrespect intended, Mister O., but that's really none of your business."

The counselor heaves a sigh while bringing his still-folded hands to his waist.

"I'm not trying to pry, Tom."

"No, you're not trying to pry at all," my brother says with a smirk. "You're *succeeding*."

"Fair enough. I just want to help. That's all."

"I know," Thomas says, shifting to a soothing tone. "But if you really want to help me," Mister O. leans in when my brother says this, "then please don't come to me for the first time in three years and pretend suddenly you're my friend. You mean well. I get that. And I do think you want to help because your wife works with my kid brother here. But I'll be gone in a year. That is, if I ever pick a college. And let's be even more honest. You're a student counselor and I'm a student who's had something pretty shitty happen to him. This is what you signed up for. It's like 'okay, Mister O., you're on…it's show time!' But I'm not a guinea pig. And I just prefer to be left alone."

The counselor opens a thick briefcase resting beside him on the bleacher that I haven't noticed until now. I tear my eyes from the pitcher's mound—he's in an early jam with bases loaded, one out, and a lefty with a .320 average at the plate—to take a quick peek. It's so stuffed with tattered files that the handle should rip off from the weight of them. "Do you know what this is?"

Thomas leans over to take a look. "Don't tell me that's my psych profile."

He laughs at that. "Call it my homework. These are the students that are under my charge here."

My brother whistles. "That's a lot of hormones."

"Tell me about it. And these are just the Q–Z kids. Mister Constantinou and Miss Bergman cover the rest of the alphabet. So that makes *S* my territory. That includes you, for those keeping score at home."

"Talk about 'take a number,' huh?"

He grins again. "It's a lot of students to follow, I admit. But, Tom, since we're in the no-bullshit zone, I'll lay it on you righteous. I don't know most of these kids. You're right about that. And most of the ones I do know are lost causes on their way to nowhere or maybe even the county pen. Messed up home lives. Crappy attitudes. Drugs. Authority issues. Some are just plain stupid in their DNA. You name it. In a word, they're royally fucked."

"Whoa!" Thomas says with a laugh and instinctively looks around to see if anyone else heard that.

"Royally fucked!" I blurt.

Mister O. looks pleased with himself and continues. "That's right, Wes. They just don't know it yet. And most of the others are just so damned boring."

"You noticed," Thomas agrees with a smile.

"But then," the counselor says while raising a finger for emphasis, "there are the kids who intrigue me. Some are very good kids, bright and talented, but with serious problems. But I genuinely maintain high hopes that they can get through their issues. I want to help them reach their true potential. Guess which category you're in."

"Well," says my brother, clearing his throat. "I don't really think prison life is for me. And I'd like to think I'm not too boring. So, I'll go with curtain number three."

The man's grin widens. "Well played, son." He reaches into the briefcase and lifts out a thin manila folder with my brother's name on the label. He slaps it on his lap and opens it. Thomas can't help but look down to see what's inside. "It's just a basic profile," Mister O. says reassuringly. "There's one for every student: screwed, boring," he flashes a wry look, "or guinea pigs."

"Wonderful," says Thomas. "My counselor's also a comedian. Kill me now."

"I'm very funny. Just ask me."

"Move along, Jimmy Fallon."

The counselor dons a pair of reading glasses, making him look professorial, and holds the paper out in front of him. "Birthday: September twenty-third, mother: Joanne, father: deceased. (That seems to hit Thomas rather hard; maybe that's his point.) Siblings: sister Rebecca and brother Wesley. I remember Rebecca when she was a student here, by the way. You'll have to tell me another time how she's doing. And I know all about young Wes here from my wife. Now let's see. Class schedule for this year. AP classes. Impressive. GPA, four-point. Never got a B?"

Thomas shrugs modestly. "The classes have been easy so far."

"So you think." He puts the paper pack into the folder, slides the folder back into the briefcase, and gestures towards it dismissively. "And that's all I know about most of the kids here. But you, Tom, I know a little more about. I've talked with your mother."

"Why?" he demands, suddenly feeling exposed and vulnerable.

"To extend my condolences, of course. But also I wanted to know what to expect from you this year. What to look out for. Forewarned is forearmed, as they say."

My brother remains guarded while I watch the pitcher shake off two of the catcher's fingering suggestions before whipping a fast ball high and inside. "Hup!"

"Hup!" I say.

Thomas stays focused on his counselor. "So what did she say about me?"

"She said you spend most of your time away from the house. Sports. Your band. Just not being around. I asked her about drugs—"

"I don't do drugs," he asserts forcefully. "I mean unless you consider alcohol...but I'm trying to chill on that ever since..." His voice trails off.

Mister O. makes a diffusing gesture with his hand. "I know that. Your mom does too."

Thomas relaxes. "I didn't think Mom even noticed anything about me. I mean, given her distracted state. She has her hands full." I don't see it but can tell he motions to me with a jerk of the head.

"I understand. I know what kind of hand you've been dealt. More than any other counselor could besides Antoinette herself. I've also asked your fellow students about you."

"Oh, wonderful," Thomas groans. "As if I don't feel awkward enough."

"C'mon kid, give me a little credit. Like you said, this is what I do."

"Okay, fine. And?"

"And...you're well-liked."

Thomas nods. "Well, that's good to know."

The counselor looks at him seriously, as if he's seen a lot over the years. "Don't take being popular for granted, Tom. A lot of kids aren't. High school can be brutal. But keeping up the whole honesty thing," the man continues, "your friends' discomfort over the subject matter of your father's passing has them unsure how to approach you."

Thomas sits back, suddenly exhausted by this conversation, which is starting to feel to him like a therapy session. I glance up at the scoreboard. Still 0–0. The parents cheer as the pitcher gets rescued by a double play. A "turn-two" players call it. "I'm still just me," he finally says.

Mister O. nods for the seventh time (I'm counting) in the meeting. "I know that. And they will too. Give it time. These things will work themselves out."

"If you say so."

Mister O. rubs his hands on his thighs. "You can't avoid how you feel, Tom. I know it's hard." Then he catches himself and raises his hand apologetically. "Forgive me. I *don't* know how hard it is. But I can tell you that coming to grips with all the issues swirling around in that large brain of yours is key to getting through the grieving process."

"Where'd you read that?"

"Shrinky-dink books," he replies, not missing a beat. I like Mister O. He suddenly shifts gears on my brother once more. He's a prober. "You playing football again?"

"Yeah."

"Good. Coach Conyers has his eye on you." He quickly adds: "And no, he didn't put me up to this. That's my own feeling on the matter."

"Sometimes I wonder if it's the right move, though. I don't want to get hurt again. I got a concussion last year when that big Stoneleigh fullback teed me up. I was counting everything by twos all week after that. So I'm playing now, but I may call it quits. We'll see."

"Seeing two-by-two," I mumble. The word concussion is familiar to me now. It's how I felt after Thomas "teed me up" as he calls it. I saw two of everything, like swimming images in front of me groping for one another. I wonder if he had to throw up too. "Toss his cookies" is what the Ord kids say.

Mister O. nods. "Well, I suppose so long as you have your music."

"I do."

"What do you like to play?"

"The blues mostly. Didn't Mom tell you? I'm a dinosaur."

"She didn't tell me *everything*. But I suppose that's an appropriate genre…given your loss."

I can feel Thomas growing fidgety at this point. "I suppose. Mister Olensky, is there anything else in particular you wanted to talk to me about? I'm here with my brother, as you can see."

"Actually, yes." His face grows serious. "I think you have an idea, considering who I'm married to." Thomas plays dumb and shakes his head. "Tom, don't bullshit me. Your brother came into my wife's school with a pretty pronounced black eye, and your mother was being very evasive when she called about it."

"Oh, shit," Thomas says. "Here we go."

"No, no. I'm not here to lecture you, son. I just want to know if everything's okay now."

"Okay?" my brother snorts. His pent-up anger suddenly comes to the fore, like he's spiked a fever. "'Okay' like how? Like I'm stuck being," he air quotes, "'the man in the house' now that Dad's…gone? 'Okay' as in I come home to a depressed mom who drinks too much and a brother who'll never talk to me or grow up? One who I gotta take down with pepper spray sometimes? 'Okay' in that our house lost our father literally one piece at a time?"

Mister O. nods with sincere compassion. "Exactly like that. I want you to know that what you're dealing with is extraordinary for a boy—man really—your age. It's normal to feel frustrated, alienated, and even pissed off."

Thomas laughs. "Gee, thanks for the stamp of approval."

A silence follows but for my humming that lets out the pressure I feel swelling around us. It's broken by the crack of the bat and sudden cheers as the left-handed hitter pulls one over the second baseman's head to drop into right field for a double. He slides into second base and then dusts himself off. The *crooosh* of his slide and brown cloud capture my attention. This game fascinates me. So many angles and measurements and numbers. I think I'll learn more. I'm glad Thomas brought me here. But he doesn't seem too happy with his visitor. Mister O., I can see, is losing patience. He turns to my brother and says:

"You better watch your tone, kid. If it wasn't for my wife being Wes's primary care instructor, it wouldn't be me sitting here chatting with you. It'd be someone from Child Services. At your front door. And the shit would come down not on you but your mother."

"What are you talking about?" says Thomas, but with a meek voice. I can tell his mouth just dried up like a raisin.

"Don't give me the innocent act, Tom. It's obvious you've gone to town on your brother. He didn't get that bruise 'roughhousing' like your mother said. Unless you want to tell me with a straight face that your mother, all hundred pounds of her, did that to him?"

"No."

"Did he slip on a bar of soap?"

Thomas closes his eyes and faces the sun low in the reddening sky. "You know he didn't."

"Okay," says Mister O. "So how long has this been going on?"

"How long? No, man. I only hit him that one night. And I was really drunk."

"It's never happened before?"

"No!" Thomas looks around, realizing how loud he said that. "I swear to God."

"Nope…nope…nope," I say, trying to support him.

The counselor heaves a relieved sigh. "Okay, son. I'm going to believe you. And you have to believe me when I tell you what a break you're getting, hashing it out this way as opposed to the police or whomever. What would've happened if your brother had an episode? You know how strong he can be."

"Yeah, I know." More silence. The runner's left stranded at second as the next batters either strike out or hit easy pop flies. I make mental notes in my head. So far this pitcher's ERA this game is zero. One hit. No RBIs. Three strikeouts. It's a strong start, but it's only the bottom of the second inning.

"Now," says Mister O. "You want to talk about what happened?"

Thomas looks at me then back to the game. "I dunno. It's like I just got so mad I wanted to hit someone. Like I feel in football sometimes."

"Who are you mad at?"

"Well, Dad for one. The guy left us holding a real bag of shit. If Grampa Frank didn't have coin, I don't know where we'd be. But my Mom's lost. I think Dad wanted to take her with him, you know?"

"Why do you say that?"

Thomas lowers his voice. "He left a round in the chamber of his pistol. I mean, shit, I dunno. Maybe he was just careless. He wasn't thinking clearly with all the meds and everything. Depression's a helluva thing. Isn't it, Mister O.?"

He nods. "Yes, it is. And it makes us do things we wouldn't normally do. It's an illness. As real as cancer. You understand your father suffered from a sickness, I hope."

"I guess. I suppose blaming him won't help anyone."

Mister O. smiles. His bushy red mustache and squinty eyes resemble the face of a garden gnome. "No, it won't. You blame anyone else?"

"Like who?"

"Your brother maybe? He's the one you seemed to have targeted."

Thomas looks back over to me as I stare at my fingers and keep track of the count (one ball, two strikes) on my fingers. He thinks I'm not listening, but I hear every word.

"I suppose. I mean, well look at him. In his own world. Oblivious to everything that's happened. It's not fair."

"What's not fair, Tom?"

"That he sucks up all the air in the house and gives us nothing back. He's a taker. Dad spent all this time with him. What good did that do Becca and me? Maybe if he'd spent more time with us, we'd have read his mood better, you know? He might still be here even."

Mister O. leans in. "Do you blame your brother for your dad's death?"

Thomas's voice goes hush. "No. Well, I guess in a way. Dad was the only one he let in."

"Let in?"

"Into his world. He's like Tommy Walker. You know who that is?"

Mister O. chuckles. "Yes, *Tommy*'s one of my favorite albums. I even have it on vinyl. But your brother's not deaf, or blind, and he's certainly not dumb. My wife can attest to that. In some ways his mind is off the charts."

My brother raises his eyebrows at that and cocks a thumb at me. "Him? Really?"

"Really. Maybe your dad saw that. Or maybe he just figured you and your sister could handle yourselves. It's hard having an autistic brother, isn't it?"

"Yeah. It's like a ride that you know's never gonna end."

"Imagine if he was your son. Think about what it did to your father. And then he comes home unable to even walk. Powerless to help his own son. I knew your dad. Talked with him once or twice at Friday night lights. He was very proud of you." Thomas nods. "He was a proud man, period. But everyone has a breaking point."

"I suppose."

"If you ever feel like you're at a breaking point, please, and I mean this, please call me day or night. Here's my number." He hands my brother a card who dutifully takes it and stuffs it into his wallet. "Because, Tom, I must be frank with you. What you did to Wes, assuming it was you, cannot, I repeat *cannot* happen again. Or next time the authorities will get involved and there'll be nothing me or Antoinette will be able to do to protect your mother. You don't want Child Services knocking on your door, believe me. It never ends well.

If you care about your brother, and I know you do, you'll keep that number handy and keep your hands off of him."

My brother takes a deep breath. "I don't know what got into me that night."

"Life, Tom. That's all. And some rocket fuel. Easy on that stuff. No one ever did anything smart when they were drunk."

Thomas thinks on that a moment. He fidgets, wrings his hands. Then he motions to the briefcase. "Who else you got in there? Any juicy bits?"

Mister O. laughs, satisfied he got his point across. "The *S* crew is the most colorful this year for some reason."

"I may have to break into your file cabinet."

"Don't bother," he replies. "It'll just depress you even more." I can tell he wishes he can suck that sentence back into his mouth but it's too late.

"Who says I'm depressed?" my brother says.

"Are you?" the counselor says, running with his gaff.

Thomas shrugs. "I haven't killed myself, have I?"

"Tom!"

"Sorry. Bad joke."

They sit back in silence. Mister O. finishes off his seltzer, folds his hands on his belly, and sizes me up, taking mental notes as I rock and moan and watch the game with hyper-focus.

"Thanks for the advice," Thomas says. "I'll hang on to the number." Then he looks at me and smiles. "Although I don't think I'm gonna need it. I guess we all have a little Ex in us."

Mister O. raises his eyebrows. "Ex?"

"It's what my dad used to call Wes. His Ex-man. His 'Extraordinary' boy."

"Ex-man," the counselor nods. "I like that. Can I use it?"

Thomas tips his head. "You'll have to ask him."

"Ex-man!" I say. This makes them both laugh which gives me a warm glow inside. I really like baseball.

"Oh, gosh. One more thing," he says, slapping his palm to his high forehead in a self-deprecating gesture. "The main thing, really. But I wanted to see how you're doing first."

Thomas nods. "Okay. So how am I doing?"

Mister O. takes a deep breath, placing both knuckles on the bleacher in front of him like a nose tackle leaning into a four-point stance. "As you alluded to before with your reality TV jibe, this is going to sound cliché but what the hell, it fits. I think you're angry, son. And I think you're confused right now. It's okay," he reassures my brother, intercepting his defensive posture. "You're a seventeen-year-old young man approaching the prime of your life and you've just lost your father. You've lost him in a way that must leave you with so many as-of-yet unanswered questions. But," he adds with a redemptive tone as he stands up straight, "you're luckier than most." My brother stands too, but I stay seated, watching the third base coach making hand signals and trying to decipher the code.

"Somehow I don't feel very lucky at the moment," Thomas says with a hint of self-pity.

"What I mean," the counselor offers with a tap to his temple, "is you're better equipped up here to make it through this than a lot of your peers. You're an exceptionally bright kid." He looks over to me. "Runs in the family." Thomas goes to say something in protest but Mister O. cuts him off with a 'talk-to-the-hand' gesture. "Don't give me the false modesty act. I've seen your grades and PSATs. And as far as you've said and as far as I can tell from watching you here, you don't do drugs, much to my relief. Don't take offense. Most mothers in this cloistered town wouldn't know if their kid's Pablo Escobar. Plus teenagers and drugs is like prison in that there's never a guilty inmate, yet someone commits all those crimes. Or in our sad case, someone keeps the dealers in business."

"I do like beer," he confesses with a smirk.

"Okay fine. You like beer. That makes two of us as you can see." He pats his gut. "I could give you the obligatory spiel about you being underaged, it's against the law, whatever, but I'm not an imbecile. I know what goes on at parties. Just go easy. Don't binge. And whatever you do, don't drink and drive. If you're ever stuck for a ride you can call me. No questions asked. You got my number. Put it in your cell. I've been to too many funerals for kids who liked beer but also liked to climb behind the wheel. One lecture at a time, though. The point is, you've got talents that keep you grounded. A family that loves you, and friends who care about you…if you let them in. And I care about you, too, Tom. Sure it's my job. But young folks like you are the reason I do what I do. And as I said," he holds up his briefcase, "half these kids I couldn't even tell you what color hair they have. But you have potential. You've just got to get through this period in your life. And you have a special challenge with your brother. My wife and I can help you with that. I take the 'guidance' part of my title very seriously. My personal phone number's a start. So is this."

From the file on Scott, Thomas J., he retrieves a glossy folder that has both an academic and bureaucratic look to it. The cover art displays American flags, happy teenagers of every race like some junior UN smiling back at my brother, and behind them faded images of soldiers sporting the uniforms of the various services, like ghosts. Thomas takes it and looks it over quizzically. The haunting apparition of the Marine in particular stares back at him.

"Son of Deceased Veteran scholarship?" he remarks, quickly getting the gist of what was, upon closer inspection, an application folder.

Mister O. nods. "The state grants it to one graduating boy and girl from each county annually. It covers children of vets who've passed away. I checked your dad's service record, and he was obviously in a combat zone given his injuries, so you qualify." My brother gives a thoughtful humph, forgetting for a moment the baseball game in front of him. "That must have been difficult for him to come home like that." Thomas just shrugs. "Anyway," the man continues, "it's purely academic. They don't care about extracurriculars because they assume you're in hardship and your family needs you home. But in your case with sports and music, it only helps your chances. It pays a full ride to in-state schools. With your report card you certainly qualify."

Thomas examines it some more, turning the folder front to back to front in his hand as if it were a rare gem he'd unearthed and was holding up to the sunlight to determine its authenticity. "Lotta kids out there," he reminds the counselor.

"You'll be okay," he assures him. "You won't have the Manhattan school system to compete with. Plus there really aren't many Mideast vets who've passed on yet."

"Lucky me," my brother says, more acerbically than intended.

Mister O. realizes his mistake and with a hoarse tone says: "You know I didn't mean it that way." I can hear the contrition in his voice as he shifts on his feet. "So…I'll fill out the forms I can and give the rest to you later this week. You can do them at home. It's all online. I'll email you my part."

"Okay," my brother says with little expression.

"Here you go." Mister O. hands over a summary pamphlet that comes with the material. "Take care of your brother now. Let's have our next chat be about the bright future you have in front of you, not the past. Deal?"

"Yeah, sure. Fine."

He leans over to me. I avoid his eyes. "Take care, Wes. My wife says you're her favorite man in her life. I'm getting jealous."

"We Scotts have a way with women," jokes Thomas. "Don't we, Wes?"

"Yesss," I say, although I'm not sure what I'm agreeing to. Whatever it is it makes them both laugh. Mister O. carefully descends the tiered bleachers as if he could topple over with every step. Thomas watches him go while he slips the laminated paper into his back pocket.

When he hops down onto the gravel, the counselor turns and looks up at us. "Tom, I know it doesn't seem like it now, but it will get better. Time does heal all wounds."

Thomas calls back to him, "Still leaves some ugly scars though, doesn't it?"

With that Mister O. turns and follows the third base line to his car parked in the high school lot. My brother watches him and then exhales. "The guy's entitled to more gratitude than that. I tell you, bro, we teenagers can be such pricks at times. Why a guy like him and his wife choose to work with kids like us, I'll never know."

Thomas doesn't even realize it. But this is the first time he's ever talked to me like an Ord.

BECCA AND THOMAS

I'm agitated tonight although I try not to show it. The dream keeps coming to me, denying me the sleep I need, and it prompts me to want to go to him. I need to see for myself where he sleeps. I need to know if he's ever coming back. I remember that word: *permanent*, and it keeps rattling through my mind like a loose coin in a tumble dryer.

I didn't go to school today. I got to wake up and watch the Von Trapps and Thomas stayed around the house shooting baskets, fiddling with his guitar, and texting friends while watching sports so it must be the weekend. The rain's been coming down in sheets all day, and now in the darkness, the black clouds flash white, hold, and then echo the distant thunderclaps. I flinch as they remind me of the rumbling explosions we heard when Dad skyped us from the faraway place before slipping away off screen. *"Love you too!"* *"Oh God please don't—"* *"I have to go now!"* Dad still had legs then.

I sit out on the porch and tap away on the iPad while my brother sits across from me with his headphones on watching a football video on his phone. The ceiling fan twirls and the alternating shadows of the blades pass across Thomas's face making him look like an apparition in strobe. The light from inside makes the rectangular screens that encase this patio and keep the bugs out look, in the contrasting darkness of the moonless, wet nighttime, like black canvases. When the lightning flashes, it briefly illuminates the world, turning deepest night into an eerie blue noon, and shows a family of racoons scurrying through the rain across the lawn before going dark again, making me wonder if I really saw anything at all. Another flash and the furry creatures freeze in place. The big one up front, the mother I bet, glances my way. Her eyes reflect like two shining pinpoints. Then blackness again and the image is gone. The rain comes down harder now and I feel like we're caught inside that waterfall of my dreams. I'm not sure where Mom is.

To my surprise Becca walks through the door from the living room and sits down. Ever since Thomas hit me, she's been visiting more. Thomas doesn't react, so I guess it's a planned visit.

"Mom still out?" she asks.

Thomas takes off his headphones. "What?"

"I said is Mom still out?"

"I guess. She's usually not home from it for a coupla more hours."

Becca nods. "It's good for her. Support groups are important."

Thomas shrugs. "Seems to be helping."

"Talking about your problems with people who've gone through the same experience never hurts."

Thomas makes a gesture of tipping a glass to his lips. "This never hurts either. They do a lot of that at these meetings too."

Becca rolls her eyes. "She's an adult. Everybody medicates in their own way."

Thomas looks down at his phone and cringes at a particularly distressing highlight. Maybe an injury. "She seems better lately. So whatever works."

"Good." I feel my sister's eyes pass over me. "How you doing, Wes?" I say nothing. "You in there, baby brother?"

"Somewhere," says Thomas.

"So," she says to my brother. "In a week you'll be eighteen. Any big plans?"

"Nope."

"No dates even?"

"Nope."

"You seeing anyone?"

"None of your business. But…nope."

"Ah," she says with a smirk. "My dear brother wears the brooding-artist hat. He celebrates with no one."

He looks at her. "Seriously, Becks? I'd say there's not much to celebrate."

She shakes her head. "How about you being young and alive? How about the fact that your counselor set you up with a nice scholarship?"

He closes his eyes as another explosion of thunder rolls overhead, hurting my ears. "Yeah. All you need is a dead father to get one."

"Whatever the reason…." She sits back. "It's a huge relief off Mom, you know. She won't see a dime of his life insurance. In case you're wondering."

"You mean Grampa Frank won't," he says. "She told me. Shit, I thought that's what people pay all that money for?"

"Most insurance doesn't pay out on a suicide."

"That's stupid."

She shakes her head no. "Think about it, Tee. If you really wanted to take care of someone, and you were a little messed up in the brain like Dad was, you could just take out a policy on Monday and kill yourself on Tuesday and they'd be rich by Friday."

"Huh. Suicide. He would have to go that way."

"Suicide!" I bark. "Suicide is painless…" I heard that in a song although I'm not sure what it means.

Thomas looks at me. I feel a smile on my shoulders. "Sometimes I think our little brother sees all."

"I know what you mean." I feel a certain vibe from Becca that I never did before Dad went away. *I have not been a good sister to you guys. I've been too wrapped up in my own affairs.*

"I was thinking I'd take you two to lunch tomorrow. After church."

Thomas raises his eyebrow. "Church? Since when do you believe in God?"

"There's a lot you don't know about me, little brother."

"You're right." Thomas's voice softens as he searches the darkness. "Can I tell you something honestly, Becks? Something that may sound corny?"

"I'm intrigued."

He looks up at her. "I'd like to learn more about you. I wish I knew you better."

She puts her palm to her lips. With a quavering voice and a smile she says, "Thank you, Tee."

My brother stands. His muscular form seems to fill the whole space. "Gotta watch the game on the big screen. HD and all that. This phone ain't cutting it. You wanna join me?"

She smiles. "No. I'll stay with Wes for a while. I forget how much I like the rain out here. Not the same as New York. It's less of a burden. More like…a friend. I'm glad I'm seeing you guys more. I only wish…"

Thomas steps over to my sister and kisses her on the top of her head. He's much larger than she is. "I know, Becks. Me too. But we're here now." He looks at me. "Aren't we, Squid?"

"Raindrops on roses!" I hum.

As Thomas tries to walk past Becca, she gently grabs his forearm. "I tried to call you earlier. You ever answer your phone?" she says.

"It died on me before. No one I really need to talk to anyway."

She looks around and notices the miniature bottles of wine Mom keeps on the little wicker shelf. Becca grabs one and twists open the cap. It makes a crackling sound. She hands it to Thomas who stops and looks at her curiously. He smiles, wraps his headphones around his cell phone before slipping it into his pocket and takes it. "Why not? It's Saturday night."

My sister takes another one and twists it open. Thomas smiles and they tap the plastic bottles together at the neck before each takes a swig and grimaces. "Damn," she says. "No wonder Mom always looks like she was weaned on a pickle." My brother laughs. Becca takes another sip and says: "Seriously, I thought boxed wine was rough."

The thunder roars and the rain comes down harder. Like a fire hose. "So, Tee," Becca continues, "happy birthday. Premature."

"Thanks."

A pause.

"How are you doing, little brother?" she finally asks.

"I'm just rosé," he says, holding up the bottle for emphasis.

"Very clever," she says, forcing a smile. Another pregnant pause. "Mom told me Wes's teacher's husband intervened before anything bad could happen. As I said. You even got a scholarship out of it."

"I still can't believe I did that," he says, staring straight ahead. "To pound down on my own kid brother like that. Especially one like him. God, I must've been shit-faced."

"It stinks. No two ways about it." She smiles down at him. "But I don't think that was you. You're a nice guy who's had a pile of shit as high as the Empire State Building stacked on him in the past few months. You seem to be getting a lot of schooling about life at a young age."

"What can I say," he smirks. He drains the bottle. "Some folks are just born lucky."

She takes a swig of the wine and winces. "This is awful."

"It gets Mom through the night," he says deadpan.

My sister gives him a warm smile. "I watched you play football last night."

He turns to her. They both stand facing one another in the rain. "I thought I saw you but figured it was my eyes playing tricks on me. Figured you'd be out at the clubs. Until I saw your bags this morning. You came a night early."

She grins sheepishly. "I may have slipped out last night when Bryce fell asleep. I'm such a rebel." She takes another swallow and coughs.

"That's pretty cool of you, big sis. So how was I?" he asks, cringing. "You see me take out that tight end before he caught the ball in the end zone? I think I broke his rib."

She gives him a sincere squeeze of his hand. "Well, if that's what passes for success in that game then yeah, you done real good, little brother. They said your name a lot over the loudspeaker. You should've won."

"Hard to win a game when your star wide receiver's in a cast," he says with indifference.

Becca takes a longer swig and forces it down. "Daddy always loved watching you play."

"I remember," he says. "He used to brag about me to all his Marine buddies right in front of me. He was drinking a lot back then. Bored the hell out of everyone. Except me." Thomas tosses his empty bottle into the plastic wastebasket. It rattles around before settling into the bottom of the container. He reaches to the shelf and grabs another.

"He had so much to live for," he says. "Why do you think he did it, Becks?"

She stares out at the blackness of the back lawn. "I don't know, Tee. I really don't. I don't think we ever will. He was a casualty of war is what I think. It just took longer to kill him. His whole future was in flux, too, which I'm sure just sprayed lighter fluid on the barbecue."

"Yeah, I remember him worrying about his future."

"The world's changing fast," she says, "and it's hard for an old-school guy like him to keep up. The Marines grounded him. And when that was gone, all those ugly ghosts from Iraq stepped in to fill the void. Do you know Dad told me once he had to identify his best friend in the platoon by his head, which the corpsmen left lying on the kid's lap?" He knows the story, he tells her. "Ugly stuff," she says, finishing her wine. "Things we'll never understand, Tee." He hands her another as she leans against the door to the house and keeps talking over the rain. "I think that gets to even the strongest man after a while. Especially one so disabled like he was. God, that was awful. I never got used to seeing him with no legs. He just hit the wall. At least that's what I keep telling myself. It's what I have to tell myself. I think I'd be consumed by it otherwise."

"Becks," he says. "A lot of people go to war and still manage not to off themselves."

She goes silent as Thomas's observation hangs in the air like a lingering toxin.

"It's so peaceful out here," she eventually says, bringing us back to this moment. She looks over to me as I fixate on the tablet. "You think he's okay?"

Thomas shrugs. "He seems happy. Hasn't had any episodes in a while."

"Grieving's exhausting," she says. "Even for someone on the spectrum, I imagine."

"Yeah," Thomas whispers. At that moment a loud crack of thunder splits the clouds and I slam my palms to my ears and moan. Becca steps over to me.

"You're okay, Wes. We're all going to be okay."

"Thanks for coming out, Becks," says Thomas.

"Sorry I can't stay longer than tomorrow. But I gotta get back to the ranch. I just thought I'd come out to check in on my wonderful, weird family."

My sister must feel so powerless to help Thomas. She knows he's still in pain. Over Dad. Over me. Over everything. As he's about to step into the house, he turns and blurts out: "I'm trying so hard not to hate him."

She sits down next to me. "I get angry at him too. It would be cold of you if you didn't feel some sense of betrayal."

"So how do you handle it?" he asks.

She looks up at him, smiles, and raises the bottle in a mock toast. "I forgive. That's all. I just tell myself I must unconditionally forgive the man. To be in so much pain to feel death is the only relief. His memory deserves better. There's a lot about him to love still. Try to hold on to the way he lived, not the way he died. I just wish you could have known him for longer."

"Me too," he says quietly.

"Me too," I mumble under my breath.

I feel them studying me again. "I wonder," Thomas says, as he leans against the door frame.

"More than meets the eye," she says.

"Becks, you want me to stay with you for a while?"

"Nah," she says. "Go enjoy your game. I'll be in in a bit. Maybe some time out here alone'll do me some good. Give me a chance to find my soul."

"Wes is still here."

"You know what I mean. Don't think too hard, Tee."

"Okay."

"Happy early birthday," she smiles while throwing him a where-have-the-years-gone sigh. "The boy is now the man. The reluctant man of the house."

Thomas says nothing more. He takes another swig and disappears into the light of the house. Then he shuts the door as I tap on the iPad while Becca, putting the wine down without drinking any more, enters a staring contest with the darkness. "You're both the men of the house now. Isn't that right, Master Scott?"

"Yesss."

A WALK IN THE RAIN

My eyes are wide open. The rain pitters against the roof shingles and I find it calling to me. The gate. Dad. The dream. I need to see him. I slide off my bed and step into the hallway. Darkness but for the barely discernible shadows in the gloom. I stand in my new Eli Manning T-shirt and sweats and let my eyes adjust. Mom tossed out my torn and blood-stained night clothes and bought me a fresh set. The old ones were small on me anyway. I keep growing. Grabbing the railing I descend the stairs and in the dead of night, it feels like I'm revisiting the scene of a crime. Thomas's crime. Thomas who's been so good to me ever since that night. Life is confusing. Or does it just confuse me? Would an Ord feel this way?

In the downstairs foyer the front door beckons. The rain comes down and an occasional flash of lightning far off in the distance shows me the way. My bare feet, now with sprouts of hair at the ankles, step one in front of the other until I'm close enough to grip the doorknob and turn. The doors are usually locked. I heard Mom tell a friend once you need a key to open them from the inside, so I don't run off. "Eloping" she calls it. I expect the same now. But when I rotate the knob, I hear a "click" like a ladyfinger popping in my ear followed by a protesting creak. The door swings open and the world, wet, dark, and windy, opens up to me. I'm scared. But my fear is overcome by my desire to go to Dad. It's been so long since I've held his hand, the only hand that isn't hot to the touch. I pound my head once to force out the screeching doubts and step into the cool waterfall coming down on the world.

❧

My bare feet step one after another over the wet gravel and mud of the shoulder. The road before me is dark with trees arching to form a hollow overhead. A black and blue tunnel gouged into my world. I'm soaked to the bone, but the rainwater's warm and soothing to my skin. The noise of the midnight shower is like a rushing creek in my ears, but I move forward with a single purpose. Occasionally a pair of white stars will appear around the bend and I'm momentarily captured in the oncoming car's headlights. I briefly look up but then back to my feet, one after another. I know where I'm going. I remember the route the long black car took from my destination to my home after Dad was put into the ground to rest. It wasn't far. At least it didn't seem far when driving. But now it's taking a long time to reach it. And the rain's getting more ferocious. I look like I've just climbed out of the ocean. The bottoms of my feet are black and now I'm starting to shiver. The rain's taken a more violent turn. A clap of thunder ricochets off the clouds like a cannon shot and I duck instinctively. I'm suddenly very afraid. I want to go home. But I can't. Not until I see Dad.

The road takes a sharp turn and crosses a narrow bridge over a rushing creek swollen to the very edge of its banks by the deluge of water from the darkness above. I know this place. Dad's home is just over the next hill beyond an abandoned barn. One step in front of the other. The barn passes by me. Rotted timber, a hole in the roof where birds nest and bats flutter in and out. Chipped paint and a collapsed rail fence. I'm close. Just over the rim of this rise.

There it is. I wipe the rain from my eyes and spot the corner of the wrought-iron gate where two country lanes intersect. Another lightning bolt flashes and the world turns a pale blue to me just in time to spot the entrance. I step off the road and move along the side of the fence, my bare feet going *squish-squish-squish* in the soggy grass. My fingers run along each metal pole, slick and shiny. Like the rib cage of a large snake.

I feel a rusted hinge and look up to see that I'm standing at the gate. The doorway to Dad's new world. When I push, it only gives a little. A chain with a padlock holds it tight. I'm getting taller, but I'm still thin enough to squeeze through. Forcing first my arm, then my shoulder, and finally my head and torso, the opening made slick by the rain gives me just enough room to pass. One leg. Then the other. And I'm on the other side.

This place looks much more frightening at night. Funny-shaped stones and statues with writing carved into their marble sides all seem to have a name on them and some numbers. A lightning flash might give me a fleeting glimpse at the life stories they tell. This one here, D. 2010, was a "loving husband." This one here, B. 1988–D. 2000 was "taken too soon." I don't think my dad's rock said anything. I know his name. Peter M. Scott. It will be hard to find him in the darkness with the rain coming down but I remember that he was put near a large maple tree and so I look for its silhouette against the lighted sky whenever the thunder smashes down on me.

Boom! Another cannon shot across the sky and flash in my eyes. Moving the hair matted to my forehead, I spy the tree. Like a charcoal drawing of a shimmering broccoli spear sticking out of the ground. Now my legs don't step gingerly over the waterlogged grass, they propel me forward to the spot where I know my dad waits for me. The stone's close enough to me now that I can read it without the spiderweb of thunderbolts to light the world for me. Some of the stones I pass are chipped, cracked, the carved writing barely legible. They sink into the ground and are ringed with determined tufts of crab grass. No one's visited these people for a long time. Forgotten ghosts in a bewildering universe. But the marble over Dad is white. Fresh. Still loved. I still love him. Someone's placed fresh flowers in the little tube that sticks out of the ground. Who? Mom? Becca maybe? Would Thomas do such a thing? He's been very nice lately so maybe.

The ground is cool and wet, and I sink my knees into it, soiling my sleeping clothes a dark brown. My exposed skin feels the dampness and it gives me a sense of oneness with the man "who left us to go six feet under," as I heard Thomas say once in his angrier days. My palm presses the wet turf and I half-expect my hand to feel Dad's reaching up through the soil to hold mine just one more time. One more time before he says good-bye to me. He never said good-bye on the pier and that's why I guess I've always expected him to come back to me. But I can read the sharp lettering on the shiny and smooth surface of his new stone.

Capt. Peter M. Scott, USMC
B. 1964–D. 2017
Husband, Father, Veteran, Friend. Semper Fidelis.

Below the inscription is a carved-out ribbon and heart with a man's profile in it. I remember Dad showing it to us once. "Purple Heart," he called it. I'm not sure what it means but I think his disappeared legs have something to do with it. I run my hand over the letters. This is all there is now. He's here with the people who'll never be seen again. That word keeps swimming through my mind. *Permanent.* He's really gone. Gone for good. I have to let him go. I just wish I could hold his hand one more time. But I'm also angry with him. He left me. Abandoned me to a family who hates me for who I am…for what I am. How could he do that? A part of me wants to scream.

But then I hear a voice. Is it a voice? Or is it just the rain playing tricks on my ears? *"No one hates you, Wesley."*

They hate me! Do you hate me too? Is that why you abandoned me, Dad?

"Please don't be upset with me, Son."

I *am* upset! And confused. Why? Why did you go when all I want to do is hold your hand again and walk with you in the surf? Why would you take that away from me? From us! Thomas isn't the only one angry with you! You ran away from me. I have no one's hand to hold now.

"Your mother has softer hands than I do, Son."

She hates me!

"Stop it, Wesley!"

The rain gets into my eyes and I close them tight while wiping my face with clammy, waterlogged hands. But Dad keeps talking.

I'm so scared. And so alone.

"You're not alone, Son. Your mother will be there for you. She carried you inside her. I gave you love, but she gave you life. Go to her. Be her Ex-man and make her as proud as you've made me. You'll be surprised what waits for you on the other side. Take her hand and don't be afraid. The world's filled with Ords who'll never be as loved as you are. Unhappy souls in a dead world. But you're so alive. You're the extraordinary in our lives. Be the son I know you can be."

I quickly whip around, still wondering if the voice I hear is someone behind me. Mocking me. But there's only the tree with its branches swaying and leaves sagging under the weight of the deluge. The voice continues. A voice I long for. A gentle voice from an otherwise rough man that would give me comfort when the night shadows closed in:

"Remember the Von Trapps. I was a captain like Georg. Maybe that's why you love that movie so much. And Maria came to him when the children thought they could never love another. They didn't like Maria, did they?"

Should I say something to him? "No," I mutter through the deafening rush of the downpour. "They were mean to her."

"Yes, they were. They teased her and pushed her away. But what happened? What did the Captain's children call her in the end?"

I look around again. There's no one else. I really am alone. Is this really Dad, or is it me? I don't know. But I know what I must do. This is when I reach deep inside, into a place I've never gone. I search for the words. Grabbing them like squirming fish in a tub. Reach, hold, pull them up. Cobble them together. Make full sentences. I have to do this. I know I can do this. I know how to talk like the Ords. I breathe in deep, and then begin to speak in a way I haven't since I was barely two, when for a reason I'll never really understand, I suddenly felt so out of place in this world and retreated to the safety and calm of my inner self. My personal safe harbor where I've ridden out the raging, terrifying storm that refuses to dissipate even after all these many years.

"Dad. I don't understand. Why did you have to leave me? Why did you leave me all alone? How can I love you for who you are, but also hate you for what you did to me?"

"Hate is a strong word, Son."

"It's how I feel."

"Now you sound like your brother."

"Maybe he's right to be so mad."

"There's no reason to hate me, Wesley. It was just my time."

I shake my head. "No, it wasn't! We had more to do still. More crabs to find together along the shore. I want you to tell me what's over the horizon, beyond the rim of the world. I need you to hold my hand. Why did you choose to leave me? Why?!"

"Oh, my dear boy. I was sick. Can't you see? I will always love you more than you can possibly know. But I am gone now."

"And I'm all alone."

"No, you aren't. Go home. Hug your mother. Talk to her."

"I don't like to talk."

"You're talking to me right now. You've never talked like this before. Not since you were very small."

"Because I love you, Dad. And I miss you. I want to hold your hand again and dig in the sand."

"You will again. I promise."

I want to cry. "You mean *we* will?"

"No, Son. My time is done. I've taken you this far. Take your mother's hand, hug your brother and sister. They can take you the rest of the way. Remember. You...are...loved."

I'm not sure, but I think this is the first time I've ever cried. Real Ord crying to go with my Ord speaking. I shed tears of loss, of missing someone I love. Of fear. My family doesn't know it, but I do look out into the wide-open world and wonder what the future brings. I can think deep thoughts, and I can love people. I love my dad. And, yes, I love Mom, Rebecca, and Thomas. I love baby Annabel too. A sister I never met. I love her because they love her. And we are all family. Dad is really gone. I see that now. But his love, his kindness to me, his decency will always live in my heart. And I can always find him there. I guess I'm ready to open up my closed spaces to the woman who has given me so much. It's okay for a son to love his mother, isn't it?

"She's the key to your happiness now. I'll wait for you on the other side. Now go live your extraordinary life and let them see who you really are."

"I love you, Dad," I say after my cry is over. "Thank you for being my biggest fan. You're my favorite Marine too. You are, to me, the most extraordinary man I'll ever know. Good-bye."

I stand under the waterfall of my incessant dream that became a premonition and then my final moments with Captain Peter Scott. I stare down at the silent marble until the bone-chilling cold forces me to move. Time to go home. To my family. I turn away and my bare feet go *squish-squish* in the grass as I find my way through the darkness back to the gate that is as unsuccessful at keeping me in as it was keeping me out.

HEADLIGHTS

I'm not sure where I am. The place with the gate and the stones was easy to find from my house but I'm lost in the storm now. Drenched, blue-lipped, shivering in the cold. I'm frightened. I don't know which way down the road to go. My feet hurt too. I think I stepped on a pine cone somewhere, and I can feel a cut filling with mud. It burns the blackened sole of my foot. Limping becomes more difficult and I soon may have to sit on the guardrail along the side of the road and rest a while. But which way to go? Which way is the bridge and beyond it the familiar streets I call home? Home where my mom waits for me. Home where people love me for who I am.

I step out into the middle of the shiny asphalt to try and get a better glimpse of what lies ahead. Nothing is familiar. I've never been down this way before. I turn and face one way then the other, shielding my eyes from the incessant downpour. All I see are two bright lights peeling around the corner. They seem to materialize out of the woods that hide the bend in the road from view. I'm fascinated by them as they grow bigger. I can hear a muffled thump of music from behind the windshield. The car weaves. I stare at it as it comes nearer. The lights hold me in place. I look down at my feet which are immersed ankle deep in water that fills a pothole gouged in the surface of the road. The engine hums, the music thumps, the lights throw a blanket of white over me. I keep my head down. There's a yellow line painted on the asphalt and I place my nearly numb toes on it and wriggle them. Now the engine roars and then I hear rubber scraping against the road, and the screeching protest of a car suddenly fishtailing before me. I finally look up again to see the headlights right in front of me.

Then a tumbling sensation to the side of the road and slamming into the gravel before rolling into the rain-soaked grass. A brief feeling of peace. Then all things growing dark. And my last thought is of my dad and how glad I am we got to talk one more time before he left my life for good.

WAKING UP

"I think he moved."

"Becks, are you sure?"

"Yeah, look. Tee, get the doctor."

"Oh, my sweet boy." This voice is close to my ear. I smell my mother's floral perfume. Her moist breath whispers to my cheek. "Please come back to us."

"Nurse says he's coming, Mom. I told you he's a tough little squid, didn't I?" Thomas says as he re-enters the room. I'd know his voice anywhere. It's so much kinder now than that night he came down on me. I try to forget it, but I can't. I don't think I ever will. But now I'm too tired to care.

"Did you bring his iPad?"

"Right here. Movie's all teed up."

"Wes," Mom says softly. Coaxing me. "Can you hear me? Can you hear this?" I hear the opening strings that take me flying high over the Austrian Alps until I swoop down to see my life's angel, Maria, spinning in a meadow under the sunlight and singing out that the hills are alive with the sound of music. That I'm alive and my family is with me.

Mom cries softly in my ear. "What were you looking for out there?"

These words through the haze. Then sleep again.

৯

Am I dreaming? Mom sits by my bed. Same clothing as the last time when I briefly saw her before sleep took over. She's on a chair pulled close to me. She flips through a magazine. I've noticed it's one of those things Ords do to pass the time. But I can tell she can't concentrate. She gives up and tosses the magazine on the chair next to hers. I'm still not sure where I am. I can only see things in the periphery. Mom sighs, checks her watch. Exhales and folds her arms tight to her frail torso. She glances down at the tablet in her lap and casually examines it. Her finger taps the screen and music blares *"…soon her mama with a gleaming gloat heard lay-ee-yodel-ay-ee-yodel-ay-hmm-hmm…what a duet for a girl and goatherd lay—"*

"Dammit!" My mother furiously tap-tap-taps the screen to make it go silent as I slip back into the void.

ം

I slowly force my eyes open. I'm more alert now, but I still have no idea where I am or how I got here. There's something tight, wet, and sticky over the crown of my head. When I try to focus, things come at me in twos, like the night Thomas hit me. My head feels like a clamp is tightened around it, but I can move my neck. Although I don't sit up in bed to look, I can feel tubes in my arms. My new Eli Manning shirt and filthy sweats are gone, replaced by a thin cotton gown of some sorts.

There are no faces hovering over me as I look up at the antiseptic fluorescent lights in the ceiling tiles. All seems white and gray. My body aches all over, but I can wiggle my toes and fingers, which I think is a good thing.

I hear a whimpering sound and think for a moment a small dog escaped someone's bag and raced into my room. This is a hospital room. I got that figured out now. How I got here is another question.

My head turns to the sound, slow and painful movement. Unable to focus, I close one eye to at least get a clear image of where the sound is coming from. Then I see it's Mom. She looks like she's been crying. Her light hair falls to her shoulders in tangles and there are dark circles under her eyes. Her cheeks are swollen and red. She cups a hand to her mouth as if to try and beat back another sob, but it pushes its way through just as I did that iron gate.

She doesn't notice that I'm awake.

"Mom, you need to go home and rest in your own bed." A familiar voice. Becca. "Just for a few hours. He'll be okay. You heard the doctor."

My mother's voice is hoarse and barely audible. She's been crying off and on for days.

"How can I just leave him here? Alone."

"He's not alone," says Thomas. "Me and Becks'll stay with him." My brother sounds so caring. Something's changed in him. Something for the better. "Seriously. You look terrible."

"Tee!" Becca snaps.

"You know what I mean," he says. "Mom, you can't help him if you get so run down you get yourself sick. We're in a zone defense now, but we don't wanna shift to man-to-man, one for his bed and one for yours."

Becca agrees. "I don't know what he means by that, but he's right. Mom, let him take you home. Take a warm bath. Have a glass of wine. Sleep in your own bed. You'll wake up refreshed. We'll get you right away and bring you back if anything changes. Promise."

I can feel my mother looking down on me, arms folded in apprehension. She doesn't want to go. But she knows it's best. "Alright. I can barely function anymore. But you two keep your cell phones handy. They tell you to turn them off in here, but I don't give a damn."

I hear the rustling noise of gathering coats and jingling car keys. Thomas says: "I'll give you a ride and then come back here."

"Don't worry, Mom," says Becca. "I'll be with him."

Thomas adds his assurance. "No one's leaving Squid alone in here." I feel a strong pressure as my brother squeezes my forearm. "Look at him. Sleeping like he just went for a stroll in the woods. Has no idea he almost got pancaked by that asshole's pickup."

"No one says life's dull with him," my sister says with a smile. "It's supposed to rain again tonight. Go already. Before you get caught in the storm like him. I've got him." Another soft hand touching mine. "Isn't that right, little brother." I want to say "yessss." But I'm too tired.

"I'll be back in a half hour," says Thomas.

The door to the room opens and shuts. My sister leans over the bed and adjusts my sheets. "What on earth were you doing out there, Wes? Going to see Dad, I bet. I know. We all miss him. Mom most of all, I think. But she's so busy worrying about us she never has time to think about herself." Becca sits down in a chair that's been dragged to the head of my bed. "I feel sad for her. We're all she's got now. Soon you'll be there with her alone. I know you'll make her happy. You make me happy. Just don't scare us like that again. You hear me?" I feel myself drifting off, like being pulled down into the abyss by the suction of a sinking ship. "We love you...."

JOANNE'S REVELATION

I don't know exactly what happens tonight. What changes in Mom to make her the parent I know. But from the things she and my family say, I think...

℘

Lightning flashes and the bedroom's momentarily lit up as if one of her children briefly flips the light switch up and down several times as a joke. The way the Von Trapp children must have tormented their many governesses before Maria. But there are no children in the house tonight. And if there were, they'd be asleep because it's 2:30 in the morning. Mom lies awake in her bed. Alone. Brooding. She still reaches out to touch her husband who now lies underground, far away on the other side of the gate I breached a few nights before on a night just like this. I once heard Mom confess to a friend while drinking wine on the porch that she still sleeps on her side of the bed.

But tonight she can't sleep. And she wonders if she should slip into the clothes that lay in a tussled heap on the floor by the dresser and join Tommy and Rebecca back at the hospital. Yes, they may be watching over her boy, who almost got killed on the road after visiting his father's grave in the rain, but who other than a mother can really care for her wounded child? And with all my quirks, my difficulties, the perpetual anxiety and stress I know I heap upon her one shovelful of surrendered dreams at a time, I'm still her son and she feels a gaping wound in her heart where my place in her life belongs. So many emotions parade before her like a cavalcade of guilt. *How could I let him be out there? Alone in the cold and rain, like it is now? How could Rebecca be so careless and leave the door unlocked? Why didn't I check the locks before I went to bed? My lonely bed. How could that irresponsible man get behind the wheel of his pickup on a night like this stone sober, let alone drunk?*

As the thunder crackles across the sky just above the rain-pelted roof, my mother contemplates whether she could've actually killed the man who hit me if more than just a severe but recoverable head injury and bruises resulted. Oh yes, she concludes. She could have easily killed him. And then she even wonders if the blow to his cracked skull rattled Wes's brain enough to shake loose the condition that's prevented her boy from really being her boy since he suddenly went silent at eighteen months. Maybe the switch that turned off his brain was flipped to the "on" position again? Maybe? *Stop it, Joanne! Listen to yourself.* But such confusing thoughts are nothing new to her lately. Becca's right. She spends so much time tending to our needs. She prunes the reeds of her children while her own garden's infiltrated and suffocated by twisted, thorny weeds. *Weeds needs, needs weeds. They are weeds, our needs.* My needs especially. Who takes care of Joanne Scott when she's sick? When she's blue, and the dog bites, the bee stings, and she's feeling sad? I wonder.

While I rest in room 1452 in the east wing of the big hospital, Mom tosses, turns, and kicks the sheets off her as if their very touch burns her legs. She can't sleep tonight. Without even thinking she says softly: "Pete?" Then she remembers he's gone and her emotions deflate. *How much more can God throw at me? What do you want, Lord? Is Daddy right? Are you just a figment of my imagination? Like Tommy's make-believe friend Jason when he was a boy?* (Grampa Frank doesn't believe in God. When Becca asks him why not, the old man smirks: "I watch the news.") *Why would you take my husband away? And do it so cruelly? Why did you force me to watch him die…piece by piece? And why did you take Annabel away from me and instead give me Wes? I'm not Mother frigging Theresa! I'm no saint of any kind and I never wanted the honor. I'm not cut out to be tested like Job. Day in and day out with the moans, the damned Von Trapps. Just once I'd like him to dress himself. Like all my friends' sons do. This will never end, will it?* "Tell me, Dammit! What have I done?" she asks the rain-pelted window as she pulls herself out of the bed, dons her robe, and makes her way into the dark hall she knows all too well. This same hall where Thomas almost killed both her and her special needs boy. *The night of the madman.* But now she's alone.

For some reason she doesn't click on the hall light. She feels a communion with the darkness. A lightning bolt rips like superheated fingers across the night sky and provides a bright blue glimpse of the stairs along with the delayed pounding that makes the China cabinet rattle. She slowly descends, all the while wondering how I'm doing. She almost lost me. And her sorrow fills her with shame as she steps down one riser at a time. *How many times did I wish Wes would just die? Would go to a better place with the angels and leave me to live my life in peace and the happiness that only being free to have a stake in just your own life can give you?* But now that my death almost came to pass, the thought of losing me is as unbearable as a blistering sore. I'm still her son. *What kind of a mother am I? What kind of a wife that I couldn't even prevent my husband from killing himself?*

And yet, for Joanne Scott, the notion of leaving this world by her own hand, a boat casting off and sailing away from a pier laden with all the chronic pressures of her life, sometimes flitters through her mind like a fleeting glimpse of a demonic mask. But then she immediately considers the devastation one man's suicide left behind to those he supposedly loved and quickly dismisses such nonsense.

"*You're not crazy, Bug,*" whispers a painfully familiar voice. "*You're just carrying a heavy field pack on an uphill hike in the rain.*" No argument there. So much weighing down on her. The financial burden of an inadequate Marine pension, Frank's bitterness and I-told-you-sos every time he writes her a check, the sudden denial of sexual release with a man she still fantasizes about in the tub, whose manly grip and musky scent still linger like phantoms of the senses. The concerns over how a father's suicide affects her two oldest children in ways they either cannot yet fathom or are unwilling to share with her to spare her from adding to her own mourning. And most overbearing of all, the constant 24/7 diligence of raising a child on the spectrum, not to mention the oppressive worry as she studies the deepening lines in her forehead and slight downward sag at the corner of once-supple lips that remind her of the relentless passage of time. *What will become of my special boy when I'm gone? Who'll watch over him in his thirties, forties, fifties, eighties perhaps? Rebecca and Thomas will have their own lives (hell, Rebecca already does). Pete, who was always Wes's champion, and the man who took so much of the role of offering our son emotional support and (yes, you can say it)* love *so I didn't have to is dead and buried. Can I be the parent he was? Do I really love my son?* She speaks honestly with herself as she brews tea while the storm hammers the saturated lawn with rain drops the size of sand crabs. *Sand crabs. Pete and Wes on the beach. How could Pete do it? How can anyone truly love someone who never shows it back? Who lives in their own churning, roiling vibration land? A land of fear of speaking and even eye contact. Of violent outbursts and pepper spray. Of strangers' judgmental, ignorant stares on boardwalks and in malls, of noises and clicks and groans and moans.* "Mommy, what's wrong with that boy?" "Don't stare, sweetie," *they say as they pull their own "normal" child closer to them.* "He's like your cousin Sam, that's all."

Actually, that mother's wrong. Wes isn't like any other boy... because no two kids on the spectrum are alike. It's a myriad of conditions. Autism is not a specific species any more than an eagle represents all birds from hummingbirds to parakeets to buzzards and ostriches. It's more like a phylum. And every one of them is special. Every one of them unique. *And yes,* she thinks as she sips her tea and stares down at the dormant iPad she's retrieved from the cupboard. *Some, like Wes, are extraordinary. At least that's what Pete always said. But then again, Pete always saw something in Wes I never did.*

My mother mindlessly taps the screen, waking it. She's about to go to *Yahoo!* and pull up the latest news and gossip when she spies a word file on the upper right corner. It has no title. Just the bland "Doc1." She taps, expecting nothing but a blank document Wes must have accidentally created through his constant fingering of the screen. But when it opens and springs to life, filling the page, Joanne Scott is astonished to find the document's filled with words. Wes's words? In a strange font. Like he's writing in his own hand. She reads:

"The waves. What do you think, Wesley?" Dad smiles. I stare down at the wet sand covering my bare feet. The cool seawater feels good against my ankles as the brine rolls over them. Dad crouches down and looks into my eyes. I look away. I don't like to meet others' stares. Not even his. Faces bother me. I don't know why. There's a lot I don't know. But there's a lot I do know too. Dad understands. He's the only one in the family who understands. He digs his thick fingers into the soupy wet sand and takes my hand. I usually don't like to be touched. I sometimes panic and it makes Mom very angry with me. Dad never gets mad. He scoops a handful of grainy porridge like a steam shovel and lays it into my palm. The salt water drips through my fingers. Something tickles. I stare at the mound as it moves. "It's a sand crab," he says with a smile. "See?" As the sand drips away, the little creature emerges. He looks panicky. I know the feeling and I feel compassion for the animal the size of an almond. Whirring legs under a soft shell. I touch it with my finger. I want to smile. But I just can't. So I stare at the crab until Dad gently removes it from my hand and lays it back *on the sand. It frantically burrows into the earth and disappears. My father puts his hands on my shoulders. I look away to the haze of the horizon. What's beyond the edge, I wonder? Dad smiles. "I thought you'd like that".*

What is *this?* Mom continues reading. She soon forgets all about the tea that goes untouched and cold. All about the raging storm over her head. All about the hospital even, and the drunk driver she could've killed. She has tunnel vision now. All she cares about are the words scrolling before her in an endless stream. This file is huge. Pages and pages. The bright light of the tablet illuminates her face, highlighting the lines and high cheek bones, the firm jawline and sharp nose that so attracted the young, freshly minted Marine officer who caught her eye at the local pub while she was doing shots with a cousin whose wedding had been called off so many years ago.

"My God," she says softly to no one.

She keeps reading. Scrolling eagerly through the digital pages like a child might rip through the wrapping paper on Christmas morning to arrive at the present hidden within an oversized box that at first appears empty but actually contains the most coveted gift on the list.

The times before school are the most confusing for me now. It's usually Dad who comes into my room and wakes me with the gentle tap of his calloused finger on my forehead. "Get up, Son," he says. Sometimes when I open my eyes and look up at his chiseled face smiling down on me, he's in his normal clothes. Jeans and T-shirt. But other times he's in his combat fatigues or dress blues and then he looks the warrior to me that he was. "Bed!" I shout in protest. And he just laughs. No pepper spray. No impatient sigh. Just a warm glow. "I know the feeling, kiddo. C'mon. Get up, Marine. Let's see what clothes match today." And then I move. But it's not like that now. Thomas comes in sometimes, but he's always in a hurry and checking his phone. "Get up, Squid, and match your clothes red-to-red, blue-to-blue, what-

ever curdles your cream." Then he's gone. None of the "Let's see what color goes where," as Dad might say. "Oh, this looks good. Come on, Ex-man. Get dressed. The Von Trapps await in the kitchen." If it isn't Thomas, and Becca's not visiting, then it's Mom. And she never smiles. She always looks like I just woke her from a bad dream she hasn't fully shaken. Tired, disheveled. Wishing her life's path had taken her anywhere else but here. I don't touch Mom like I do Dad, because she doesn't love me like Dad. Love is touch...touch is love. All I care about now is what's at my feet. I wriggle my toes over the edge of the bed though now I notice my feet meet the floor. Am I as big as Dad now? I wish I could see him to find out. Maybe someday when he wakes up. Maybe I'll try to visit him. I haven't given up on Mom. If I could talk to her I'd tell her I'm sorry for being me. I don't always like being me either. So here, I guess, we have something in common. I'd like to think we have more. But I need her to take a step forward. Be my Mommy like when I was a baby. She says I could talk then. I don't know what happened. I wish I did. I want to love her. But I need to know she loves me. The way she still loves Annabel. And I don't know if she does. It makes me sad to write this. What son doesn't want to hold his own mother? But does she see me as her son? The way Dad does? I just want it to stop burning...I want to take her hand. Mommy, where are you? I feel so lonely.

The more she reads, the more the thunder booming and shaking the house as the worst of the storm passes directly overhead fades into the background, to the point where she doesn't even hear it. Her finger frantically scrolls the words on the screen. More and more. Like a thirsty urchin suddenly doused by a fire hose. One large paragraph that goes on for pages, thousands of words. No breaks. No indentations. Just one continuous thought unleashed from its cage to pour out the heart of her boy she realizes she doesn't know at all into the confusing, cruel world around him. *How long has he been writing this?*

"I'm sorry," she says in a cracked voice as the tangerine light of dawn peeking around the breaking clouds peers through the foggy sheen of the kitchen window. She's not even aware she's been crying. Nor does she realize it's morning and the rain has gone and sunlight splashes across her face, replacing the glow of my thoughts on the page. "I'm so sorry, baby."

SECRET OF
THE TABLET

I open my eyes briefly and spot Mom sitting on the chair across from me. She looks like she's been crying again. Sunbeams pierce the window, so I know it's daytime. Last night's angry storm's over. She's too engrossed in whatever's released such a floodgate of emotions to notice I'm watching her. She comes into focus. Then I see. It's my tablet. Her fingers whip in sharp upward motions to keep scrolling. Keep reading.

I close my eyes again and soon I hear the *clickety-clack* of heels on linoleum flooring.

Mom whispers. "Did you ever know all this?"

"No, Missus Scott. I suspected there was something more to him, but this…this is astounding." I know that voice. Antoinette.

Becca's with them too. "Mom, I had no clue he could even read at such a high level. Let alone to write something so…deep."

"Listen to this," my mother says in a quavering voice. *"Faces bother me. I don't know why. There's a lot I don't know. But there's a lot I do know too. Dad understands. He's the only one in the family who under-stands. He digs his thick fingers into the soupy wet sand and takes my hand. I usually don't like to be touched. I sometimes panic, and it makes Mom very angry with me. Dad never gets mad."*

Mom stops and says to herself in a hush tone. "Dad never gets mad."

Antoinette sits down in the chair next to Mom. "He misses his father very much."

Mom nods. "The accident was near the cemetery. On Linton Road by the bridge. We figure he must've been trying to find Pete there. In the middle of the night. During that awful storm."

Becca's voice is contrite. "I left the door unlocked when I went out. Idiot. He could've been killed."

"It's not your fault," Mom says, trying to soothe her daughter's guilt. "He never eloped before. Antoinette, you never had any problems with him wandering off, right?"

"None," she confirms to my sister. "Even when we'd go to the store together. I was shocked when I heard. But he's apparently filled with surprises."

Mom says: "That's an understatement. I guess God smiled down on us."

"He smiled down on Wes," Becca says softly.

Mom turns to Antoinette: "I feel so foolish. I really didn't know he was so…"

"Aware?"

"Alive."

Through my closed lids but sharp ears I hear another set of footsteps. These sound more purposeful. Official. A deep, confident voice.

"How's our patient today?" I feel movement on the bed. Strong hands pressing down on my belly, my arms, my legs. "I understand he's conscious now. Very good. He wasn't in a coma longer than what, two days?"

"He looks unconscious to me," Mom says.

I feel his hands against my forehead and flinch. "See? He's with us. Just resting. Aren't you, Wes? You've had a busy few days. Just try to sleep. My shift is over, but Doctor Angeli will be back in an hour to check up on him. She's very good with kids. Especially those on the spectrum."

"Thank you, Doctor."

"You're welcome. He's a lucky young man."

"I know," Mom says. "That damned drunk could've killed him. He weaved at the last second. A glancing blow."

"Yes. He certainly is lucky he didn't suffer more than a severe concussion and some bruised ribs and femur. But what I mean is he's lucky to have a family that obviously cares for him as much as you all do." A pause. I can sense his embarrassment. "Well, I've said too much. Have a good day." His footfalls fade down the hall.

Becca's voice. "Cute. And a doctor. Mom, you should—"

"Not now, please. I have enough on my plate."

Antoinette chimes in. "A little more never hurts if it's good for what ails you."

After a quiet chuckle, Becca's voice again. This time serious. "He wrote all that?"

"Pages and pages," says Mom. She continues reading aloud. *"My room is like one of those Picasso paintings Antoinette at the special school shows me. His 'blue period' she calls it. 'Wes, do you know what "blue" is?' Of course, I do. It's the color of Dad's dress uniform when he parades at the camp or attends weddings, funerals, and parties with Mom in her evening best. The color of the ocean and the sky and the canvas of my world. I look up to him and then turn away. It almost burns to look at him in the dimness of the shadow world. Don't go."*

Now it's Antoinette's turn to fight back a sob. "I've been so *condescending* towards him. He knows so much more than I realize. And this is what I do. Missus Scott, I'm so sorry I've been underestimating your son."

"We've all been," Mom says. "Well. Almost all of us. Peter never did."

I hear movement. The crunch of the fabric as Mom pushes herself off the chair. She moves close to me. The back of her hand caresses my cheek. It's not hot anymore. I like it.

"And there he lies," she says. "Mommy's little man. Mommy's lucky little man."

❦

Today Doctor Angeli tells Mom I can leave the hospital. She says my head's better now. I still ache when I move but I can tell that I'm doing better than I was the day before. And they took all the tubes out of my arm and rolled the machines away, so I guess I'm healing. I don't even wear a bandage anymore. Becca and Thomas are in the room with me too. I glance up from my hand to see smiles all around. Then I scooch out from under the thin sheet and sit on the edge of the bed.

"Tough kid," Thomas says.

"Smart kid," adds Becca.

"Come on," says Mom. "Out of bed with you, young man. We're taking you home." I look up from my wriggling fingers to see clothes laid out on the chair. Mom picks up one set and brings the shirt and sweatpants over to me. She lays them on my lap. I stare down at what looks like a football jersey. "No more hospital gowns for you. Back to street clothes. I brought you a few sets. I think you'll like this one. Red-to-red. What do you think, Wes?"

I grab the shirt which is really a brand-new football jersey and hold it up. It's white with red stripes on the sleeve and a big red *10* on the back. I read the name. **MANNING.** I throw it on eagerly.

"Told you he'd dig it," Thomas says in triumph. "You can wear it when we take you to the Meadowlands to see them. Would you like that, Wes?"

I would. I like football. I like Thomas again. "Yesssss," I say.

After I put the clothes on, I stay seated on the bed. Mom approaches me. "Come on, Wes. It's time to go home. Time to take my Ex-man home."

Ex-man. Extraordinary. It's the first time I've ever heard Mom use that word about me.

"Ex-man," I say. "Mommy's Ex-man."

She lets out a squeak and cups her hand to her mouth. "That's right," she says softly. A grin peeks out from either side of her trembling fingers. "You're my Ex-man too. My beautiful, warm, brilliant, thoughtful, loving Ex-man." There's silence as I stare at my wriggling feet. I feel a warm pressure against me. Body-to-body. The smell of floral perfume. Soft skin. Not like Dad's. Smooth like a baby. Mom hesitantly presses while folding her arms around me. It doesn't burn now. Dad says it's okay. I don't feel like flinching. I want to... hold her back.

"Hugsss," I say.

"Hugs," Mom says back in a whisper. I reach around and she's so thin my arms overlap across her bony back. I squeeze tight. I've never held my mother before. She's never held me.

She says through tears. "All my life, this is all I've ever wanted to do. I'm so sorry I didn't try sooner. But we have a long life together. I'm looking forward to knowing you more. I'm so sorry it's taken me this long."

"So sorry," I repeat. I'm just saying what she says, but it makes her cry.

I hear Becca whisper to Thomas. "God, now I feel like crying too." Silence. "Tee? Are you choking up?"

"No," he clears his throat.

"Oh my gosh, yes you are!"

"I just got some dust in my eye, okay?"

"In a hospital?"

"Shut up."

"The big man has a heart," she laughs. "It's okay. This is as good a reason as it gets to let your guard down."

Mom and I continue to hold each other. "I never want to let go," she says. "Please tell me you'll let me hold you again."

"Yesss…" I say. And I bury my face in her shoulder. The fabric of her blouse soaks up my tears.

"Mommy loves her Ex-man."

The nurse arrives with a wheelchair. And Mom disengages from me reluctantly. "I hear our special patient be leaving us today?" she says. "We gonna miss you around here, Meestah Scott."

"Why?" says Thomas, breaking the moment. "He just laid there."

"Tee!" says Becca.

"Nah," says the nurse. She has a strong Caribbean accent. She taps her temple. "He got a lot going on up dere. Don't he, Meesus Scott?"

Mom nods. "Yes, he does."

"And we always happy when de children leave here in one piece. He gots a long life ahead of him. We glad he okay."

"Thank you," says Becca.

"What's with the wheelchair?" asks my brother. "Can I sit in it?"

"Hospital policy. De patients have to be wheeled out. So hop in, Meestah Scott. Let Annabel take you for a ride, okay?"

Mom looks up. A brief flash of sorrow passes over her face before she regains her poise. Some wounds, I'm learning, can only scab over. They never heal. I wonder if it will be the same with me and Dad.

"Annabel?" Mom reads the nurse's name plate on her pocket. *Annabel Maraj, RN.*

"Yes. Momma name me dat when she first see me as a babe in her arms. Annabel means—"

"Beautiful," Mom says. "It means 'beautiful.' I do love that name."

"Well dis young man you have here's beautiful too. Aren't you, Wesley?"

"Yes," Mom says. "He certainly is. Come on, Wes. Hop in. Let Nurse Annabel take you out."

I pull on my sweats, slide down off the bed, and slip into the chair. My fingers twirl in my vision and as we move I focus on the hospital floor tiles. *One...two...three...four...five...*I guess I'll always like to count.

SAND CRABS

"The waves. What do you think, Wes?" Mom says with a smile. "Doesn't it feel good against your ankles? Especially on a hot day like this?"

She holds the broad-brimmed hat to prevent the sea breeze from blowing it away and the white cover to her bathing suit presses up against a body that's filled in the skeletal gaps from the year before. She stands by my side, barefoot as well. Her feet next to mine. Mine are much bigger now. Our shoes are back on the blanket laid out across the white sands halfway to the crest of the dunes topped by the swaying marram grass, *Ammophila arenaria*. My brother and sister sit on their beach chairs under a multicolored umbrella like a swirled lollipop. Becca's engrossed in a novel about a lawyer on the run while Thomas listens to iTunes through his earbuds and flips through his Binghamton University incoming freshman handbook.

It's been a year since Dad went away. I'm getting used to it now. I still think of him at night and sometimes, when the wind blows just right through the leaves outside my window, I'll hear him calling to me. Calling me his Ex-man. His favorite Marine.

But now as I stare down at the wet dun-colored sand covering my feet, I'm drawn to my mother's legs, tanned and shapely after a year of Yoga and other hobbies she pursues to get past her lost husband. She sleeps in the middle of the bed now. But I still sometimes catch her puffy-eyed on the porch, sipping morning tea, in deep reflection over her life as she stares out to the lawn and distant tree line. It's as if she's waiting for him to emerge out of the misty sunrise and take her hand one last time. But he's gone. And now I really understand what *permanent* means. Never ever again.

Another wave breaks ten yards out, and its remnant of cool seawater rolls over my feet and I wriggle my toes in the rushing foam. Mom crouches down and looks into my eyes. I don't look away from them. I still don't like to meet others' stares…but Mom's eyes, light blue like a robin's egg, are different now. They're somehow softer, more in sync with my swirling, roiling existence within myself, and I don't know why that is. There's a lot I don't know. But there's a lot I do know too. Mom understands. The whole family understands now. She digs her delicate fingers into the soupy wet sand and takes my hand. I don't panic. Now I welcome her touch. Soft, feminine, comforting…*loving*. I know I can be frustrating to live with and to care for, but it's not the way it used to be with us. Mom rarely gets mad at me anymore. She scoops a handful of grainy porridge and lays it into my palm. The salt water drips through my fingers. Something tickles. I stare at the mound as it moves. "It's a sand crab," she says with a smile. "You know what they are. I know you do. I know you know a lot of things, Wesley Scott. I know we can learn from each other. I know I love you very much…and you love me."

As the sand drips away, the little creature scrambles around in the bowl of my curved fingers. It's terrified. And I can understand. I feel that way about the world still. I always will. But now I have a whole family to help me seek shelter from the storm. My mother, my sister, my brother. They are my breakwaters. My inner harbor. *Don't be afraid, little crab. I'm not going to hurt you. Here, let's get you home.* I want to smile. But I can't. Mom gently removes it from my hand and lays it back on the sand at the edge of the waterline. It furiously burrows down into the porridge until only an air bubble remains as any evidence of its subterranean existence. Then *pop!* All trace of it's gone.

My mother takes my hand in hers and I squeeze. Then I look away to the haze of the horizon. I still wonder what's beyond the edge?

Mom smiles. "You love those little guys, don't you? Someday I hope you'll write down why. I want to know all about you. All about my Ex-man."

We both stand up tall and straight. I have two inches on her now and I'm growing every day. I briefly glance down at her. I'm fifteen, and almost as tall as Dad is—Dad was—when we last dug for crabs on the beach. My mom tells me she's always wanted to do this with me. Today makes her very happy. Me too. "I know you hear me. I know what's in there. Thank you for this, Wes. Thank you for being my son."

The emotion of the moment prompts me to moan, but Mom knows it's not despair. It's just the way I deal with the complexities of the world. Although I've learned that the most beautiful things in life are the simple things. A sand crab on the beach. A brother's thumbs-up at me in the stands while he hustles back to the sidelines on the football field below after making a crucial tackle. A sister's weekender bag in the vestibule that tells me she's going to stay a while. A mother's pure devotion. And a son's love. Even if I can't express it, it's there. Like a bass note to a symphony of my life whose absence is only noticed when it hits a dissonant note or stops playing altogether.

People walk past us on the water's edge and glance my way as I utter my release of emotions. I'll never be an Ord. But Mom pays them little attention. She's no longer embarrassed by me. She's inspired, she says. I'm her Extraordinary Boy.

Now I'm calm again. My moan is carried away by the salty air to the far shore beyond the edge of the world.

"Come on," she says, taking my hand and walking me away from the surf that crashes behind me like a roaring freight train. But I ignore it. I'm focusing on my mother. My hand in hers. Warm to the touch. "Let's go back to the house. I'm hungry. Aren't you?"

No, I think. I'm loved.

THE END

ABOUT THE AUTHOR

B rad Schaeffer is an author, columnist, commodities trader, and musician. His eclectic writings, covering a broad spectrum of topics including history, the arts, politics, science, business, pop culture, and general observations on life, have appeared in *The Wall Street Journal*, *New York Daily News*, *National Review*, *Daily Wire*, and others. He is the author of the historical novel *Of Another Time and Place*, about a German flying ace who chooses to commit treason to rescue a family of Jews from the Nazis during the height of World War II. His second novel, *The Extraordinary*, tells the story of a family struggling with a war veteran father's PTSD as told through the words of his autistic teenage son. He currently lives in New Jersey.